THE PRICE YOU PAY

Somnath Batabyal worked for a decade in journalism, covering crime and criminality, hobnobbing with politicians and policemen, before entering the quieter world of Western academia. His first book, *Making News in India: Star News and Star Ananda*, was published in 2011. He has also edited a volume, *Indian Mass Media and the Politics of Change* (2010). Somnath now lives in London where he teaches at the School of Oriental and African Studies. *The Price You Pay* is his first novel.

THE PRICE YOU PAY

SOMNATH BATABYAL

HarperCollins *Publishers* India

First published in India in 2013 by
HarperCollins *Publishers* India

Copyright © Somnath Batabyal 2013

ISBN: 978-93-5029-425-3

2 4 6 8 10 9 7 5 3 1

Somnath Batabyal asserts the moral right
to be identified as the author of this work.

This is a work of fiction and all characters and incidents described in this book
are the product of the author's imagination. Any resemblance to actual persons,
living or dead, is entirely coincidental.

HarperCollins *Publishers*
A-53, Sector 57, Noida, Uttar Pradesh 201301, India
77-85 Fulham Palace Road, London W6 8JB, United Kingdom
Hazelton Lanes, 55 Avenue Road, Suite 2900, Toronto, Ontario M5R 3L2
and 1995 Markham Road, Scarborough, Ontario M1B 5M8, Canada
25 Ryde Road, Pymble, Sydney, NSW 2073, Australia
31 View Road, Glenfield, Auckland 10, New Zealand
10 East 53rd Street, New York NY 10022, USA

Typeset in 11/14 Dante MT by
R. Ajith Kumar

Printed and bound at
Thomson Press (India) Ltd.

To MKB, first-class raconteur

and

to Georgie Pope, superwoman, best friend

1

❦

'Good morning, sir. The commissioner would like to speak to you.'

'Yes, of course. Morning.' Uday Kumar tried to sound more awake than he felt. The clock on the bedside table showed a little past 6 a.m. and an uneasy feeling crept into his drowsy head, merging with the canned music that said he was on hold.

It was not the timing that bothered him. As a deputy commissioner in Delhi Police, Uday was used to answering his political and professional bosses at all hours but a direct call from Delhi's top policeman brought a sense of impending trouble. Not the kind of trouble that had won him a president's medal or got him suspended twice, but the irksome variety, like the hostility he felt from his wife, sleeping beside him: neither acute enough for a showdown, nor mild enough to ignore.

'Uday,' he heard the commissioner's measured voice, 'have you seen the *Times*?'

'No, sir, I haven't, but I'll call for it immediately. Good morning, sir.'

'Please get back to me.' His boss did not bother with salutations.

Uday scrambled out of bed and pulled on his track bottoms,

calling to the guard to bring the morning newspapers. His wife Alka peered out of the covers irritably, refusing to return his apologetic smile.

The photograph on the front page of the *Times of India* jolted him awake. It showed a figure strung upside down from a tree. The caption informed that this man, accused of petty theft, had been publicly thrashed by Ranbir Singh, a station house officer in Uday's charge. The headline read: 'Delhi Police Abuse Human Rights. Again.'

Ranbir Singh, who must have been waiting for the call, answered it at the first ring.

'Is this true, Ranbir? Have you done this?' Uday heard himself shouting.

'Yes, sir, but I was …'

Uday was not in the mood for explanations. 'My office. In an hour,' he said, and hung up.

Dressing hurriedly, Uday returned the commissioner's call, assuring him he was investigating the matter and would prepare a full report that afternoon. He ignored Alka's sullen presence at breakfast and silently chewed on his aaloo parantha, wondering how to avoid a media frenzy over this minor issue. He had a big day ahead and he wasn't going to let it be spoilt by some small-time crook and a fool of a policewallah.

Uday was still contemplating strategy as he lowered his bulky frame into the back of the white Ambassador car when the first journalist phoned. It was television reporter Arvind Rao, possibly the last person Uday wanted to hear from that morning. He thought for a moment, then decided to take the call – Arvind had a knack for becoming inventive when stalled.

'Hello, Arvind, how are you?' Uday began in his damage-control voice.

'Namashkar, sir. Congratulations. Your officers are front-page news.'

'Shouldn't be. You guys have strange priorities. This is a minor disciplinary matter.'

'Are you joking? Ranbir will be dragged through mud. I think this will become big. What action are you taking?'

'Arvind, there is nothing in this story. Wait; I might give you a bigger one today.'

Uday had plans for this evening's news, and had scheduled a press conference. His team, along with the Special Cell, had just busted an international cricket-betting syndicate. Cricket, crime and cash – that was prime-time television; not this thief-thrashing bullshit.

'Boss, we know the evening story. Police PR. No one is interested in a solved case. I need a comment on this one. You have to tell me something.' Arvind's persistence was annoying.

'I am on my way to the office and I will look into the matter,' Uday responded sharply. 'I cannot say anything before I know the facts.'

The journalist hung up, surprising Uday who had expected more of a contest.

He had reached Chanakyapuri and, if the traffic held off, would be at his office in half an hour. He wound down the window as the vehicle sped past the embassies on Nyaya Marg, savouring the start of the winter and claiming a few moments of calm to collect his thoughts. There were very few streets left in Delhi where one could breathe the early morning air, and this particular stretch, with its broad and empty roads, orderly tree-lined pavements and ostentatious architecture, was Uday's favourite. He rearranged the cushions on the car seat, trying to find a comfortable position.

The back pain, which had started with a slipped disc ten years ago, increased in intensity each winter.

The car came to a halt outside his office. Sunil Mishra, Uday's immensely capable personal assistant, was standing at the entrance, his attentive eyes on his boss as he struggled to get out of the seat, grimacing with the effort. Mishra, Uday knew, would require no prompting to schedule a doctor's appointment.

'Good morning, sir. Ranbir Singh is here.'

'Give me five minutes,' Uday replied, as he pulled himself up the steps.

As soon as he was in his office, Uday received a call from the genial and garrulous press officer of Delhi Police, Vikram Singh, whose Machiavellian dealings would have extracted a nod of approval from the philosopher himself.

'Boss, what is going on? You should not give comments to journalists without at least telling me, no?'

'Why, what happened, sardarji? I haven't said a word to anyone,' Uday replied, both indignant and worried.

'Watch Nayi Khabar. I will call you back.'

Uday switched on the television set and searched for the Hindi news channel. Within moments, the earnest voice of Arvind Rao could be heard. He listened incredulously as the journalist claimed that in an exclusive interview, the deputy commissioner of police, north district, Uday Kumar, had told the news channel that an inquiry would be conducted against Ranbir Singh and appropriate action taken.

Uday swore as he phoned the press officer back. 'Vikram, if this is what that bhenchod understood from our conversation, then maybe *he* needs to be hung upside down and thrashed!'

'You know how it is, boss man.' Vikram chuckled. 'It's a circus and I'm the ringmaster without a whip. I can guarantee, within ten minutes every news channel will be saying the same thing. Anyway, don't worry; I will handle it from here. You just get ready for the evening show. You have a big day ahead.'

Uday pulled out his crumpled copy of the *Times*. How had this happened? Ranbir might be corrupt, but he was also efficient and certainly not stupid. From a station house officer, Uday did not expect more. There were no honest SHOs in Delhi, he knew that. To get the posting in the first place, one had to pay hefty bribes that had to be recovered later. The more lucrative the area, the bigger the bribe; and Ranbir's terrain, Chandni Chowk, was practically a gold mine. Part of Old Delhi, it still housed some of the city's earliest and biggest entrepreneurs. There might be no flashy glass-front air-conditioned offices, but millions changed hands in cash in those narrow congested streets every day. It was also communally volatile. Ranbir Singh was not posted there for his honesty – or lack thereof – but for his competence.

There was a knock at the door and the man who had ruined Uday's morning walked in gingerly, followed by Assistant Commissioner Dilip Tandon.

'Ranbir, what were you thinking?' Uday began immediately. 'I can understand you thrashing the fucker, but to do it with a press photographer around? Are you blind? Have you gone mad?' His voice rose and Ranbir remained quiet, eyes on the floor, waiting for his boss to let off steam.

'Go on, tell me,' Uday said impatiently.

'Sir, I caught the guy red-handed. He is a local nuisance. I wanted to teach him a lesson, sir, and also make an example of him for the residents.' Ranbir paused for a moment and looked at Uday. 'But I swear, sir, there was no photographer around. I told my men to watch out even for mobile phones. Take my uniform off if you like, sir, send me to the Lines, suspend me, but I can swear by it.'

Uday watched Ranbir for a few moments and decided he was not lying. There was no point ticking him off for administering a few slaps: that was accepted practice, though this tree business was definitely innovative. The police could not afford to open a case against every petty criminal caught. To send a person to jail took time and effort, and ate into other policing duties.

'Okay, you can go. I'll call you later,' Uday told Ranbir. 'Tandon, one minute,' he said to the other policeman, who had been standing by silently during the exchange. 'Start a departmental inquiry and take your time with this,' Uday instructed him, unnecessarily he realized. He knew Ranbir and Tandon worked hand in glove to make money and one would hardly jeopardize the other. 'I don't want to be bothered with this any more. That's all for now,' he said with barely controlled distaste.

'Yes, sir.' Tandon saluted and hurried out.

The Tandons of the force were the worst sort: notoriously corrupt and absolutely incompetent. By Uday's reckoning, the best policemen were those like himself: middling corrupt, but efficient. Absolute unbending honesty was no less problematic than heartless corruption. If used effectively, Uday always said, amorality could be a policeman's weapon.

'Mishra-ji,' Uday told his PA on the intercom, 'get Ashwin, the *Times* guy.' He wanted the mystery of the newspaper photograph solved. Uday knew the journalist, Ashwin Pandey, who had done the story, and quite liked him.

The reporter came on the line.

'Good morning, Ashwin. What is this that you keep doing?'

'Ha ha, sir, good morning. Nothing much, just a small story to keep the job,' the voice at the other end was flush with victory.

'Come and have tea with me,' Uday said. 'If you are free, come now.'

Mishra-ji walked in with the morning files. For the next half- hour, Uday busied himself with the tedious administrative side of policing a district: sanctioning leave; penning formalized begging letters to headquarters for equipment, manpower and money; examining the progress of pending cases and attending to personal requests. An orderly knocked and told him that Ashwin Pandey was waiting to see him.

'Yes, send him in,' Uday said, and asked for tea.

Ashwin seemed bulkier, Uday thought. He was also without the trademark thick glasses.

'Arre, what happened, your vision has suddenly cleared?' Uday exclaimed, getting up to shake hands.

'What to do, sir?' Ashwin replied. 'There is so much to see in this city of yours that I decided to get 20/20 vision. Got this laser treatment done,' he said, sitting down.

'Really?' Uday thought of his wife's deteriorating vision. 'Must be expensive, no?'

'Yes, a bit, but I have a friend who has started this facility. Got a discount.'

'Did you also do a friendly story for your friend?'

'Unlike your fellows who get free treatment and if not, threaten to slap false cases.'

The retort was instant and Uday laughed. 'I will take the doctor's name and address from you later. But for now, tell me boss, how did you do this?' He waved his copy of the *Times*. 'I called Ranbir in today and screwed him over. He swears that there was no photographer around.'

'Your man is right.' Ashwin grinned. 'We were not there. Not when the thief was being thrashed, anyway.'

'Then?'

'Well, I got to hear about the incident from this guy who lives in the neighbourhood and went to the spot. The thief was still around, screaming about police torture to anyone who cared to listen. We strung the chap up again and took his photo. He was only too ready to oblige.'

'What!' Uday exclaimed, shocked. 'Ashwin, what are you saying? You are worse than my constables. You really put that guy up again?' He began to laugh.

Ashwin nodded, smiling sheepishly.

'What a crook!' The cop chuckled. 'He shafted Ranbir right back.'

After tea, the reporter rose to leave. He shook Uday's hand. 'No hard feelings I hope, sir.'

'None from my side, but do not go towards Chandni Chowk. I cannot guarantee your safety. See you at the press conference.'

As Ashwin left, Mishra-ji walked in. 'Sir, there have been phone calls from the news channels asking for comments. They are all running the morning story.'

'These journalists, Mishra-ji,' Uday said to his PA, 'they have no mothers, no sisters. Any hole they get, they'll park their dirty dicks. Compared to them, we are angels.'

He related Ashwin's story and Mishra-ji, who had served his boss for over twenty years, shared his outrage and amusement.

After lunch, delivered by special arrangement with the nearby Oberoi Maidens Hotel, Uday settled down to read his notes once more. Through months of phone taps, his team had established links between the cricket-betting syndicate in central Delhi and the organized crime gangs in Dubai, Hong Kong and

Malaysia and, most importantly, Pakistan. That always got the headlines, Uday thought. He was convinced that two players in the national team were involved with the syndicate but the evidence was inconclusive.

Years ago, he had been part of the team responsible for unearthing the Hansiegate scandal, where top international players were implicated in organized betting. Although the police had telephone conversations between South African skipper Hansie Cronje, his teammates and bookies on tape, they were nervous about breaking the story. Governments got involved and the whole thing turned nasty. Out of the blue, Hansie confessed, professing that his Christian roots had pushed him to tell the truth.

Uday never met Hansie, and a couple of years later, when the cricketer died in a plane crash, he was depressed for weeks. There was something graceful about how Hansie had found the courage to own up to his crime, knowing the consequences. A career built through hard work and graft would now lie in tatters, forever to be ridiculed.

Unlike our motherfuckers, Uday grimaced inwardly. The whole country knew they were guilty, but they still had the nerve to behave as if nothing had happened. Half of them were television commentators and the rest were in Parliament.

It was not the investigation, nor its coverage that worried Uday, but the announcement to be made afterwards by the police commissioner. He was hoping nothing would change the man's mind. That a so-called human rights' abuse in his jurisdiction should have cropped up on this of all days was just plain bad luck. Uday was to be transferred from his present position to take over as deputy commissioner of police, Crime Branch. Technically the new posting was not a promotion, nor was it a more glamorous assignment. But it afforded Uday the opportunity to be a real policeman again. He'd had enough of districts. Most of the time, it seemed to him, he was like a counsellor, negotiating between warring factions. No more playing community cop to criminal politicians and their hoodlums, and eating cheap sweets at their gatherings. Now he could go arrest the bastards.

And then there was the tip-off, not really concrete information but a sort of murmur that Uday had picked up. If true, he would need the resources of the Crime Branch. The final chapter of his policing career had arrived. How he would be remembered depended on what happened in the next few months. Uday Kumar was not planning on a quiet exit.

2

'Is the boy still there?' Amir Akhtar asked the receptionist. It was 2.15, and the chief reporter of the *Express* was thinking of lunch.

'Yes,' came the reply over the phone. 'He hasn't left the sofa at all.'

'In half an hour, if he is around, send him in.'

Amir stepped out of his cramped cabin into the reporting section, now empty. Even if they were not working on stories, he encouraged his team to be out during the day. The reporters were his eyes and ears, and Amir encouraged their presence on the city's streets. 'If you want to fool around, do it outside,' he would say.

He bent down and touched his toes, feeling the hamstring stretch. As he walked towards the toilets, Amir could see the boy ... what was his name ... sitting on a sofa, reading the newspapers. He paused and stared at the face – young and earnest – and felt a stab of irritation. The editorial meeting in the morning had not gone smoothly and on top of that, the editor, Mihir Ghosh, was trying to saddle him with this boy. He wanted experienced hands; not eager faces, fresh out of college, wanting a revolution. 'I want to make a difference' or such claptrap during an interview meant instant rejection in Amir's mind.

Apart from Vivek Sethi, his senior crime reporter who had

recently put in his papers, for two years now there had been
zero defections from Amir's team, which finally resembled a
settled unit.

He liked Vivek, but the notice period was a strain for both
men. He was infuriated to discover that Vivek had failed to visit
the site of a double murder in south Delhi last night. His report
read like it had been filched from a TV bulletin: short, sketchy
and sensational.

This sort of sloppiness stood out in a newspaper known for
its sound investigative journalism. The *Express*'s reputation had
been built on the back of the city reporting team, which Amir
had headed for the past six years. His benchmark for a story
was simple. 'If your article catches the eye of the editor of the
Times of India, you have done your job,' Amir told his reporters.
'Only fools write for ordinary people. You want to be read by
journalists; not shopkeepers.'

Amir came out of the toilet, turned to see the boy still sitting
there, and headed for his cabin, feeling guilty. The chap probably
hadn't eaten.

Settling back in his chair, Amir picked up the CV he had been
ignoring on his desk. Abhishek Dutta was twenty-four. His early
education had been in Benares, at the government-run Kendriya
Vidyalaya. To get through those institutions you need to be
tough, Amir thought, and examined the photograph. This one
looked like a softie: wide-set eyes, narrow angular face, a mop
of jet-black hair and a fair complexion. Abhishek had graduated
with honours in history from Delhi University's Hindu College.
'Ah, my alma mater,' Amir noted. Work experience … a subeditor
at *Secure Now* … what was that … a security magazine? He
tossed the CV to one side, losing interest, and turned back to
his computer.

'Good afternoon, sir.'

Amir jumped. He turned to see Abhishek Dutta standing by the entrance to his cabin. The receptionist should have warned him before sending the boy in.

Abhishek was taller than he had expected, with a vulnerable look about him. Chicks must dig this guy, was Amir's first thought. He looks like he needs mothering.

'Yes?' he said aloud.

'I am Abhishek Dutta, sir. Mr Ghosh asked me to meet you.'

'Yes, yes. He told me. Sorry, it took me a while. I have looked at your CV. I don't have anything for you right now, but perhaps in a while. I shall keep the CV with me.' He reached for the document on the table. 'Your number is here, right? I will call you if something comes up.' Amir avoided eye contact, wishing that the boy would leave.

'Sir, if I could just have a moment,' Abhishek said, refusing to disappear.

Amir was forced to look up, and felt guilty again. 'Sit, sit,' he said resignedly. 'Tell me.'

The boy spoke in a rushed eager voice, persistent and believable. He described his stint at the security magazine and how, though designated a subeditor, he handled virtually all the production. He researched, edited and proofread stories and even made the pages. There was just no one else. But he felt he was stagnating. There was not much more he could learn at the magazine and anyway, he really, really wanted to be a reporter; not sit at a desk.

Amir knew he should not encourage this keen young man. He should just hear him out and let him leave. 'So what do you think is the difference between a subeditor and a reporter?' he heard himself say. 'Not the technical difference – one goes out and reports, the other produces. Tell me why you feel that you are more suited to being a reporter.' He couldn't believe he was engaging in this conversation; he had no intention of hiring the boy.

'You know, sir,' Abhishek began tentatively, 'I think there is one fundamental difference between subeditors and reporters. A subeditor gets life insurance, pays bills on time, checks for the best mortgage rates. A reporter is a bit more reckless.'

The old journalist laughed loudly. What cheek! 'Did you think of this line before you came here? Or did you hear it in a trashy Hollywood war reporters' film?' he asked, not in an unfriendly manner.

Abhishek, embarrassed, was beginning to explain himself when he was cut short by the appearance of a man in his mid-thirties, with a round amiable face, a receding hairline and a slight paunch. He leaned against the flimsy wooden partition that marked Amir's domain from the rest of the reporting room.

'What, boss?' The man addressed Amir, holding out a piece of paper between finger and thumb with obvious disdain. 'I am your senior crime reporter and you assign me regular press conferences. What will everyone think? The paper's image – you must think of the paper's image.'

Amir, who had been leaning back in his chair, sprang up, surprising Abhishek with his agility. 'Do they tell you how bad the paper looks when our senior crime reporter fails to get to the spot of a double murder, Vivek?' Amir towered over the man.

'I didn't miss the story, no?' Vivek smirked. 'Young reporters are enthusiastic. We are getting old.'

'You are also getting fat. Now leave me alone,' Amir said, snatching the paper from him and handing it to Abhishek as Vivek retreated. 'Go, cover this and file a report. I'll see you in the evening,' he told the surprised boy, and turned back to his computer screen.

The young man stepped out into the reporting area feeling light-headed. He tried to make sense of the words on the paper in his hands: press conference ... police headquarters ... betting. He needed to sit down and gather his thoughts, but he wasn't sure where. The reporting room had started to fill up. Vivek was lounging in front of a computer, a game of Pac-Man playing on auto mode on his screen. A female reporter, about the same age as Vivek, was reading the newspapers, feet up on a chair. Another woman, not much older than himself, was writing in her notepad. She looked up and smiled.

'Hello. So you got an assignment?' she asked kindly.

Abhishek nodded.

'Let's see.' She took the paper. 'Take a seat. By the way, I am Maya,' she muttered.

Abhishek turned to pull up a chair and said an awkward hello. He sat and looked around, savouring the feeling of being in a reporting unit. He took in everything: the dozen worn chairs; the desks burdened with hundreds of newspapers; the bags, books, notepads, pens and pencils strewn chaotically, belonging to no one in particular. The room was badly lit and there were no windows, but to Abhishek, rejoicing in the prospect of covering an event, infrastructural flaws which reporters bitched about every day simply didn't exist.

'It's easy,' Maya was telling him. 'Just go to the police headquarters and meet the PRO, Vikram Singh. He will tell you what to do. Do you know where the building is?'

'No,' Abhishek said quietly, 'I don't.'

'Ai boss, you don't know where the police headquarters is and you are being asked to cover crime?' Vivek laughed, swivelling his chair to face them. Abhishek, smiling hesitantly, was wondering how to answer him when Amir shouted from his cabin, 'Vivek, have you changed your mind? You want to cover the PC?'

'Arre boss, no, no,' Vivek shouted back merrily. 'Just wondering at my replacements.'

'Maya, you come into my cabin and let that boy be. Let him figure it out,' Amir called again.

She jumped up, winking at Abhishek, and walked off, her long skirt trailing only slightly on the floor.

Setting off to cover his first press conference, the morning's five-hour wait no longer mattered. At the start of the day, Abhishek had told himself he would not leave without meeting Amir Akhtar. He had met the editor of the newspaper, Mihir Ghosh, the day before when he had come to the office, clutching a letter of reference from his father's friend, a correspondent at the *Times*. Mr Ghosh had called him in and after a chat told him that in most cases he didn't hire Bengalis, fearing charges of nepotism, nor anyone who came to him with reference letters.

'I cannot give you a job but you will meet the chief reporter, Amir Akhtar. Come tomorrow at nine,' he had said.

Abhishek felt grateful for the opportunity and was determined to make it work. After graduating, he had spent a year selling washing machines, before joining *Secure Now*. He had stuck at the mind-numbing job for two years – he needed the money – but in an India changing at a frenetic pace, he was afraid of being left behind.

It was past three in the afternoon, the winter sun shining weakly through central Delhi's smog-filled air, when Abhishek Dutta stepped out of the newspaper office into the street's cacophony and started walking the short distance to the police headquarters.

His stomach, acquiescent all day, now protested at the lack of attention. Until just a few months back, Bahadur Shah Zafar Marg, like most of Delhi's working districts, had offered a delectable array of affordable street food. In the run up to the Commonwealth Games, in their sanitizing zeal, the government had managed to rinse away most of these eateries, and Abhishek searched in vain for a samosa or a kulche-chhole stall. People hurried along, their recently retrieved woollen jumpers – pink, blue, scarlet and green – adding a splash of gaiety to this office stretch.

Buses raged past, unmindful of the limitations of lane driving or the cars and bikes that wove between. Auto drivers casually blocked the road, their necks craning out of their vehicles, negotiating prices with potential passengers. Having only recently left the quiet environs of the university where he was camping in a friend's hostel room, Abhishek was keenly alive to the bustling exchanges of central Delhi.

He turned left at the ITO intersection. A hundred metres ahead, thrusting into the sky like a giant phallus, was the police headquarters; and across the road, shorter and stockier, stood the income tax office. In the by-lane adjoining it, Abhishek spotted a few surviving food stalls. He stood with others at the traffic light, waiting for the crowd to reach a critical mass that would then surge forward, arms outstretched, to stop the rush of speeding vehicles with a collective willpower.

Once across, Abhishek approached a man sitting on a wooden cart, frying omelettes and serving them with sliced white bread.

'What will you have?' the man asked, looking up.

'There's not much choice, is there?' Abhishek replied with a smile. 'I'll have the bread and omelette.'

'Ah, but you must look closely, my friend. I have a deep-fried omelette, a lightly fried one, a spicy omelette that will make your loins tingle, and a bland one that will cure your stomach bug. The list is long. My menu is like the human body, babu – you see one man, but the soul has many colours.'

'You are right,' Abhishek told the street philosopher. 'So let me have the spicy one.'

'Sure.' The omelettewallah seemed happy with his order. 'It is a young man's choice. Where are you from?'

'Benares.'

'I knew it.' The vendor's smile widened. 'Me too. There is a smell of the old city and something of the River Ganga in you.' He joined his hands and touched them to his forehead at the mention of the sacred river, then continued, 'I never talk to Dilliwallahs. Their soul has only one colour – that of money.'

The sandwich was soon ready and Abhishek ate quickly.

'You haven't eaten all morning, have you?' the vendor asked. Abhishek nodded with his mouth full. 'I'll make another for you. It will be quick. I know you're in a rush.'

Abhishek looked at the man again, hunched over his stove, and tried to guess his age. His hair was jet-black, but the streaks of white in his stubble and the lines across his face gave an impression of years. Oblivious to the cold, he was dressed in a singlet and a faded lungi.

As he ate the second sandwich, Abhishek asked the man how long he had been in Delhi.

'Seven months. But I am going back soon. My family is still in Benares.'

Abhishek wanted to ask more, but refrained. He knew the story anyway; only the particulars would be new. It could be a daughter's wedding or a wife's illness. Sometimes the debts were inherited: a father's bereavement forcing a son's hand.

'You remind me of my son,' the omelettewallah told Abhishek as he paid. 'Come again.'

'Yes.' Abhishek nodded shyly and walked away, joining the mass effort to cross the road and heading for the police headquarters.

After a routine frisking at the fortified entrance for pedestrians, Abhishek entered a forecourt where official white Ambassadors, festooned with red lights and flags, were parked in a row. The two guards, in full police regalia and striking turbans, were clearly stationed there for ornamental purposes and paid the newcomer no attention as he headed for the door marked 'Public Relations'.

Inside the long press room, under fluorescent lights, dozens of noisy journalists lounged on fake leather sofas, awaiting the press conference. Several stood clustered around the two flat-screen televisions which shared the wall with photographs of smiling old men in khaki caps.

'Yes, sir, what can I do for you?' boomed press officer Vikram Singh, ushering Abhishek to his cabin. 'Ah,' he said after Abhishek introduced himself, 'so Vivek is too big for press conferences these days? He sends the young guns. Is this your first job?'

'Yes,' Abhishek replied, deciding neither to press the security magazine stint, nor the fact that this might be a one-assignment show.

'Excellent.' Vikram nodded at him happily.

Abhishek was unsure why his inexperience was a matter for such jubilation.

'There is an old Chinese curse, Abhishek-ji,' the PRO continued. 'It says, "May you live in interesting times." Have you heard it? No? Well, my friend, you are cursed. Anyone planning a career in media now is cursed.' The smile never left the man's face. 'Ten, perhaps fifteen, at a stretch – that was the number of journalists I used to see in a day. Now, before I get up in the morning, I have that many missed calls. But you will see the circus for yourself,' he said with an exaggerated sigh. 'Today's conference is important. You will meet a lot of people.'

One of the several phones on Vikram's desk rang and he looked displeased at being cut off mid-flow. Shrugging his shoulders at Abhishek to indicate the demands of his job, he picked up the receiver.

An orderly handed Abhishek a glass of water and as he drank, he became aware of a dangerous gurgling in his belly.

The police officer put the phone down. 'It's time. Let's get everyone to the main building for the conference. Come.' He led Abhishek back to the press room. 'The television cameras increase every day,' he said. 'Look at this crowd. Until last year we operated from a dingy one-room affair on the first floor. Then we shifted down here. But now even this doesn't seem enough. Reporters are more important than officers these days. Soon we'll have to vacate our cabins for you guys.'

At the next entrance, the guards let Abhishek through without a frisk. He did not know it then, it meant he had just entered the privileged domain of the press, which at the lower end allows for free parking, waiving of traffic fines and reserved tickets for box office hits, and at the higher end, government housing, foreign junkets and customized holidays for two.

Inside the conference room, the PRO strode to the front as Abhishek found himself a place at the back. Several dozen television teams were frenetically jostling, trying to negotiate the best possible position for their equipment. Cameramen yelled at their assistants to display channel logos prominently while placing the mikes. The reporters congregated in smaller groups.

Abhishek sat down and felt the rumble in his stomach return with increasing urgency. He cursed the vendor and the food he had so hungrily consumed a short while ago. 'That's how he gets the money to dye his hair black – cheap oil and rotten eggs. All these bloody Benarasis are the same – sweet talk and nothing else,' he thought moodily as he stared at the press handout.

The police officers arrived and Abhishek noted the ease with which the journalists mingled with them, shaking hands, slapping backs and exchanging pleasantries as they made their way towards the stage. A few minutes later, Police Commissioner V.N. Pratap made his entrance through a door adjoining the platform. The journalists immediately settled into their chairs and the cameramen conceded that no more vantage would be secured today. The press conference started a prompt ten minutes later than scheduled.

As the commissioner began speaking about Uday Kumar and his team's splendid investigation into a cricket-betting syndicate, Abhishek realized that he could hold on no longer and would have to find a loo. He rushed out of the back door and, in his hurry, collided with a young man running in from the opposite direction.

Mayank Sharma stood at the back of the conference room, trying to catch his breath. He'd left his driver at the traffic lights and sprinted all the way, hoping to catch Uday Kumar before the press conference began but the constable at the gate had held him up to check his ID. Of average height, with a pleasant unmemorable face, and body language designed to deflect attention from himself, Mayank was remembered by few. The young assistant commissioner of police, Crime Branch, preferred it that way.

'The team displayed exceptional patience in their investigation. It was thorough and meticulous,' the commissioner was telling the assembled journalists. 'They waited for months to ensure the case was watertight before making arrests.'

From the dais, Uday noticed Mayank. He whispered something to the officer by his side and slipped out of the hall.

'Sir, you were right,' Mayank said the moment they met in the corridor.

'Wait, not here.' The second floor housed the police control room, the nerve centre that monitored the 60,000-plus force, and was not the best place for a discreet conversation. Taking the young officer's arm, Uday headed towards the toilets.

Abhishek had been suffering the indignities of an upset stomach for some time and was finally emerging from his cubicle when he heard hushed voices coming from the far end of the toilet. Something in their tone made him stop, his hand on the slightly open door.

'Your tip-off … it seems that it's true,' Mayank was telling the senior police officer as they entered.

Uday held up a hand, frowning. 'Just a moment,' he warned, quickly scanning the rows of open cubicle doors. 'How are you so sure?' He looked back at Mayank sharply.

'Sir, three things. First, word has been put out for a safe house for him. I don't know where, but definitely somewhere in the city. Second, his central Delhi associates have recently been receiving unusually large sums of back-channel hawala money. Third, his operations in Singapore are winding down. It all adds up to what you had told me: Babloo Shankar is planning a comeback.'

There was a pause. Abhishek remained still. Instinct told him that he couldn't afford to be discovered.

'Okay.' He heard the other voice again. 'Control your excitement. This must not get out. Absolutely no one in the police should hear of this. Do you understand, Mayank?'

'Yes, sir.'

'I'll be posted to the Crime Branch within a week and we'll work on this together. Come, I have to get back now.'

Once sure that he was alone, Abhishek emerged from the toilets and returned to the conference room. He tried to appear nonchalant as he reclaimed his seat in the back row. On stage, the commissioner was holding forth on the menace of cricket betting and the virtues of his officers. Abhishek made a few notes.

Policemen: Uday Kumar, Mayank (confirmed tip-off)

Babloo Shankar planning a comeback.

Half an hour later the press conference concluded and refreshments were served. Abhishek, mindful of his belly, left quietly. There would be ample time to meet his fellow reporters, if he could keep this job. And with the information he had, he thought he just might.

On the street, Abhishek hunched his shoulders against the early evening chill. If something came of this, he would buy that grimy omelettewallah a bottle of hair dye himself.

3

Uday Kumar sped away from the police headquarters, satisfied with the evening's outcome: his new posting was confirmed, the press conference had gone off without any glitches, and Ranbir's indiscretion seemed buried. To top it all, three weeks after the first tip-off, Mayank Sharma had told him that Babloo Shankar was indeed coming back.

Uday was glad he had asked Mayank to work with him. The boy had trained under him and was efficient and hard-working. He was also scrupulously honest, but one could work around that. Within a very short time in the Crime Branch, Mayank had earned a reputation for keeping his mouth shut and his ear to the ground. But what should Uday tell him to listen for?

He made a phone call to a friend in Mumbai, Sunil Shinde, who worked with the Research and Analysis Wing, the government's external intelligence unit. As part of its varied remit, from masterminding bomb blasts in Karachi to fiddling with governments in Nepal, the RAW also kept an eye on expatriate underworld dons. Uday told Shinde what he had just heard from Mayank.

'Let me call you back. I'll see what I can find,' his friend told him.

Uday stretched himself out on the back seat, trying to soothe the nagging ache in his lower spine when he heard his call sign.

The radio operator sitting in the front told him that the deputy commissioner of the neighbouring district, Vishnu Gupta, was asking for him. 'Sir, Charlie 1 calling, sir.'

'Charlie 1, November 1, please go ahead. Over,' Uday replied.

'November 1, Charlie 1,' began Gupta, 'I have a demonstration tomorrow which will pass Golcha cinema and move towards Red Fort. They should reach your district by afternoon. Over.'

'Roger. Arrangements made. Out.'

Uday returned the handset, cursing Gupta under his breath. 'Worthless. All this man does is police procession and weigh his options for better postings.'

Even mundane exchanges with officers from the Central services irritated Uday. Many of them, peers and seniors included, had trained under him, a man from a state cadre, the perennial second rung. He knew their worth well, including this bhenchod Gupta, twenty years younger, but today holding the same rank. In a year or two, Uday would have to report to the dimwit.

'Yesterday's kids,' he would thunder to his junior officers, 'chhokras, here with their smart English accents and degrees in history and sociology, talking down to me, Uday Kumar! Half of these motherfuckers begged me to train them.'

In his early pursuit of a career in the Central services, Uday was no different from the objects of his derision. In Nehru's India of the previous century, such a career was one of the few ways to avoid social obscurity. For those who got through, a world of opportunity awaited. The public school–educated envisioned a life of wining and dining diplomacy, while entry to the administrative or police services was the small-town boy's wet dream. As a reward for years of swotting history books and memorizing obscure events and facts, young men – and the occasional woman – were allowed to rule the lives of thousands.

Uday did not make it to this top tier and, instead, had to settle for the state services. The going rate for his dowry tripled nevertheless and his father, a clerk in a district court in Bihar, could not understand his son's disappointment. 'There is money in this service too. After all, it's the same uniform, no?' he ranted.

'Yes, same khaki uniform,' Uday used to think bitterly, 'just not the same respect. We are the untouchables, the scheduled castes, and these bastards from the Central services are the Brahmins.'

Uday was known as the Dirty Harry of Delhi Police; to be called upon when things needed cleaning up. What was in college a derogatory reference to his Bihari background – 'Fucking Hari' – now evoked Hollywood's most notorious cop. His humble origin and natural flamboyance found resonance in a nickname that both shamed and pleased him.

Back at the office, Uday took a shower and changed into civvies. He helped himself to the pakore Mishra-ji laid out for him and started surfing the news channels.

'Did they use my bytes?' he asked his PA.

'Yes, sir, most channels have used at least one.'

'And the Ranbir story? Any channel running that?'

'Three of the Hindi ones, sir. But that's all.'

Uday nodded. Good. 'I want to finish all pending files tonight,' he said. Seeing his PA's stricken face, Uday added, 'You can go home. From tomorrow we have other work to do.'

Shortly after Mishra-ji had left, Shinde called back with information: Babloo Shankar would send in associates first. Uday had a hunch he would. Putting the phone down, he sat for a while, thinking through what he had just heard. For now his quarry had changed. Still lethal, but at least she was easy on the eye. Better to run after a Madame X than that old cripple, Babloo.

It had been a quiet news day and Amir was looking forward to an evening at the Press Club. He would do one final check of the city pages, and then leave.

'But how can you change Proteas to Protease,' Rajat Sharma, the sports reporter, was demanding of a young subeditor at the desk.

'I did a spellcheck and that is what was suggested.' The girl shrugged.

'Proteas is the South African cricket team. What the fuck is Protease?'

'I don't know. The spellcheck suggested it,' the girl explained patiently.

Amir suppressed a laugh as he ambled over. Two of the pages were done and he signed the printed copies, marking his approval.

'Call me if you need anything. I'll be at the club,' he told the desk editor.

'This is the only desk which inserts mistakes,' Rajat said as he walked outside with Amir. 'Perfectly clean copy, man, and look at what they do. It had my byline on it. I look like a fool and I am beginning to feel like one.'

'That's what happens when you get interns for free. They protease you,' Amir said, grinning. 'Come to the club. I'll buy you a drink.'

Amir had reached the stairs when Abhishek caught up with him. 'Sir,' he called out.

'Oh, yes, hi.' Amir looked back without stopping. 'Quite a good report. It's being carried.'

'Thank you, sir. But I was going to ask you what time to come in tomorrow.'

Horribly persistent, Amir thought as they descended the

stairs. 'Look, there's no vacancy right now. Why don't I let you know when something comes up?'

The night air was crisp. A parking attendant brought the car out and Amir was just getting in when Abhishek lightly touched him on the arm. 'Sir, I think I've got a big story.'

Oh Christ, he is one of those, Amir thought, impatiently making to close the door. 'What is it? I am getting late.'

'Sir, I've heard that someone called Babloo Shankar is coming back.'

Amir looked away and stared ahead at the road. This was a joke; this boy was a joke. His mind reeled. How did he know? What did he know? Who was this boy? Amir tried to calm himself and took a deep breath. He saw that his knuckles were white from clutching the steering wheel. He turned to look at the young man and registered the slightly quizzical expression on his face. He had no idea, Amir decided. 'Get in,' he told Abhishek, feeling an overwhelming urge to smoke.

Another vehicle started honking behind them. Amir put the car into gear and slid away, and then turned into the first side alley.

'Yes, tell me,' he said, stopping the car.

Abhishek related the information precisely, detailing in particular the snatches of conversation between the two policemen. Amir did not smile at the indelicate reason for his eavesdropping, the young man noted.

Amir heard him out to the end of his story. A bike was coming towards them down the alley, its headlights on full glare, blinding both of them. Amir waited for it to pass. Then he spoke slowly, carefully. 'If anyone – and I mean anyone – gets to know of this, your career in journalism in this city is over. Rest assured about that. For now, come to the office tomorrow. No promises, but perhaps an internship can be arranged.'

Abhishek got out of the car and Amir drove straight to the Press Club where his two pegs of rum and water were waiting.

The young man went back for his scooter, wondering what he had stumbled across. He was certain Amir Akhtar had looked scared.

Uday Kumar's office was situated in a part of Delhi where the frenzy of the new city had yet to invade. The area was protected by a large green buffer, the Ridge, and the aged buildings of the university slowed the onslaught of development, their oldness shaming even the most heartless bulldozer. Until recently, the chief minister's offices were situated here and the area remained close to the corridors of power. But it moved at a pace that suggested scepticism towards the world-class city baying at its borders.

Sunil Mishra had enjoyed his three-year posting here and was sorry it was coming to an end. He did not like the police headquarters where his boss Uday Kumar would now be based as DCP, Crime Branch. The intrigues of that monstrous ten-storey building, with its tiny cubicle-like offices for people of his rank, suffocated him. He was thinking despondently of his future in a cramped room, the inevitable media glare of the posting and his boss's penchant for it, when somebody knocked at the door.

Mishra jumped up and extended his hand, smiling broadly at the man who walked in. 'The sun has arrived from the west today. You have come to our humble abode,' he told a beaming Amir Akhtar.

'Mishra-ji, it is you who have forgotten us, the downtrodden of this world,' Amir replied, seizing the proffered hand with both of his.

'Please sit. What can I get you? Some tea or coffee?'

Amir liked the diminutive mild-mannered man, and on another day would have gladly sat down to tea. But this was not the moment. 'No, Mishra-ji. Thanks. I need to meet Uday immediately.'

The deputy commissioner was in a good mood that morning. Two new trainees had landed up and he was giving them his initiatory talk with relish. He loved doing this: shaking up the young men, shocking their sensibilities, knocking off some of the official jargon they were fed at the academy. He had asked them the three things required to be a good policeman, and was roaring with laughter at their replies. 'Which motherfucker told you that?' Uday howled, doubling up and slapping the table. 'Keen eye? Did you say keen eye? Keen eye for what, you idiots?' He loved to see them squirm. 'In Uday Kumar's school you will be trained in only one exercise: how to extend the length of your tongue. Ask me why.'

The trainees remained silent.

'Go on, ask me,' Uday encouraged.

'Why, sir?' one of them murmured.

'So that you can lick the asses of your senior officers well!' Before he could enjoy their shocked reactions, the phone rang. 'Amir Akhtar? Yes, send him in.'

The timing was uncanny. Uday had not met Amir in a long time. He could not possibly know anything.

'Akhtar mian, you look good. What magic potion do you take and who administers it?' Despite his anxiety, Uday grinned with the pleasure of seeing an old associate.

'The good fortune of bachelorhood. Keeps you fit and running. How are you?' Amir said, settling himself down on a chair and crossing his legs. He always did this, Uday thought, as he watched Amir make himself comfortable. It was his way of dealing with power, this easy casualness. Uday remembered the first time he had met Amir at the residence of a senior policeman. While he, a young officer, had sat on the edge of the sofa, ill at ease, Amir had sat just like this, smoking a cigarette.

'Chai?' Uday asked, and Amir nodded. 'Two teas. One without milk for sahab,' Uday instructed the orderly.

Amir looked at the trainee officers who were still standing to attention.

Uday noted the look. 'Okay, dismissed, boys. Your first class is over. The sooner you forget your academy manuals, the better.'

He was shaking his head in silent laughter as they stepped out, expecting Amir to share his amusement. It was a universal phenomenon: the contempt the experienced had for the young, and the derision with which the youth regarded the old.

'Is Babloo back?' Amir's voice cut through Uday's attempt at hilarity.

Uday, caught by surprise, looked blankly at Amir. Tea was brought in at that moment, giving the cop time to gather his thoughts. He concentrated on preparing it, while his guest sat observing him.

Amir knew from his friend's reaction that it was true; Abhishek Dutta was right.

'Don't get into it again, Amir,' Uday said finally, handing him a cup.

'That's not possible, Uday. We both know that.'

'Why?' Uday snapped. 'It's not your job. I would not go after him either if I were not in this damned uniform. We have both spent too many years on this. Look at what it has done to you and your marriage. And now you want more? Let it go, man.'

Amir quietly sipped his tea as Uday went on. Arguing with

a man who had already lost the argument was pointless. It was easier to let him say his piece and feel the better for it. Amir's gaze shifted to the board behind Uday as he spoke. It displayed the names of all the officers who had held the post since 1946, a year before India gained Independence. He knew all the serving policemen and quite a few of those who had retired.

'You are not listening, are you, Amir?' Uday asked.

'I am,' Amir replied. 'Thank you very much for your concern about my soul and my family life, but stop the bullshit, Uday. If I don't get involved, every presswallah in this city will. How will you get Babloo Shankar then?'

'So, it's blackmail, Amir?' Uday said softly. 'You know the consequences of blackmailing a Delhi Police officer?'

Amir kept silent.

'So what do you want?' Uday finally gave in.

'For now, a promise that you will share with me every detail of what is happening. I will activate my people too. I haven't lost my source base completely,' the newsman replied.

Uday paused for a while, working out how much to say. 'We know very little. We have heard a rumour that he is coming back. Still unconfirmed. I have put someone on the job. But really, we don't know much right now,' he said, hoping he sounded truthful. 'By the way, how do you know this?' Uday added, after a pause.

'In case you have forgotten, I am still a reporter,' Amir said, smiling now. Even after three decades in the job, he enjoyed flummoxing a police officer.

The phone rang.

'Five minutes,' Uday said before turning back to Amir. 'Okay. You find out what you can and get back to me. I'll see what comes up.'

'Who is this new young man you have put on the job? Mayank is the name, if I am not mistaken,' Amir said casually, standing up.

Uday looked surprised, then smiled. 'Your sources are very good indeed. Come, I'll see you out now.' He led the journalist to the door. 'Just one thing, Amir,' he said as they shook hands, 'I hope we've both realized that there is no point being brave. It leads to mistakes.'

Amir smiled. 'Bravery was your baby, Uday. I'm glad you've grown up. I'll call you. Bye.'

Abhishek had been in the office since 10 a.m. but, without Amir's presence, was not allowed into the editorial meeting. Maya, kind and mildly flirtatious, found him a desktop on which he was trying to figure out the mystery of Babloo Shankar.

A Wikipedia page provided the basics: Babloo was wanted by the police of three Indian states for several high-profile kidnappings in the 1980s and '90s. The Central Bureau of Investigation had issued letter rogatories against him and he was on Interpol's most-wanted list. He fled the country in 1996 after a shootout with the police in which he was severely injured. A bullet, still lodged in his spine, had paralysed him permanently from the waist down. He was reported to be staying on a yacht off the Singapore coastline. Not much was known about his present activities.

Other websites detailed the kidnappings, Babloo's background and the profiles of his victims. Abhishek made notes.

The notorious kidnapper was born in eastern Uttar Pradesh in 1963, Abhishek read in a mildly hagiographical website, indiasmostwanted.com. His brother was the violent and dreaded gangster, Arun Shankar. Their father was a policeman in Azamgarh, a town where the distinction between cops and robbers vanished in the business of extortions, political kidnappings and gunrunning. Given his lineage, Babloo's choice of career was unremarkable, though his crimes were not.

In his early years he had fought against what seemed preordained. To Abhishek's surprise, Babloo had studied aeronautical engineering in Soviet Russia, had a Lebanese girlfriend and was hoping to get a job in Cairo when things took a turn. 'Destiny,' the web page stated, 'would not be denied.'

In the winter of 1984, Babloo returned from Moscow to visit his family. As he came out of Lucknow airport, six gunmen fired at him. Although he was unarmed, Babloo managed to escape, crawling through drainpipes that were laid outside the airport.

He never returned to Russia. Instead, he moved to Delhi the following year. Six kidnappings later, Babloo Shankar was the first organized gangster Delhi Police had encountered.

Just when he had made a name for himself, Babloo vanished. His brother was killed in gang warfare and was found in his car with five bullets pumped into his chest and two in the head. One eye was gouged out and three fingers of his left hand were chopped off. The police started to believe that without Arun's protection, Babloo too might have been killed.

He re-emerged in 1993 and in just three years carried out a dozen recorded kidnappings in Delhi and Mumbai. His victims included hoteliers, politicians, diamond merchants and film producers. The crimes unnerved the police, but they were even more worried that many were paying ransom to avoid being kidnapped.

By 1996, when Babloo fled the country, such was his repute

that several small-time criminals were collecting protection money by pretending to be part of his gang.

Babloo's character, Abhishek read, had one remarkable trait: despite his fairly prolific run, he apparently never used physical violence. His victims, except in the last and final kidnapping, had always returned unharmed once the ransom amount was delivered. And they always refused to give a police statement.

'Lunch?' Maya Srivastava was standing by his side. Abhishek hurriedly closed the page.

'Yes, please,' he answered. 'I'm quite hungry.'

'Good. Do you like south Indian food?' she asked and he nodded, quickly erasing his viewing history and shutting down the computer.

'Arre boss,' Vivek exclaimed as they walked past the reception. 'Second day and you are out with the girls. Reporter or Romeo?'

'Fuck off, Vivek,' Maya laughed at him. 'Why don't you do some work.' She turned to Abhishek. 'Don't mind him. He is a bastard. All journalists generally are – the good ones, at least,' she said, as they descended the steps and headed towards the restaurant.

They had barely settled down at a table when Maya called out to a young man whom Abhishek had met briefly in the reporting room the day before.

'Rahul!'

Rahul walked up to their table and dropped his bag. 'I will order some food and be back,' he said.

'He is the nicest guy in our department,' Maya told Abhishek. 'Not my type, a bit rustic, but has a refreshing honesty. You should become friends with him.'

'Is the food good?' Rahul asked, squeezing into the seat beside Abhishek who was enjoying his lemon rice with curd.

'Yes.' He nodded.

'Okay, first rule of survival in journalism. When your seniors ask you about food and it's good, hand over the fork.'

'Learn some manners, Rahul,' Maya teased.

'You learn manners,' he retorted through a mouthful of rice. 'I am hungry.'

As they ate, Maya and Rahul discussed the dismal facilities and pay at the *Express*, perhaps for Abhishek's benefit; a sort of performance to warn the wannabe.

Journalists kept approaching their table to say hello. 'What's happening? Is everything routine? Any exclusives?'

Neither side gave anything away. 'Nope, nothing new. You?'

After the third such drill, Rahul turned to Abhishek and said, 'I can bet that at least one of these bastards will file an exclusive story tomorrow, and knows it. But look at their innocent faces.'

'Rahul,' Maya retorted, 'would you tell them if you were doing one?'

'No,' he admitted and then laughed. 'We're a bunch of liars. We only tell the truth to the world.'

Maya rose to leave. 'I have an interview in twenty minutes. See you guys at the office.'

Over coffee, Rahul gave Abhishek some advice. 'You could tell boss that you want to cover crime. Vivek is leaving.'

'Really? Can I?'

'No harm in trying. Mind you, you'll have to fill Vivek's shoes and he is absolutely the best when he wants to be. But talk to Amir. See how he responds.'

As they walked back to the office, Abhishek mulled over Rahul's frank advice. If Babloo Shankar's impending return could secure him an internship, might it not make him a crime reporter?

4

In 1982, when Delhi was preparing to host the Asian Games, workers from across the country and beyond its borders had swarmed to the city to meet the construction demands. After a week or two of national euphoria and pride, the athletes left. The event was declared a success by the state, the officials packed their bags, the guests and spectators returned home, and the everyday business of the city resumed. But there were many who could not go back.

The invisible workers stayed on, tackling different hurdles and running other races, building their uncertain lives on the banks of a moribund river, not very far from the newspaper offices. Known as Yamuna Pushta, a shanty town grew, housing at its peak, over a hundred thousand people.

Thirty years later, another sporting event, the Commonwealth Games, displaced them. A six-lane expressway and multi-storey buildings now stood like forgotten memorials to the tin and tarpaulin shacks and the kachcha roads. What took three decades to build vanished in four years of bulldozing, authorized by numerous court orders and choreographed by a powerful state.

The evicted residents of the Yamuna Pushta scattered to the city's outskirts. Shorn of a protective community, raucous neighbours, the mindful eyes of uncles and aunts, and robbed of livelihoods, the poor became poorer, petty thieves became criminals and criminals aspired to be gangsters.

Matera was born in the Pushta and lived there for twenty-five years with his parents and six siblings before their exile to the eastern stretches of the city, in a wretched, dark room where his mother cursed all day and cried through the night. But he wasn't the sort of young man to be deterred by a bit of bad kismet or government brutality. His last eight years of work – from running errands to enforcing orders and acting as part-time strongman – had finally resulted in a promotion. He and two associates were now in charge of daily operations at the satta – the betting centre at Kucha Chalan in Chandni Chowk. It was the business hub of gambling in the city and Salim Khan, the boss, dropped by regularly. Matera's hard work was being noticed. For this small-time crook, things were starting to happen.

Today, he was looking forward to seeing Amir bhai and had taken an hour off from work to meet him at a tea stall opposite Jama Masjid. He walked towards the mosque through the lanes of the old city, eager to tell his benefactor the stories of his dazzling rise.

Amir headed to the meeting place, thinking about his meeting with Uday. His old friend was hiding something, he was sure, but perhaps not very much.

After what he had heard from Abhishek the previous night, Amir had called Matera. If there was anyone in Delhi who would know of Babloo's return, it was Salim Khan, Matera's boss and satta king of north India.

Amir decided to take the metro. In the early afternoon, the crowds were thin and the ride would give him time to decide how much he could tell Matera. He liked the boy, but was well aware that young criminals were boastful.

Amir had first met Matera, then barely out of his teens, at a police station in south Delhi. The journalist, serving out his stint in television, was researching a story on gangs that specialized in car theft. Matera and four others had been arrested by the Special Cell, and Amir had arranged to meet them in the lock-up to find out about their modus operandi.

Unlike the sullen hardened criminals who surrounded him, Matera was a born storyteller and Amir enjoyed his company. After his release from Tihar Jail a year later, Matera sought out Amir and took the journalist to his chawl in Yamuna Pushta, introducing him to his extended family. He later told Amir, 'Your coming made me a hero. Everyone knew you from television.'

Amir kept in touch with Matera, advising him and once in a while intervening on his behalf with the police. While not exactly an informant, Matera kept him regaled with stories of the dark underbelly of Old Delhi whenever they met. His requests were never outlandish and Amir accommodated most. This was the first time the reporter was going to ask for payback.

After the calm interiors of the metro, Chandni Chowk was a medley of a thousand clashing tunes, each playing to an oblivious audience. Amir stood fascinated, remembering it all. The road was jammed with rickshaws, cycles, scooters and bikes. Two cars had strayed in and their drivers leaned out of the side windows, urging on the traffic through which children dodged. Amir watched a group of schoolgirls walking along the middle of the street, engrossed in conversation, paying no heed to the indignation they caused. An auto-rickshaw came up behind them and honked. One of the girls turned around and wagged her finger at him imperiously before turning back to her friends and their gossip. Amir smiled at the audacity.

On both sides of the street, there were shops laden with food, utensils, items of clothing. Several hawkers pushed their wares. Cobblers, locksmiths and booksellers fought over pavement space for which pedestrians had long ago abandoned hope. Amid the spectacle Amir observed the generational traders, assured of the value of their wares, sedate and unmindful to the demands of a quick sell.

Suddenly a shifty-eyed man wrapped in a shawl appeared at his side. 'Dollar, sir? Dollar change?' he whispered conspiratorially, flashing a few bills. Amir shrugged him off and walked briskly towards Jama Masjid.

There was a time not so long ago when Amir frequented these parts after nightfall, once other restaurants in the city closed their doors. The street that led from the old mosque towards the Red Fort served meat and fluffy white naans at prices unthinkable anywhere else in the capital. They catered to the city's night prowlers who sat on roadside benches devouring spicy lamb keema and tandoori chicken, washing it down with rum and Coke.

These days, Amir made it a point to be home before midnight and rationed his drinking to not more than three pegs of his favourite Old Monk rum. 'I hardly get out any more,' he thought as he hurried through a lane barely three metres wide. A boy grabbed at his ankle. 'Shoeshine, sir?' Amir pulled away and kept walking, weaving through the men and women, the children returning from school and the occasional auto that muscled past.

On the increasingly rare occasions that Amir crossed the invisible line of the society he inhabited – from the cappuccino chains to the five-rupee tea stalls – he felt a pang of disgust with himself. In bureau meetings he bitterly complained about reporters who viewed the city from a bird's-eye perspective,

and yet he risked joining their ranks. 'If you don't know
what ordinary people feel when bus fares go up, do television
journalism. I need reporters, not Honda owners,' he would rage.
Amir knew that he too was losing touch and his outbursts were
perhaps as much against himself as at his reporting unit. 'Maybe,
Mihir-da,' he confided in his editor, 'the real city is the one which
my journalists operate in. I am the one who is in the wrong.'

He spotted Matera through the flow of traffic and waved.
The boy's hair grew longer every month, even as he got skinnier,
Amir thought. By the time he crossed the street, his tea was ready
and Matera was standing next to him, proffering a Classic Mild.

'No ... Given up smoking,' Amir said, holding the boy
affectionately by the shoulders.

Matera was astonished. 'Getting old, bhai?'

'Keeping young.' Amir took the cup of tea and greeted the
shop owner as Matera and he sat down. 'How are you?' he asked
Matera.

'I am fine,' Matera replied, and quickly launched into details
of his new job and career prospects.

Amir listened, enjoying the stories and waiting for the right
opening.

Matera began to speak about Salim Khan. 'He comes regularly,
in fact almost every day. I report directly to him now. I'd never
realized how much running a satta business could teach you.
Things you would never get to learn in banks or in the software
business. It teaches you about human beings, you know, people
– ordinary people and also the big people. All types come.'

'Tell me about Salim,' Amir stepped in.

'First-class human being, Amir bhai. But also very dangerous.
He is respected in all circles, you know. Even by the police.
People know him.'

'Matera,' Amir interjected, 'has anything changed in recent times? Anyone new coming?'

Matera looked at Amir, one eyebrow raised. 'New? No. What do you mean?'

'Nothing,' Amir replied. 'Listen to me and listen carefully. 'Who has kept you out of jail all these years? Who has protected you?'

'You have,' Matera replied without a pause. 'I live because you have your hand on my head. What is it, Amir bhai?' he asked, concern spreading over his face.

'I don't know yet.' Amir drained his cup and stood up. 'I want you to be with Salim as much as you can and just let me know if there's anything out of the ordinary. Anything. Can you do that?'

'I can, but tell me what's going on.' His curiosity was piqued and Amir knew that if not checked immediately, the boy would spread rumours.

'If even a word of this gets out, Matera, I will cut your tongue off,' the newsman warned.

Ever dramatic, Matera stuck out his tongue and made a slicing gesture. 'If I speak a word, Amir bhai, I'll bring it to you myself.'

Amir tried to pay for the tea, but the stall owner waved a hand. 'No, no, sir. Our honour that you have come.'

'I'll go with you to the metro station,' Matera offered, but Amir shook his head. 'You are a big criminal now, bastard. Can't be seen with the likes of you.'

'Amir bhai, take care. Khuda hafiz,' Matera said, his face flushed with pride at the compliment.

Mayank Sharma gathered the papers and files he would need for his presentation that afternoon, then stood in front of the mirror, carefully checking his police uniform. Satisfied, he headed downstairs to join his parents for breakfast.

'Morning, Baba,' he said, pulling up a chair opposite his father.

'Good morning, Mayank. You're ready earlier than usual?'

'Yes. New boss has taken over and I have to make a presentation.'

'Oh, has Uday Kumar joined?'

'Yes,' he replied shortly. Mayank liked to keep office matters discreet. But his father, by reading every article on the police force in four newspapers and diligently watching the crime-obsessed television news, kept himself informed.

'You know you have to meet a girl this Thursday,' his mother said, bringing in the teapot.

'Yes, I remember that.' Mayank had completely forgotten and tried to think through his diary for that day. 'What time do we have to be there?'

'At seven thirty p.m., Andrews Ganj.'

'Okay. If nothing comes up, I will be there.'

For the next twenty minutes, Mayank Sharma, assistant commissioner, Crime Branch, tried to forget his office and the stress of having to choose a girl to marry, and listened to his father talk about the floundering family business. His parents shielded him from the situation as far as possible, but the last two months had seen an alarming decline in their fortunes.

In the late 1990s, as multinational companies started to set up shop in India and the rigid state control on production monopoly was dented, Mayank's father, Madhukar Sharma, had set up a factory that produced fibreglass body parts for motorcycles. With demand peaking in the 1990s, the business did well. Now, with a slowdown in the global economy, companies were trying to cut corners. Cheaper plastic was replacing his father's more durable but costlier products.

While he never voiced it, of course, his father perhaps hoped that Mayank would help. But even if he wanted to, the young man did not see how. Being a policeman did not give you the power to secure a contract or force plastic manufacturers to stop producing. Most people outside of the state's power matrix believed that the police could do anything; these days, even his father.

'Did you speak to Batra Uncle?' Mayank asked, once he'd heard about the latest desertion of clients.

'Yes, but he has no time these days. He never had any difficulty coming and asking for campaign funds. Now he keeps making excuses,' his father replied. Ravinder Batra was his mother's first cousin and an up-and-coming politician in the ruling Congress party.

'I'll speak to him,' his mother intervened. 'Mayank beta, you have to go, no?'

'Yes,' he replied gratefully.

His mother handed him his wallet and lunch box. 'The driver is waiting downstairs. He refuses to come up and have tea. I keep telling him,' she said.

'Okay, will tell him. Bye Ma, bye Baba.'

Mayank descended the narrow staircase of their house in Karol Bagh thoughtfully, wondering how a wife would fit into this family situation. Two years after joining the police service, he still handed over his entire salary to his mother, who saw to it that there was enough in his wallet each morning. They continued to live in their congested west Delhi residence even though he was entitled to official quarters. He was the only son, and as such family life revolved around him. 'How will a woman

I like – a modern working girl – fit into this scenario?' he would ask his counsellor.

'Morning, Balbir,' Mayank greeted his driver and settled into the office jeep with his diary open on his knees. Besides meeting Uday Kumar in the afternoon, his day seemed relatively free. There were two departmental inquiries that he could postpone; only a case file due in court next week would need examination. Good, he thought to himself. He could go through the Babloo case file once more.

Ever since Uday Kumar had given him the tip-off three weeks ago, Mayank had been researching the notorious kidnapper. The secrecy bothered him. Ideally, he would have contacted his counterparts in Mumbai and Uttar Pradesh where cases were registered against Babloo. He would have spoken with former and serving policemen who knew the man's background. But Uday refused permission. 'Half the police were on his payroll. You ask questions and he gets to know.'

What caught Mayank's eye was how simple Babloo's operations were. The criminal stuck to what he knew. He specialized in kidnappings. His victims were always successful, prominent middle-aged men over fifty or youths aged between fourteen and twenty. The one time he deviated from this and kidnapped a six-year-old girl, the police tracked him down. Sex, or the promise of it, was the trap. Middle-aged men are worried about their waning virility and the young ones are anxious to discover it. Never fails, Mayank smiled.

Uday had told him to think like Babloo. 'Get inside his head. Why do you want to come back? You know you could be jailed for life on past crimes alone. What is your motivation?'

For three weeks, Mayank had asked himself the same question. He was no closer to an answer.

'I liked your report on the cricket-betting syndicate,' Vikram said to Abhishek.

'I just put down what you gave in the press release, sir,' Abhishek replied, surprised at the compliment.

'Boss, that is more than you can ask of reporters these days,' Vikram snorted.

Abhishek was at the police PRO's office, waiting to be called in for a meeting with the police commissioner; an honour accorded to few fledgling reporters. He knew that his predecessor's reputation had much to do with this privilege. Abhishek had been surprised when Vivek had taken him aside three days earlier to advise him on how to use the opportunity. 'Don't treat it as a PR exercise. Get the upper hand,' he had explained.

Amir's only advice, while agreeing to allow Abhishek to cover crime, had been to keep his trap shut. Agreeing was perhaps not the word – Amir Akhtar had been forced, blackmailed almost, into letting the boy have his way, and Abhishek knew he would not be able to repeat the madness that had gripped him in Amir's office. It had got him the job, but also earned the ire of the man he most wanted to please.

'I'll tell everyone that Babloo Shankar is coming back,' he had blurted out after the chief reporter had contemptuously dismissed his request for covering crime. Perhaps it was the unpredictability, the hint of machismo, which had swayed Amir. 'He must know that I don't have the balls,' the young man thought.

Yet, here he was, twelve days after first walking into the office of the *Express*, waiting to meet Delhi's most senior policeman.

'I am a bit surprised that the commissioner is meeting you,' Vikram said to Abhishek. 'Given what happened the other day with the cricket comment, he is pretty upset with the press.'

'Why, what happened, sir?'

'Oh, don't ask.' Vikram shook his head before continuing, 'Three weeks back, an old couple was murdered at their south Delhi residence. The press went to town with it – saturation coverage. A day later, this television reporter, new chap, cornered the commissioner and asked him for an update. Boss got irritated and snapped that police investigations are not a cricket match that you can keep giving live updates. The channel used the byte to suggest that the police equate murders to cricket matches. Others picked it up, and soon it seemed like we were playing cricket in the afternoons while murderers roamed Delhi's streets looking for victims.'

Abhishek laughed. Vikram Singh had a way of putting things that made you complicit in his indignation.

'We got the murderer three days later. The story was buried on page four and television reports just about mentioned it. That's our press.'

It was Abhishek's turn to shake his head.

An attendant came in to inform them that the commissioner was ready to meet Abhishek.

Commissioner V. N. Pratap was poring over a file on a desk at the end of an enormous room when Abhishek knocked. With a quick upward glance, he waved the reporter in. 'Please sit,' he said. 'I'll just take a minute.'

This must have been the largest room Abhishek had ever entered. And definitely the most powerful. He sat on the edge of a well-upholstered chair, trying not to look nervous.

'Good afternoon, Abhishek-ji. Sorry to have kept you waiting.' Pratap's voice was as warm and friendly as his smile.

'Not at all, sir,' Abhishek replied, overawed.

'So, what can we do for you?' The commissioner took off his reading glasses and sat back in his chair.

'Sir, I am just starting off on the crime beat and thought it would be a good idea to meet you. That's why I placed the request.'

'Yes, of course. My door is always open for journalists, and you have Vikram Singh, of course, for any immediate queries. Is this your first job? You look very young.'

On his own turf, Pratap was adept at dealing with young reporters and Abhishek, he quickly surmised, was a rookie. This would not take long. He was careful, however, not to appear dismissive and patiently went through the spiel he reserved for newcomers: The police were public servants and were certainly accountable to the press. The fourth estate was doing an important job and he had the highest respect for it. If the police were wrong – as they often were – it was the duty of the press to pull them up, but the media too must cross-check facts before broadcasting or publishing them. They also had a duty towards their readers and viewers. Pratap smiled at the polite young man drinking his tea, and decided that their meeting was over.

'I am sorry, Abhishek, but I do have to get on now. I am really glad to see young people like you venturing into journalism, and I'm always available.' Pratap's mind was already drifting.

'Thank you very much, sir. I am very grateful for your support,' Abhishek said, adding, 'I was just wondering if I could get a quote from you for a story.'

'Yes, of course. Go ahead.' The commissioner was busy checking messages on his mobile phone.

'Sir, the Delhi Police security wing has not employed a single person of Sikh origin since 1984, after Prime Minister Indira Gandhi was assassinated by her Sikh bodyguards. It seems that there was an unwritten missive from the home ministry about this.' Pratap's eyes were now fixed on him and Abhishek felt increasingly nervous. 'Is this true and if it is, isn't it unconstitutional?' He finished his question in a rush, embarrassed and surprised at of his own audacity, and forced himself to meet the police commissioner's gaze.

The smug, patronizing look had vanished. Vivek was right, he thought; he had the man's attention.

A hesitant smile now played on Pratap's lips. 'I don't know about this,' he finally managed to say. 'I'll definitely check and get back to you.'

'Sir, we are running the story tomorrow. My first story … I hope you understand. So if you can just find out … I can wait.'

One of the phones on the desk rang.

'Yes? Ask them to sit,' Pratap snapped. 'Abhishek, you are new to the profession and, of course, will quickly understand.' He tried to sound brisk and in command. 'There are some things that are just not written about, you see. Sometimes, in the interest of the nation, we ask the press for embargoes on certain matters.'

'My editor has approved the story, sir, and I have been asked to get a comment from you,' Abhishek replied, sticking to what Vivek had told him to say. Abhishek's admiration for his senior colleague grew as he watched Pratap's reaction.

'Okay, Abhishek, I am older than you and I'll ask you for a favour. We must be together on this.'

The young man wondered at how quickly equations change. The police commissioner of Delhi was invoking age as a shield against a novice reporter.

'I must request you – no, ask you – not to do this story.'

Abhishek tried to say something, but the policeman put his hand up. 'Look, you have years ahead of you. Having the police commissioner as your friend is an advantage. Ask any of your colleagues. I'll assure you open access to this office.'

Vivek had cautioned him against prolonging the moment of victory. 'Sir, if it is your wish, of course I cannot do the story. The problem will be explaining this to the office,' Abhishek said gracefully.

'Your office has intelligent people. Tell Amir it's a personal request from me. He'll understand. But in the meantime, is there anything I can do for you?'

Abhishek thought for a while and then hesitantly said, 'Sir, I would like to meet Uday Kumar.'

'But of course.' Pratap was relieved. 'He's an excellent officer. I'll call him this evening.'

As he stood up to shake hands with the commissioner, Abhishek made sure that he appeared grateful.

5

Imran observed her as she stood at the window taking photographs of the street below. She clicked several times before turning back to him. The subtlety of her transformations always unnerved him. They were never drastic, a change in gait perhaps or in her manner of speech, but she certainly seemed different today. No longer the coy housewife he had seen her play to the landlord just moments ago, she had returned to the steely professional he knew.

'This is a good location,' she said. 'The hotel next door is ideal. Makes us less noticeable.'

Imran was gladdened by the praise. It had taken him two weeks to find the right place, and before settling on it, she had made him drive between the property and a farmhouse in Mehrauli at different times of the day to observe traffic patterns and check for police barriers.

It was a two-bedroom flat on the second floor, unspectacularly furnished and located in one of the early neighbourhoods of south Delhi: Panchsheel Enclave. Built in the early 1970s, this was an affluent colony in the midst of a construction boom. The government had changed the housing regulations in Delhi and privately owned homes could now be built up to four storeys, one storey higher than what the previous decade's bureaucrats had sanctioned. To the comfortably retired residents of the area, the lure of selling a floor in an overpriced market justified the sacrifice of peace and obscurity.

Four properties were being reconstructed around the couple's chosen hideout. Chopra, their new landlord, had complained bitterly about the hotel next door, which was also adding an extra floor.

'They have not left an inch between my wall and theirs. There's seepage in the bathrooms, my bedroom has cracks. We can't do anything. The owner has bribed the police.'

They had nodded sympathetically.

'Good,' she told Imran now. 'The police are busy making money here. It will keep them occupied.'

'You really charmed the old landlord,' Imran said admiringly. 'He was ready in a moment. No talk of police verification once he met you.'

Two days before Uday Kumar got his tip-off from Mumbai that Babloo's long-time paramour and cohort, the infamous Madame X, had entered India, a couple had checked into the Imperial Hotel in New Delhi. Imran Tahir had arrived from Malaysia and Monika Mathur came in from the United States via Singapore. They were moving back to India after spending a decade abroad, in Alabama, USA.

They had been married for the past four years and it was, Monika had explained shyly to their would-be landlord, time to start a family. Chopra uncle, as she immediately started referring to the man, had nodded appreciatively at her words and her well-rounded breasts.

'The house is ready, my dear. I was sure you would like it, so I got it cleaned. You just have to move in.'

After they had made the final checks, they drove to the

The Price You Pay   53

Imperial to check out and settle the bill. As Monika got out of
the car and walked down the hallway towards the reception,
Imran marvelled again at the ease with which she slid back into
character: the banker in town on business with her husband.

'Have you heard from Sadiq today?' she asked him.

'No, nothing. He said he might call later this evening,' Imran
replied.

'How many spotters do we have now?'

'Including Sadiq, three. Two for the boy and one for the
family, mostly following the father when he is in town.'

'Okay. I have to call Babloo tonight. Is there anything you
think we might need?'

'No, not right now,' he answered.

The bill came and Imran paid; sixty per cent in cash and the
rest with an American Express card. They left a tip, not miserly
but nothing to remark on. To anyone who might have seen them
during their stay at the hotel, the couple would have appeared
no different from the hundreds of young, successful people who
checked in every month.

'Is there a different route to the house?' she asked Imran,
who instructed the driver to avoid the BRT corridor and go via
India Gate, taking the road through Deer Park and Hauz Khas
to their new home.

The beat constable would write in the police diary later that
week that in C Block, Panchsheel Enclave, a young couple had
moved in. The landlord knew the tenants and would not be
asking for police verification.

Monika Mathur alias Archana Pandey, known in police circles
as Madame X, had arrived in Delhi.

'I am struggling to make a list, sir,' Mayank told Uday. 'In the '90s, Babloo was targeting only politicians and top industrialists. He never went for someone who couldn't pay, or asked for an amount beyond the victim's capacity. Today, Delhi has several thousand millionaires and kidnapping is the most lucrative crime. With the Commonwealth Games, even small-time contractors have acquired Swiss accounts. Half of Delhi can afford to be kidnapped. How can we monitor such numbers?' He paused and looked at his boss.

'You can't think from the angle of potential victims, Mayank,' Uday said slowly. 'I told you to think like Babloo. Why is he coming back? It cannot be for money. That's not the motivation; there is something else. Let's start with the assumption that he wants to make a statement by carrying out another kidnapping. Right?'

'Right, sir.'

'If that is what he plans, he won't kidnap just anyone. He'll go for someone big.' Uday paused and thought for a while. 'What about his associates here? Just Salim Khan?'

'Yes, sir,' Mayank replied. 'The other two whom he worked with ... Suleiman is dead and Mohan Sharma is in Lucknow jail.'

'I know the jail superintendent there. Let's get a fix on Mohan's mobile phone. Most of these bastards have several SIM cards, but let's see.' Uday made a note in his diary. 'What do you know about Archana Pandey?' he asked, looking up.

'From the police records, sir, she lives and works with Babloo in Singapore. He first used her for that hotelier kidnapping in '92.'

'Yes.' Uday smiled. 'That motherfucker got horny and walked straight into Babloo's trap. She's quite sexy, I am told. What else?'

'Not much, sir. She used to play bit parts in Bollywood before she met Babloo. She got a break as the leading lady in a film financed by him. *Mobster*, I think it was called. It flopped. After that she took up this alternative acting career with our man, and it has proved far more lucrative. I am told that in police circles she goes by the name Madame X.'

'That's right. Now, Mayank, listen very carefully. Forget Babloo for now. Your Madame X is either already here or on her way.'

Uday took a videocassette from one of the desk drawers and handed it to his junior colleague. 'Here you go – your homework. *Mobster*. Watch the film. It was hard to find a copy. In the next three days,' Uday continued, 'talk to the deputy commissioners of all twelve districts. Get a list of the important people in their area from each. Don't give them any specifics. Once you get that going, we can start pruning it down. Then …' The phone on Uday's desk rang.

'Hello … Who?' he asked impatiently. 'Oh yes, yes. Send him in after five minutes, Mishra-ji.' He put the phone down and turned towards Mayank. 'Some new reporter wants to meet me. Comes with the commissioner's reference. Anyway, what was I saying? Yes, so we tap the phones of those on top of the list. Work on the Archana angle. We also need to put a tap on Salim Khan. I'll alert the international airports to look out for a man in a wheelchair. Okay?'

Mayank nodded.

'Good. Now let's meet this new boy.'

'Come in, Abhishek.' Uday appraised the tall young man who stood hesitating at the door. 'Please sit. This is Assistant Commissioner Mayank Sharma. So, how can I help?'

'Good afternoon, sir. I have just joined the *Express* as a crime reporter and thought I should introduce myself. I have heard a lot about you,' Abhishek said.

'Where has Vivek Sethi gone?'

'He is leaving, sir, joining News Today.'

'Give him my regards and tell him to drop in,' Uday said. 'Haven't seen him in a while. Now tell me something – who are you, young man? Should we be afraid of you? You come with the commissioner's reference.'

Abhishek smiled. 'Just a coincidence, sir. I met Commissioner Pratap and happened to mention that I would like to meet you. He offered to call.'

'Boss, in thirty years, no commissioner has ever sent any reporter to me without a reason. There's something you're not telling me.' Uday looked keenly at the boy in front of him. 'Anyway, you work with Amir?'

'Yes, sir.'

'The best in the business. We're contemporaries. You'll learn a lot from him.'

'I hope to, sir,' Abhishek replied politely.

The tea came, and Mayank handed out the cups.

'So why did you ask for me, Abhishek?' Uday enquired. 'Why not go to the senior officers here? They would all have met you. After all, you are the commissioner's man.'

Mayank knew the drill. He had witnessed it intermittently for two years now. His boss would start with a few self-deprecatory phrases and then, once mollified, would launch into a list of colourful achievements. Mayank's privileged Delhi background and his assured status as a Central services' officer did not blind him to the everyday frustrations of a rural man from the state services.

Today, however, something else was on the veteran cop's mind. Uday was trying to piece together a puzzle even as he kept Abhishek entertained with his stories.

'People my age want easy postings. All these big men you will meet in the building,' Uday said, waving his arms, 'with their fancy designations; all they do is look at files for an hour a day and then have lunch at the India International Centre. On weekends they play golf.'

Abhishek and Mayank, as expected of them, smiled.

'I might be small fry, bachche, but the commissioner insisted I join the Crime Branch. I told him, "Sir, my married life is in doldrums. My wife beats me every night. This means she will go home to her parents." He said, "I have been trying to make my wife do that for years!" So here I am, Abhishek babu, fifty-five years old and still working the streets.'

Uday played the part of the bragging cop to perfection. But his mind was working away. Amir Akhtar came to him knowing something he should not have. Now this boy, working with Amir, had dropped in to see him with the commissioner's reference. Uday Kumar did not believe in coincidences; he knew something was up.

Ten minutes later, he decided to wind down the act. 'So, Abhishek, since you have come to me and given me the honour, I will help you. You are from Benares; my father grew up there. You fall into my relationship circle. We Biharis go by our hearts. Ask Amir. I trained him when he first started out. Now that you have me as your guru, I want payment – guru-dakshina.' Uday grinned.

'Whatever you say, sir,' Abhishek replied. He understood the game: Defer to the man, flatter him and grovel slightly.

'Arre bachche, you think you can give Uday Kumar anything? Big people of this city want to bestow gifts on Uday Kumar. By the grace of God, I lack nothing. I am a simple man and I intend to stay that way. But what I want,' he continued with another intense look at Abhishek, 'is that you work hard and you learn.

The press are our colleagues. They work alongside us; they tell the people what we do. So you have to know, understand, and be responsible. I will teach you if you promise to work hard. OK?'

'Yes, sir, of course.' Abhishek nodded enthusiastically.

'First thing you have to do is understand the city. You are an outsider like I once was. You have to feel its pulse; know it at different times of the day and night.'

Uday turned to Mayank. 'Do you still go out on night patrol?'

'Not since I have been posted here, sir. It is not required at the Crime Branch,' the officer replied.

Uday slapped the desk in disgust. 'Not required? It is not required that an old man like me slave away with no hope of promotion or perks. But I do it, no?'

Mayank looked suitably chastened.

'Right! Abhishek, Mayank will take you out on night patrol, a night gasht. Go this Friday. Take him to your office and fix the details. And you, Abhishek, you must tell me what you saw in the city. Write me two pages, OK? I want to see what you observe. Don't worry; I will give you stories. Uday Kumar will make you a star.' He smiled. The act was over.

'Thank you for your help, sir.' Abhishek was genuinely grateful.

The deputy commissioner nodded at both men, indicating dismissal.

'Maya,' Amir called from his cabin.

'Coming, just a minute,' she yelled. Walking across the reporting room towards the boss's cabin, she was aware of Abhishek's eyes on her.

'Sit,' Amir said, his eyes on the computer screen. 'Please tell me something. Why does every news story become a feature with you? "Government poised to grant minority status to Jamia Millia Islamia University." That's enough. Why add colour to this news item?' He sounded exasperated. 'You want to be a writer, write for the features page whenever you like. City pages require reporters.'

'I never get time to write for anyone else, Amir.' Maya sounded hurt.

'How will you get time? You are too busy flirting with the new boy,' he said, now grinning.

'Shush!' She giggled. 'What are you saying, Amir? You are such a gossip.'

'OK, listen, take everyone's order. I'm calling the club. And tonight will be a late one; it's Vivek's farewell too.'

Maya left his cabin and called out loudly, 'Place your orders, guys. Who is having what?'

Every second Friday, Amir made it a point to gather the reporting unit at the Press Club. When the management offered to pick up the tab, terming it a 'bonding exercise', the chief reporter refused. 'Just gossip and bitching, Mihir-da,' he said to his editor later. 'Can't have those bastards intruding. Next they will ration our drinking and make me draw pie charts.'

Rahul said he could not make it. He had been married a month now to his long-time girlfriend and reporter at *Sunday Times*, Madhumita Biswas, and was avoiding the club.

Amir laughed at him over the partition. 'Rahul, stop being ridiculous. People start drinking after marriage and you are trying to give up? Won't work. Call Madhumita too. Drinks are on me.' He paused and looked at Abhishek, sitting quietly amid the loud drinks' orders. 'And you are coming too. Vivek's farewell should be your initiation.'

Although he must have passed it several times, Abhishek had never really noticed the derelict, almost decrepit two-storey building on Raisina Road. Located opposite the ostentatious Chelmsford Club and a stone's throw from various national symbols – Parliament, Rashtrapati Bhavan and India Gate – the Press Club was not an architectural marvel. There were no liveried doormen at the gates, and the men's urinal was situated unashamedly close to the entrance. A tiny glass-panelled enclosure served as a reception where Amir signed in the new recruit.

As he pushed open the door to the main dining hall, Abhishek was surprised at the smell of cigarettes that clung to the air. The smoking ban in restaurants and clubs had been in place for years, but the journalists decreed that the law was an ass and wrote their own in great plumes that lingered in the air.

The neon strip lights contributed to the Press Club's seedy, shabby feel. The sunmica-covered tables, the cheap whisky in thick tall glasses, and the well-used plates completed the scene.

Abhishek mentioned his observations to Rahul, who replied brusquely: 'This bunch of people is one of the most powerful in the country. Don't be fooled by the decor.'

Maya, Abhishek noticed, had conspired to sit next to him. 'Great food. The rum tastes like fertilizer, but it's thirty rupees a peg,' she said, and told him to try the shammi kebabs. Abhishek caught Amir winking at her and wondered at the joke.

Twenty minutes later, Vivek joined them. Amir got up to give him a hug. 'You come late even for a drink?' he said, slapping Vivek's back.

'And you keep time even when you are drunk,' Vivek shot back. 'Good evening, guys.' He pulled up a chair next to Abhishek. 'How was the meeting with the big boss?' he whispered.

'Went really well. Can't thank you enough.'

'Don't worry about thanking me. I extract my dues.' Vivek's eyes shone with mischief. 'So, give me details.'

Abhishek, in a low voice, summarized his meeting with the commissioner.

'Excellent. Well done. Now go easy and never tell anyone I gave you the tip-off. I don't want to appear soft in my middle age.'

Abhishek nodded, basking in Vivek's praise and obvious delight.

'But you should know that you have failed as a reporter,' Vivek added, taking a gulp of his whisky. 'You trusted what I said. How did you know that I was not setting you up? You are, after all, my competition now. Never trust anyone in this profession.'

'I didn't. I went to the Security Lines and checked out what you'd told me.'

Vivek's smugness dropped momentarily. 'What?' he spluttered. 'You went there?'

'Yes, I went the very next day.' Abhishek told Vivek that at the Delhi Police Security Lines, he had asked for Constable Balbinder Singh.

'Who Balbinder Singh?' a guard at the reception desk had queried.

'Balbinder Singh, the sardarji, the Sikh gentleman … ?' Abhishek had nervously replied.

The guard was dismissive. 'No, we don't have sardars here. You are mistaken.'

'I apologized and left immediately,' continued Abhishek. 'Your information was one hundred per cent correct, Vivek sir. Sorry, I did not mean any offence.'

'I will watch out for you, Abhishek Dutta,' Vivek said slowly, staring at him. 'You're going to be a handful.'

Rahul left soon after, Madhumita in tow, sparking off derisive laughter from the table. 'He is such a mouse in front of her. It is funny … his bravado in the office and then, Madhumita shows up and he becomes all silly,' Maya smirked to Abhishek.

The bell rang for the final orders and there was a scramble towards the bar. Amir took orders for another round. Abhishek refused. From this world of loud gestures and casual claims, the new reporter slipped out for his night gasht unobserved.

6

'**M**y parents feel that the coming of the Maruti car changed Delhi in the '80s,' Mayank told Abhishek. 'My father is emphatic that it took away the stability of the Ambassador and the Fiat with a flimsiness that, over time, started to reflect in us.'

It was past 1 a.m. The awkwardness of two young men meeting in a forced context was being mitigated by a glass of sweet milky tea at a roadside stall, the heat generated from the flickering gas burner providing some relief from the mid-November cold. They were in Seemapuri, a district at the outer extremities of north-east Delhi. Abhishek lived close by, in Mayur Vihar, an area dotted with unimaginative but adequate concrete blocks for the city's middle class. On learning this, Mayank had decided that they should start their night's journey there. 'Let me introduce you to your neighbours,' he had said.

When he met Abhishek outside the Press Club, Mayank had offered him two choices. He could either spend the night in a police station to see how things operated, or they could roam the city: go to various police checkpoints, see the positions of the Police Control Room vans, get a feel – as Uday Kumar had said – of Delhi. For Abhishek, the choice had been obvious.

'Good, I like driving,' Mayank said, and they'd climbed into his jeep.

It had taken fifty minutes to drive from New Delhi to Seemapuri. On the way, Mayank had stopped to inspect three PCR vans. Abhishek was amused by the dozing policemen, their initial irritation at being disturbed and then their clumsy, snappy efforts to come to attention. In the first van, the policemen had taken off their belts and shoes and were sharing what looked like a bottle of alcohol. Mayank patiently waited with Abhishek as the policemen dressed. He'd then asked to see their night logbooks.

'Shanti hai, sir. All quiet. We just did two rounds,' one of the policemen had muttered. Mayank checked the book, nodded and left.

After they'd found the constables in the third van asleep, one with his head on the wheel and the other in the back, Mayank felt he should explain. 'The inspector and his deputies have fixed nights for patrolling. These policemen know the duty patterns. They were not expecting us tonight.'

The two young men finished their tea, ordered another round and moved towards the footpath, close to a fire made from cardboard boxes, newspapers, a few pieces of wood and bicycle tyres. The warmth compensated for the stench of burning rubber as they squatted on the pavement next to three crouching men gazing into the fire.

'At the police academy,' Mayank continued, 'I was obsessed with understanding crime patterns in cities. For example, a port city like Mumbai or Chennai is very different to Delhi. There is hardly any organized crime here; no Dawood Ibrahim or Chhota Rajan.'

Abhishek was tempted to ask his new friend about Babloo Shankar, but resisted.

'I should qualify that,' Mayank added quickly. 'Delhi saw terrorism much before Mumbai. I can't remember the exact date, but it was definitely sometime in 1980 when the first terrorist strike happened. The chief of the Nirankari sect was killed. What was the name?' He pondered for a moment. 'Yes, Baba Gurbachan Singh and his bodyguard Pratap Singh.'

A boy brought the tea and both men fell silent, enjoying its comfort. Lighting a cigarette, Abhishek cued Mayank: 'You were saying about Delhi in the '80s.'

'Yes ... Actually everything really changed after 1984. Indira Gandhi's murder and the anti-Sikh riots destroyed the city. I was too young, but my parents still talk about the horror. So many Sikhs were killed, men burnt, women raped. And look at our criminal justice system. The court cases go on even now and the guilty roam openly, especially the politicians. I am sure you know.'

'I know the basic facts, but not much,' Abhishek admitted.

'Yes, too recent history to be taught in classrooms. After the riots, there was a spurt of terrorist strikes. In 1985, there were bomb blasts on three consecutive days: 10, 11 and 12 May. Transistor radios were used as set-off devices. Then, on 31 July, a member of Parliament, Lalit Maken, and his wife were killed along with another party colleague.'

'You have some memory, Mayank,' Abhishek said appreciatively, stubbing out his cigarette.

'Sorry, maybe I am showing off now.' Mayank sounded embarrassed. 'But Uday sir instructed me to give you a bit of background.'

'It's fascinating. Please go on.'

'Well, several other political leaders were killed in the following months. My mother's family is very well connected in the Congress party, so these are all familiar names. After Maken, on 4 September Arjun Das, a member of the Metropolitan Council, was killed in Laxmi Bai Nagar ... Look, I could go on but we should head off now if you want to check out the police station.' Mayank looked at his watch. 'It's one thirty.'

'Yes, let's go. Thanks, this has been really educative.' Abhishek stood up. 'I thought policemen were kind of ... you know ... like constables on the road, taking bribes and harassing people.'

'That's our public image and quite rightly too,' Mayank said, paying for the tea. 'Do you want to walk a bit?' he asked. 'The police station is just five minutes away, we can then go towards central Delhi where I was posted earlier and maybe, if we have time, I will show you some interesting things that happen in the posh parts of our diplomatic enclaves. What do you say?'

'All sounds very good to me, Mayank. Thank you again.'

As they stepped into the by-lanes of Seemapuri, Abhishek was surprised by all the activity. Despite the winter night and the late hour, carts crunched the potholed roads, people lurched by carrying sacks on their backs, an old Hindi song floated down from an upstairs window and a group of children played hopscotch under a street light.

A few auto drivers slept in their tiny open vehicles. Others, finding the cold impossible to bear, congregated in silence around small fires. The narrow lanes and the houses haphazardly constructed on top of one another reminded Abhishek of home. 'Quite like Benares,' he remarked to Mayank.

'Nothing holy about this place though. Most of these guys are smack addicts.' Mayank indicated the crouching silhouettes.

'Who said anything about holy? It's exactly the same in Benares. Charas addicts are everywhere in the old town. My parents made sure to keep me away.'

'Where did you live in Benares?' Mayank asked.

Abhishek had grown up in the campus of the Benares Hindu University where his father was a professor of English.

He went to the Central School quite close to home. 'Protected, government-coddled existence. I then went to Kolkata for my higher secondary. All my relatives amassed in that city, so I suffered another kind of coddling. And then Delhi University for graduation. I was at Hindu College. I bet you were a Stephenian?'

Mayank smiled at the reference to the decades of rivalry between Delhi University students from every other college and those from the decidedly superior – a fact grudgingly admitted – St Stephen's. 'No such chance. Went to IIT Delhi. I was a computer geek,' he replied. 'This way,' he said, turning left onto a main street, where the lights of the police station became visible. 'I studied computer-science engineering. My doctoral thesis was on cyber crime. I submitted it only after I joined the force. That was tough. IIT does not take things lightly,' he said.

Abhishek wasn't surprised to hear that Mayank was a product of the prestigious Indian Institutes of Technology that came up as pillars of modernity under Nehru in the 1950s and still retained their edge, despite the continued privatization of higher education.

At the police station, the duty officer had to be summoned and he arrived looking dishevelled; a mousy, sad-mouthed man with small eyes and a thin moustache on a flat face. He was apologetic, and Mayank, despite his status, seemed even more so.

'I was on a random patrol, Om Prakash-ji. So just dropped by. Don't bother yourself.'

'No-no, sir, not at all,' he protested. 'It is a privilege; an officer like you coming by. What can I get, sir – something to eat, tea, coffee?'

'Nothing, nothing,' they both insisted.

Ten minutes later, after their third round of tea, the two young men managed to leave the police station. Om Prakash pleaded to be allowed to drive them to Mayank's jeep or at least have it brought to the police station. In the end, they let him accompany them to the vehicle.

'Good night, sir. Please come again,' Om Prakash said, bending forward to clasp Mayank's hand between his own. He circled the jeep and shook hands with Abhishek, saluting as they drove away.

'I know the policeman is a hated figure,' Mayank said, driving carefully through the narrow lanes, 'but imagine this: Om Prakash stays away from his family for four to five nights a week, patrolling these streets in the cold; he lives in really inhospitable barracks with others like him; goes home briefly and then back to work again within hours. For years on end, it's the same routine. We officers have ambitions. We have cars, houses, family lives. What do these men have? Oh yes, they are corrupt and I do not condone corruption. But over the last two years, I have started to understand some of it.'

They turned onto the near-empty highway towards ITO, the jeep's headlights carving columns of light through the smoky mist. Mayank stepped on the accelerator. 'You know who piss me off? The officers, people like me, who conduct daylight robberies. The constable takes money from a truck driver; you see it – the officer gets his cut behind closed doors; you miss it. As you were saying, your view of police is that of the corrupt constable on the street. But I can assure you, the officers are far worse.'

They turned right onto Laxmi Nagar, heading towards the Yamuna Pushta bridge.

'Are you married?' Abhishek asked.

'Not yet. But looking.' Seeing Abhishek's quizzical look, Mayank added, 'I mean I am seeing girls. Like, you know, arranged stuff.'

'Really? Found anyone?'

'Don't know yet,' Mayank said, thinking of Ritika Tytler, whom he'd met the day before. She did seem nice and he had told his mother he wasn't averse to another meeting. If Ritika wanted to, of course.

Mayank Sharma had jotted down his priorities – what he was looking for in a woman – in bullet points, as advised by the marriage counsellor. On first impression, Ritika seemed to measure up rather well. She was educated (point one), she came from a respectable family (point two), she was definitely beautiful (point four). Now he had to find out whether she could manage point three: could she adjust to his surroundings? There were other things to consider too: her desire to have an occupation, children, her likes, dislikes … but those could come later.

'Hungry?' Mayank asked Abhishek. 'If you are, we are going to the right place.'

Her outfit for the evening was the first thing she needed to consider: provocative, but not slutty. She chose a long black silk dress with thin shoulder straps and a silver choker to set it off. The ostentatious diamond engagement ring completed the picture. Very little make-up; just a few strokes of mascara. Simple, elegant, not too unapproachable – Archana had looked at the mirror and was proud of what she saw.

She and Imran went to the nightclub together. Inside, Archana immediately spotted the boy. He appeared younger than his years, almost someone the bouncer should have ejected. She ordered two shots of Glenmorangie, enough to let her slip into the role, and then kept to a Margarita for the rest of the evening. Stepping onto the dance floor, she made sure that the boy saw her. Their eyes met for the briefest of moments, nothing to let him assume that she had noticed him. Then she spent the next hour devoting her attention to Imran as they gyrated to the music. Not once did she glance back at the boy who was sitting with a group of his friends, unable to take his eyes off her.

Archana was flirting with him, Imran thought, indeed somewhat aggressively. But he knew the act. She ground her hips against him on the dance floor, letting his groin feel her curvaceous behind. When he did not know how to respond, she grabbed his hands and crossed them around her body, pulling him closer. Her hips moved to the repetitive beat, her soft buttocks making his cock ache. Whenever she turned to face him he enjoyed the plunging neckline of her dress, which revealed a glimpse of those ample breasts that had kept him awake at nights on the hotel room sofa. Despite her candid presence these past weeks, Imran had never dreamt of making a move on her. You do not sleep with Babloo Shankar's woman.

Suddenly Archana asked him to go to the car, saying she would join him in a minute, and strode away. Though taken aback and disappointed, he knew better than to argue and headed towards the basement. He was just beginning to drop off, the effects of alcohol taking over, when she opened the door at his side. He started. 'Do you want to drive?' he asked.

Archana smiled, pushed the seat back, and put her leg across him. He tried to utter something, but her right hand covered his mouth. With her left, she unzipped his trousers. He became hard in a moment and she deftly pulled out his penis. Her hand now circled his throat as she expertly lowered herself onto him. He realized – the corner of his lips later twitched at the memory – that she was wearing no panties. Had she gone to remove them when she sent him to the car?

As Archana thrust onto him, at first gently and then in rapid motions, she put her mouth close to his ear, whispering, 'Don't come.' She did though, moments later, in a violent frenzy, pushing his face between her breasts.

She moved off just as suddenly and climbed onto the passenger seat. Smoothing her dress, she lit a cigarette and waited for him to zip up. 'Shall we go?' she asked, not unkindly.

Imran drove out of the basement, and immediately Archana had other things on her mind. Tonight was crucial. The first contact had been made and though she was not absolutely sure, she felt it had worked. She opened the car window and let the chill of the night air hit her uncovered shoulders. 'How far?' she asked Imran.

'Twenty more minutes.'

Archana rummaged in her bag for the mouth freshener spray. She reapplied her lipstick; the first coat now visible on Imran's shirt collar.

Matera was enjoying his evening. He rarely had free time these days, what with family duties and his responsibilities at the satta den. But tonight Salim Bhai had invited the staff of all his betting centres for a party, and Matera and his two associates were in charge. Rum, whisky and vodka flowed freely. There was changezi chicken from the shop next to Golcha cinema and mutton barra kebabs from Karim's. Two floodlights harshly illuminated a large room on the second floor of a decrepit old building in Kucha Chalan, where some forty tables and three hundred chairs stood pushed against the paan juice–spattered walls. Salim Bhai had warned Matera: They must be back in place by 9 a.m. the next day. Business must not suffer.

Loud music blared from the hired stereo system and the more enthusiastic revellers were pulling filmi moves to a popular Hindi song: *'Beedi jalai le jigar se piya …'*

Matera lip-synced silently, sprawled flat across a charpai. Yes, a great night. He had outdone himself and even Salim Bhai had appreciated his efforts.

'Ai Matera, get up, you bastard!' Someone was pulling his arm.

He opened his eyes and smiled at Bunty Master. 'Na, yaar,' he slurred.

'Ai, come and dance, you lazy fuck,' another voice suggested.

'OK, OK,' he groaned, smiling. 'Give me two minutes.'

Matera staggered to the loo. He leaned against the wall and struggled to unbutton his trousers. Somebody had opened the window and the breeze on his face felt pleasant. He finished peeing but stood awhile, enjoying the fresh air. Then, forcing his eyes open, he peered outside. It was a cloudless night and, despite the late hour, the sky was illuminated. His gaze shifted to the street below where a blue Lexus was parked. Salim Bhai was talking to someone through the car window. Matera watched, trying to remember why this was significant.

'After my training I was posted to central Delhi, at the Darya Ganj police station,' Mayank carried on with his personalized tour for Abhishek.

'My posting surprised many. This is a communally sensitive area and there is a minor mafia operating in betting and prostitution. But the commissioner called me to his office and told me he was taking a personal interest in my career and I shouldn't let him down. Uday sir, he said, had recommended me.' Mayank paused and smiled. 'I was chased out in six months.'

'Why?' Abhishek asked, amazed.

'Long story. Can you pass the water please?'

They were eating mutton biryani inside the jeep, parked near Jama Masjid. Mayank had refused to sit on the benches placed on the street. Abhishek noted, not without some concern, that just before entering the area his companion had taken a pistol from the dashboard and tucked it into the back of his trousers.

'I was posted under Vishnu Gupta, the deputy commissioner of this area,' Mayank continued. 'After working with Uday sir, this man was a revelation. He was the stereotype of the bad policeman – absolutely, resolutely corrupt. But more than that, he was also offended by anyone else in the force getting work done. Investigations were continually scuttled. I could not trust my own people. The moment I would start planning a raid, word would leak out and I would come back empty-handed. It was extremely awkward.'

Mayank had started to gather intelligence on the satta mafia in the area. 'There was one major guy, Salim Khan. He ran his operations out of an old building in Kucha Chalan, quite close to here. I was planning a raid on the place and one morning went on an impromptu recce with my radio operator, Surinder. I was in civvies; did not even carry a gun. It was foolish.'

Abhishek had stopped eating.

'Don't like the food?'

'No-no; I like it. Go on,' he urged.

'It was badly planned. The moment I went near the building, the spotters started screaming, "ACP is here, ACP is here!" On the spur of the moment, I told Surinder, "Let's go in." We just ran into the building. Boss, there was pandemonium. People were running helter-skelter. We couldn't run after everyone. So Surinder and I just started bolting the doors from outside. Whoever managed to run out, we let them go. My plan was to lock as many inside as I possibly could. People started jumping out of a first-floor window. So I stood there, just below it. All I had as a weapon – you won't believe this – was a broom with a long handle that I'd found there. Every time someone looked out, I poked him. Thinking back now, it was farcical. But somehow it worked. All those guys were thinking that if the area assistant commissioner was there, he must have come with a force. That saved us. I couldn't carry that on for very long, of course, and had to send Surinder to get reinforcements. I couldn't get a signal on my radio and mobile phone so Surinder had to run all the way to the police station for back-up. Finally the local SHO arrived with some men. We arrested one hundred and sixty-three people that day.'

'Unbelievable. Congratulations,' Abhishek gushed.

'Yes,' Mayank said happily. 'You know what the commissioner did? He called my boss and said, "For two years you have been jerking off. A boy comes and arrests everyone under your bloody nose. You should be ashamed."'

'Is that why you were kicked out?'

'Well, the real drama started after the arrests. What happened taught me things the academy never bothers with. We took these one hundred and sixty-three to court. But the metropolitan magistrate let them go with a fine of five hundred rupees each. Can you believe that?'

'You are kidding,' Abhishek was indignant.

'Wait, it doesn't end here. A month later, Salim filed a case against me in the court of the same magistrate. He said that I'd been taking monthly pay-offs from the manager of his so-called garment factory. They'd deferred payments for one month and that's supposedly why I cooked up the case.' Mayank paused. 'But we should move on now. Let's pay. I will tell you the rest of the story on the way.'

As they drove away from Jama Masjid towards their final destination, Delhi's diplomatic enclave, Chanakyapuri, Mayank promised Abhishek a final surprise.

'So what happened next?' Abhishek asked, impatient to hear the rest of the story.

'Uday sir saved me,' Mayank replied. 'It could have got very nasty. After the case was registered, the magistrate called to fix a meeting at a five-star hotel. I was immediately suspicious, but I went. He told me that the SHO who'd registered the arrests that morning was on Salim's payroll and had doctored the case report in a way that could easily implicate me. He asked what he should do. I asked him what could be done. He suggested that I drop the case and Salim would drop his. I refused and went straight to Uday Kumar, telling him everything. Uday sir called that bloody SHO. I was there. He said to the man, "Next time Salim steps out of his area, arrest him and place a gun on him. Register a case under the Arms Act. There will be no bail. We will sort him out in the lock-up." The SHO got the message and he must have told Salim. Two days later, Salim withdrew the allegations.' Mayank smiled. 'End of story.'

'But you were still transferred?'

'Ah, yes. My boss, Vishnu Gupta, and his associates used their connections in the home ministry. The commissioner said I should be proud that the home ministry was asking for my removal – I must be doing something right. He ensured that I got this posting. The Crime Branch is the best if you want to learn investigations.'

Twenty minutes later, they arrived at Chanakyapuri. Mayank parked the jeep and walked Abhishek towards the Pakistan High Commission. 'What we're about to see is quite brutal. Don't say anything. I will explain later.'

7

'Corruption and the Commonwealth Games saga continues. In a fresh development, officers of the Central Bureau of Investigation last night raided the residences of two senior officials in the sports ministry. The prime minister stated that the guilty shall not be spared. In other developments, the city police ...'

Amir woke up as the television news, set as an alarm, invaded the silence. He stayed for a minute, face buried into the pillow, half listening to the unnecessarily excited news anchor before rolling over, stretching his hands above his head and arching his back. Prior to the days of cable TV, it had been the thud of the newspapers falling on the balcony that woke him. Now, his life patterns were dictated by new technologies. He got up quickly, flung the covers off and in two long strides reached the window overlooking his first-floor balcony. The newspapers had not yet arrived.

'It gets later every day,' he thought irritably. 'People watch news before getting to the office, and no one harangues their newspaper vendors any more.' He made a mental note to call his, before heading towards the kitchen to make coffee.

Amir was particularly eager to read the lead story from the reporting unit. It should be a good start to the week, he felt. He had seen the proofs the previous night, but you never got the feel of a front page from a miniature PDF version. For that, you needed to smooth the rough edges of a newspaper, unfold it, flatten it, glance at the headlines and then go to your story. Run through it briskly the first time, then read every other news item on the page. Read it a second time, slowly, and evaluate it against the other reports. Later, after you have gone through all the other newspapers that are part of your morning routine, go back to your story. That was how, for three decades now, Amir had been savouring his scoops.

He might not have climbed the editorial ladder as quickly as others in his trade, but few could claim the satisfaction this journalist got from a good news story. A byline was its own reward and sometimes when a story was really, really good – as this one definitely was – it could lead to a question in parliament, perhaps even an inquiry commission. A kick up the establishment's arse – the thought thrilled Amir.

This morning's report carried an added excitement: the introduction of his newest recruit, Abhishek Dutta. When Amir had announced the story, he'd seen the jaws of the other reporters drop. Even the editor had been surprised. The response from the police and the government would be fun to watch.

Hearing the thud, Amir walked out to the balcony and picked up the newspaper bundle. From the pile, he took out the *Express*. 'Policemen snore as crime rates soar.' Three explicit photographs complemented the bad poetry of the headline. Amir liked the one with the policeman's head on the steering wheel, a blanket wrapped around him. The story was dynamite, coming at a time when a series of rapes had forced the commissioner to put three thousand more policemen on night patrol.

Amir sat down on the easy chair in the balcony, enjoying the soft morning light on his face. He scanned the headlines of all the other newspapers. Easily the best story today, he thought to himself, delighted. He had been taken aback not only by the audacity of the story, but also by how quietly the young reporter had gone about his job. 'One story proves nothing,' he reminded himself. 'But the signs are good. The boy has news sense.' He decided to call Abhishek.

'Good morning. Still sleeping?'

'Hello, yes. Sorry sir, just getting up.'

'Don't worry,' Amir said. 'Just wanted to congratulate you on your first byline. It is a very good story. I will see you later at the office.'

'Thank you, sir. Thank you very much.'

Amir looked onto the street below. Despite the thousand things that had changed over the years here, this remained: the reluctant early morning pilgrimage of students. 'But they certainly dress better than we did,' he thought, appraising a group. He headed for the shower.

By 8.30, Amir was ready to leave. His room, now a mess of strewn clothes, crumpled sheets and discarded newspapers, would be spotless by the time he returned. His mother and a maid, both of whom lived downstairs, indulged Amir's love for cleanliness and singular inability to achieve it. But, besides taking care of domestic matters like washing clothes and catering to his sporadic demands for dinner, his mother had limited involvement in his life. Amir liked his space and she, now almost eighty, wanted the reassurance of hearing the soft padding of his feet above her ceiling late at night. It was a mutually beneficial arrangement.

Even after Shobha left him, Amir had felt no urge to live anywhere else. Friends had advised a change of place; even his mother had tentatively suggested a move. But Amir refused. He liked the easy familiarity of the house he had grown up in: the large window of his room overlooking the garden; the rounded staircase with wooden banisters his father had designed after a trip to Europe; and the short, diagonal path that led from the driveway to the gate, lined with seasonal flowers. Most of all, he treasured the neighbourhood. In a city incessantly tearing down to build again, the university's land laws offered protection against the cardboard modernity doled out in matchbox housings all over Delhi.

As he stepped onto the driveway, Amir met Ram Sharan. The vendor was waiting for him sheepishly, a mound of undelivered newspapers on his bicycle rack.

'So you come to meet me only for money these days?' Amir upbraided him. Both men were veterans of the news business and they treated each other with as much familiarity as age and class divisions allowed. 'This late?' Amir looked dramatically at his watch. 'Your newspapers are becoming waste papers.'

Ram Sharan mumbled about printing delays, the laziness of truck drivers and early morning fog, all conniving to keep him from his mission.

'Take the money from Ma,' Amir said over his shoulder as he walked away. 'We will talk about your son's job next week.'

He drove his car out of the quiet neighbourhood, turned onto the already busy main road and passed the new metro station. The addition of the metro rail to the city's crumbling public transport system was an initiative he fully supported in the newspaper. Yet, Amir was saddened by how the trees had suddenly vanished. All over Delhi familiar landmarks were disappearing, leaving him disorientated. Just beyond the station, with its functional concrete and white, there used to be a tiny tree-lined courtyard where students could while away their summer afternoons. This had given way to a large neon advertising board with changing loyalties.

Despite being prone to the occasional road rage, Amir enjoyed driving. It put him in touch with the city and offered him its pulse. On days like this, when he managed to leave home early, he took a right at Raj Ghat and turned towards Delhi Gate. It was a narrower road, but Amir liked the drive past the Feroze Shah Kotla grounds where he used to play cricket for the university. Now it was being readied for the World Cup. He would send a reporter later to check on the progress.

Amir waited at the Delhi Gate traffic lights impatiently, drumming his fingers on the wheel and fidgeting. The left lane was notionally open, but several auto-rickshaws had arranged themselves in such a way as to completely block his path. He honked a few times out of habit, but would have been surprised had it borne any effect. Since he'd stopped smoking, traffic lights made him edgy. When his family physician and childhood friend Kabir Azam told him that it was time to quit, Amir's first reaction had been incredulity. 'Look, it's true that when I smoke, my lungs complain. They ask, "Why this miserly diet? Take us to ITO!" You think cigarettes affect me? Do you ever step out of your bloody air-conditioned clinic?' But he did quit when shown the cloud patch in his lungs.

In spite of his erratic daily habits and a not-so-rationed alcohol intake, Amir craved fitness. On most mornings he ran up the two flights of stairs to his office, and played weekend cricket at the local club. Envious overweight colleagues asked him the secret of his lean sinewy frame and Amir would reply wryly, 'I have a dog's stomach. It consumes butter but does not accept it.'

He reached his office at 9.15. The narrow street that ran past the newspaper buildings would soon be clogged like a smoker's artery. The impossibly full parking lots would spit out cars and bikes, roadside tea stalls would muscle in on space, long queues and incessant honking would replace this relative calm. But for now, anyone standing at either end of Bahadur Shah Zafar Marg had an unimpeded view down this influential street.

Chhote Lal, office driver and parking attendant for the favoured few, was at the door before Amir could switch the engine off.

'Don't park it too far inside,' Amir told him. 'Takes the whole day to get it out. I might have to leave for lunch.'

'Sir, you are not taking the loan? Everyone is getting a new car. You get a big car and then we will not be able to push it inside,' Chhote Lal said as he took the keys.

'Yeah-yeah, this is running fine, na? No problem with this car. You just park it,' Amir said tetchily, heading for the stairs.

Chhote Lal and the other office drivers knew the latest management scheme to stem the flow of journalists leaving to join television. The idea was to induce them to buy cars, the more unaffordable the better, with one hundred per cent financing by the company. It would then make minor monthly deductions from their salaries. The longer it took to repay the loan, the longer a journalist was forced to stay. Or at least that was the idea; Vivek Sethi had simply told his prospective employer to buy off his loan.

Amir never applied for the scheme, partly because he liked his car of six years and partly from the fear that his application might be rejected. Even the peons knew of the disaster he had been on television a few years back. It was no secret that Amir

Akhtar, the well-known chief reporter of the *Express*, was tied to his job. No one, not even a paranoid management, was expecting an imminent departure.

Abhishek picked up the newspaper from the front door of his small one-room tenement, originally meant as servants' quarters, at the back of a third-floor apartment in east Delhi. Yes, there it was – his name on the front page. Like a junkie on a first hit, he sat down and let the wave of unexpected elation sweep over him. He read the story slowly, trying to concentrate, but found it difficult to keep his eyes from the byline in bold letters: Abhishek Dutta. At that moment he was absolutely certain that nothing in his short, unremarkable life compared to this feeling. He wanted to call his parents, his relatives. He wanted to tell them not to worry; he would not be a failure. And just like a junkie, minutes later, Abhishek started to worry about the next hit, his next story.

His cellphone rang, breaking the reverie. It was Mayank Sharma.

'Hi, Mayank.'

'Good morning, Abhishek,' came the friendly voice. 'How did you do this?'

'I am really sorry. Should have told you. I …'

'No-no, don't apologize. I meant when did you take the pictures? I never saw the camera.'

'Oh, it was my phone camera. I got it recently. Works well even without a flash. But really, I am sorry.'

'Don't be. You didn't mention my name. The control room guys get shafted. But it's an excellent story. Your first, isn't it? Congratulations.'

Abhishek was relieved. 'Thanks, Mayank. I really enjoyed our night out.'

'Me too. Come to the headquarters soon. Bye.'

Vivek called next. 'Boss, you have fucked them. What a story,' he exclaimed.

Abhishek laughed, delighting in the affirmation.

'But you are quite a crook, you know?' Vivek added. 'You were going out that night and you didn't say a word. Now tell me, who was your man? Which cop did you go with?'

'No one. I went alone, Vivek. I stay in Mayur Vihar and thought I'd take a detour to see a bit of the city.'

'I see.' Vivek sounded amused. 'You will go far, my boy.'

Abhishek hurriedly got ready. He had another idea and this might be even bigger.

In a mediated world of sponsored news, rehashed fillers, cricket and cinema gossip, Abhishek Dutta was discovering how valued a good news story is – and how heady and intoxicating its aftermath.

'Sixty thousand criminals vanish worldwide every year. What does the Interpol do? Nothing,' Uday told Mayank vehemently. The younger policeman was giving him an update on his investigations and urging him to involve intelligence agencies. It had been reconfirmed by Uday's sources that Archana could not be traced in Singapore. Babloo's current whereabouts was also ambiguous.

'But should we not at least send her photos to the local agencies?' Mayank persisted.

'She is a chameleon, Mayank. Have you not read the files? Twice she walked out of police traps even when they had her mug shots.' Uday looked out of his fifth-floor window and after a short silence said, 'Our best hope is ground-level intelligence. Talk to the police stations. Find out what the beat constables are hearing – who has moved in, who has moved out. Concentrate on south and south-west Delhi. That is where they will strike.'

Mayank had grave doubts about the way his boss was handling this case. Not to send out a red alert for a known criminal who was planning an operation in your city contravened every rule he knew. He was almost certain that the DCP was not preventing a crime, but allowing it to happen.

'Have you seen the morning papers? Was this on your night gasht?' Uday asked, pointing at the *Express*, and changing the subject.

'Yes, sir, I was there,' Mayank replied, trying to gauge his boss's reaction to Abhishek's story. 'But I had no idea that he was taking photos. I called him this morning as soon as I saw the report. He said he had used a phone camera. I am sorry, sir, I should have been more careful.'

Uday burst out laughing. 'I hear the commissioner has already asked for an explanation. The control room idiots are running around trying to blame each other. One second, let me call our press officer,' Uday chuckled, reaching for the phone. 'Hello, Vikram. Bad morning for you, I hear. This new boy is good. He has screwed us.' Uday listened for a while, the smile on his face getting bigger. 'Ha ha, yes, I have met him. He dropped in the other day.'

Mayank, wondering at the pleasure officers got from seeing each other screwed, suppressed his own grin.

'OK, next time Abhishek comes, send him up. Bye … Fun start to the week,' Uday said, turning to Mayank. 'OK, get on with it. Get me some ground information.'

As Mayank walked out of the office, he had the distinct feeling that he was being set up for a fall. Secrecy the young officer understood, but this was surely irresponsible.

'If you can cross the hurdle which will come in your mid-sixties, you have a long life. I cannot exactly see it, but an accident perhaps.'

Abhishek was sitting with six other journalists in Uday Kumar's room and the policeman was holding court, demonstrating his palm-reading skills. These gatherings at Uday's office were an evening ritual, regularly attended by every crime reporter in the city. In spite of the fierce competition among journalists, the DCP had found a way to keep everyone happy, doling out stories equally, and occasionally implicating troublesome fellow officers. But for such generosity, he demanded a fawning loyalty.

Inspecting Abhishek's upwardly turned hands, Uday continued, 'Maybe an illness. But otherwise, good steady life, excellent prospects. Your career really takes off in your thirties. How old are you now?'

'I am twenty-three, sir. Any particular illness that you foresee? My father has diabetes. You think it could be that?' Abhishek asked.

'There you go,' Uday exclaimed loudly. He dropped the reporter's hands and hit his desk in triumph. 'You have fallen for the classic conman's trap – you ask a question, he knows you are hooked. This is the moment he was waiting for.' Uday laughed at the mildly embarrassed Abhishek, and the other journalists joined in. Ridiculing the new upstart was a crucial part of the initiation.

Abhishek didn't mind. He had just come from the PRO's

office where he had revelled in his fellow crime reporters' praise all afternoon: 'Great story, boss. Screwed them.' 'I have heard the commissioner is livid. Good story.' 'Hey Abhishek, yaar, what a story. Fucked them over. They deserve it, the fuckers.'

Abhishek also noted that it was the senior journalists who seemed more appreciative. Mathur sahab was the oldest of the lot. Almost seventy, short, silver-haired and missing most of his front teeth, he worked as a freelancer for the only Urdu newspaper still surviving in Delhi. He had been their crime reporter for four decades. Five years ago they retired him, only to realize that he would not stop coming.

The veteran had sat next to Abhishek and told him, 'Very good story. It will shake the bosses upstairs.' He flashed the young man a toothless grin. 'Remember one thing: Never take bylines for positive stories. They will think you are a lackey. Only when you screw them, file negative stories, will they take notice of you.'

Abhishek had nodded, not sure he comprehended.

Three news channels had showed his story in their morning newspaper round-ups. A television journalist told Abhishek his channel had asked the commissioner for an official response. The press was going for the jugular, as Amir had predicted in the morning meeting.

'You see, the moment you have turned your palm upwards and are sitting opposite me, you are assuming a vulnerable position,' Uday, in his element now, continued. 'Of course, I am conning you and so is the motherfucker of an astrologer who has absolutely nothing to offer. So, kid, remember: You are your own God. Uday Kumar, bhenchod, is a swindler.' He finished and smiled at the journalists, seeking their approval.

They responded enthusiastically.

Suddenly two of the reporters' phones began to ring almost simultaneously. As they stepped out of the office to answer them, Abhishek's mobile also started vibrating.

Amir was on the line. 'Where are you?'

'At the police headquarters, sir,' Abhishek replied.

'OK, I'm sending a car. It will reach you in five minutes. Be downstairs. There has been a blast in a firecracker factory in Faridabad. Seems quite big. Photographer Praveen Tyagi will be going with you. He has the address. All the best.'

Abhishek joined the rush of departing journalists. His photographer was already at the gates, and he jumped into the car.

'You know there was a fight over this assignment in the office?' Praveen immediately volunteered.

'No. What do you mean?' Abhishek frowned.

'Kavita Joshi is the night reporter. So technically any incident after five p.m. is her duty. But Amir insisted that you be sent.'

Abhishek was quiet, and then asked, 'Are you the night photographer, Praveen?'

'Yes,' he replied. 'For this whole week.'

Praveen Tyagi was nearly forty, but had only recently been designated junior photographer. He had worked at the *Express* for fourteen years, he told Abhishek, the first ten as a darkroom boy and then as an assistant to the chief photographer, Kabir Jain. 'I have been working with Kabir-ji for a long time. He taught me everything I know.'

Abhishek found Praveen's tale heart-warming. He had grown up in a poor household in east Delhi, joining his father in his early teens at their small workshop for bike and car repairs. 'I know everything about vehicles. Give me parts, and I can build a car from scratch,' he told Abhishek candidly. After marriage, his wife resented his being a mere mechanic. He was also tired of the gasoline and grease. 'Kabir-ji was a regular customer at the workshop and I used to attend to his scooter. He secured me the apprenticeship at the *Express*. The pay was very bad but I learnt a new trade and at night and during off days, I continued to help my father at the workshop.'

It was the evening rush hour and the traffic lurched forward in short bursts; drivers impatiently leaning on their horns and drowning out Praveen's narrative.

'How long will this take?' Abhishek asked his.

'Depends,' he replied non-committally, waving at the traffic.

'Don't worry too much,' Praveen offered. 'You will still get your story. Where can the burnt go? You can find them in the nearest hospital. The problem is mine. If the fire is put out, I might not get a good photo.' After a pause, he added, 'But it is a firecracker factory. The blaze should continue.'

Amir decided to wait for Abhishek to return from the assignment before leaving for the day. The fire had killed eighteen children and left thirty-two with severe burns. Amir knew the scenes would be horrifying, especially for a newcomer.

A little after 10 p.m., when he was editing the last story in his drop box and thinking about ordering food, Amir's phone rang. 'Matera. All well?'

'Salaam, sir,' the young criminal's cheerful voice came on the line. 'I have some news.'

'Yes?'

Amir listened carefully as Matera told him about Friday night's party and the car on the street.

'I was drunk, Amir Bhai. I went right up to the car. Salim Bhai was there and he got very angry on seeing me. He immediately sent me off.'

'Did you see who was in the car, Matera?'

'A man and a woman, sir. I saw that. Top-notch woman that too.'

Amir kept prodding, but couldn't get any more details. 'I'll call soon. And in the meantime, keep that paan-chewing mouth of yours shut.'

Amir looked up as Abhishek, still wearing his overcoat, arrived back in the office. As soon as she saw him, Kavita Joshi stomped out.

'File two copies,' Amir told the pale young man. 'One with all essential details: how many dead, how many injured, where, what, how. Then file a personal account: what you saw, people you spoke to, their reactions. OK?'

Abhishek nodded.

'I am here if you need any help,' Amir added gently.

'Write a straight report,' Abhishek told himself, switching on the computer.

More than fifty children were working in an illegal firecracker factory in Faridabad. Aged between nine and fourteen, they came from Sivakasi in the state of Tamil Nadu, a place whose only stamp on modern India was to provide it with firecrackers for celebrating festivals, victories in cricket matches and weddings. No-no, that is commentary; Abhishek checked himself and tried again.

Sivakasi is famous for producing firecrackers, and its children, because of their familiarity with the trade, are regularly sent to factories in different Indian cities. The cause of the fire was not yet confirmed, but the police suspect a short circuit in the wiring. It took six hours to bring the blaze under control, the area superintendent of police said, 'because of the highly inflammable goods kept in the factory, the fire spread rapidly and was difficult to contain'. The death count now stands at twenty but is certain to rise. Of the thirty injured some have suffered one hundred per cent burns, but for some reason are refusing to die. No-no – just that they have suffered one hundred per cent burns, and the doctors attending to them have said that there is little they can do.

Should he write about that girl who, covered with a white sheet, her face completely burnt, had stared at him mutely? Or should he leave that for the personal account? Should he write about the television crew that had insisted on using their harsh lights in the dim corridors of the provincial hospital, inflicting even more suffering on those children? The doctors had pleaded with the cameramen and their assistants, and then given up.

Abhishek got up and went to the toilet. He splashed water on his face and looked at himself in the mirror. He'd thought that he would have cried, maybe vomited out the horrors he had seen that evening. But nothing happened. He remained calm. The pressman's immunity was beginning to cloak itself around him.

He came back to his desk, finished the reports, and took them to Amir.

His boss was flipping through the photographs of the fire. 'Fucker can't get a decent shot. Sorry I sent him with you. He should have remained a darkroom assistant, stupid mechanic. No bloody news sense.'

Abhishek waited till both copies were cleared before speaking to Amir. 'Sir, I have a story idea.'

'Aren't you tired?' Amir asked, surprised. 'Sit. Tell me.'

Without mentioning his friend's name, Abhishek described what Mayank had shown him at the Pakistan High Commission at the end of their night tour.

'It's an excellent story.' Amir nodded thoughtfully, then proceeded to describe to his attentive new recruit how it should be done.

Long after the reporter left, Amir remained sitting in his cabin.

Archana's mobile rang at midnight. Babloo was, as a rule, punctual.

'Tell me,' he said. He did not like small talk on the phone and conversations were rare. He insisted that she use a new SIM card every time he called. She could never call him.

Archana spoke briefly about the evening with Imran, of the boy, and his return to the nightclub on the subsequent two nights. 'The spotter said that on Saturday he went alone,' she added.

'Go next Friday. Not before. All else well?' Babloo asked.

She wanted to tell him about other developments: the meeting with Salim Khan, the renting of the Mehrauli farmhouse, the progress on infiltrating the security team of the boy's father and the house staff – and that she missed him. Knowing Babloo, she resisted. 'All fine,' she said instead, and the line went dead.

Archana liked interaction and hated the wait. In company, she was sparkling. Alone, she was listless. This, she knew, was to be one of those long-drawn-out games. She took out the previous night's pizza and a beer from the fridge, and went out to the terrace. The neighbours next door were having a barbecue, and their laughter floated above the noise of traffic. Someone was singing a song, but Archana couldn't catch the lyrics. She looked at the flower bed. The gardener had promised her a bloom of roses by March. She wouldn't be here then, she thought. She sat on a chair and wrapped a shawl around her. The years in Singapore had made her susceptible to cold. And yet, once upon a time, a winter evening in Delhi had been among her favourite things.

8

At the Pakistan High Commission in Chanakyapuri, a policeman shoved Abhishek. 'Back, back. Get back!' Abhishek stepped away compliantly.

A man tried to say something to the cop, who waved his thick wooden stick at him: 'Sit down. Keep sitting down!'

Abhishek had brought a blanket, which he now laid out on the dewy grass. He sat next to a family of five: three daughters, husband and wife. It was 3 a.m.; two hours more before they would be allowed to queue.

'Where are you from?' the father asked Abhishek.

'Dilli. And you?'

'We are from Chandigarh. Going to Lahore. My sister-in-law is getting married. Where are you going?'

'Karachi,' Abhishek replied. 'My maternal family is from there. I am going on a short visit.'

'Have you got a letter from them?' the man asked, somewhat urgently. 'I hear that you need a letter signed by the local municipal councillor.' He rummaged through a large bag and extracted an envelope. 'Do you know if this will work?' He held the paper up to Abhishek who tried to read it by the light of his mobile phone. It was a short letter, written in the Urdu script.

'Oh, I don't know how to read this,' he said apologetically.

The man, crestfallen, turned back to his wife and did not speak to Abhishek again.

For lack of anything better to do, the journalist lit his fourth cigarette. The street lights, insufficient against the winter fog, spread an eerie glow which threw indistinct shadows in every direction. People slept or just sat listlessly; some huddled together to keep warm.

He made a rough head count: nearly two hundred now – the crowd had doubled in an hour. Nine policemen ensured that no one stepped off the lawns or approached the counter situated at the back of the high commission.

Kabir Jain was crouching at a distance, his camera bag nowhere in sight. Amir had said that there was no one better at covert work than the chief photographer of the *Express*. 'Don't talk to or approach him,' he had instructed Abhishek. 'You are going alone.' What the new reporter did not know was that Amir had also requested the senior cameraman to keep an eye on his ward.

The auto-rickshaws Abhishek had been told to expect emerged out of the thick fog, just before 5 a.m., like a juddering green and yellow cavalry, rounding the corner en masse, disgorging dozens of young men who immediately formed a queue in front of the counter. After their placid acceptance of the night's incarceration, the men and women now jostled and fought each other to secure a place in queues that had already conspired to eliminate them. He slowly approached the crowd pleading with the men in uniform.

'Those applying for a Pakistani visa are required to get coupons first,' Mayank had explained two nights earlier. 'They arrive in the middle of the night, hoping to queue early, but the counters open only at seven a.m. Look,' Mayank had shown

Abhishek, 'they are being held in that field and won't be let loose until five. By that time, hired men will have already formed a long queue.' Only a limited number of coupons were issued each day. 'Most of these people will be disappointed.'

Abhishek now observed a family that was trying to tell two cops that they had to leave for Lahore immediately. 'Urgent, sir. Her father is dead,' the man said, gesturing towards his wife.

'Get in line,' one policeman responded indifferently.

'Maybe you will get lucky,' said the other.

As the policemen turned enquiringly towards him, Abhishek knew that he looked different from most of the men and women gathered there.

'Sir,' he said deferentially, 'I wanted to stand in the line. Up at the front.'

They pointed him to a tout standing next to the counter.

The man seemed to be in his early forties. Despite the cold, he wore no warm clothes, appearing perfectly at ease in his Michael Jackson T-shirt, jeans and fake Nike shoes. He was talking animatedly with his colleagues in front.

'What?' He turned to Abhishek, who repeated his request.

'First eight places, three thousand rupees; next twelve, two thousand. Where do you want?' he said.

'And behind that?' Abhishek asked.

'There is nothing behind that. You never know how many coupons come. Sometimes they just give ten. You don't want to come back again, do you?' Those around him agreed in unison.

'OK, I will take the one in front,' Abhishek said, reaching for his wallet.

'No-no,' the man said hurriedly. 'Not here. Come.'

Abhishek followed him away from the crowd.

'The police, you know … they want all the money.' The

tout smiled. 'Bhenchods, all of them. We do all the hard work; they take the cream. Nothing remains for us.' He looked almost apologetic as he counted the money Abhishek gave him. 'Thank you,' he said, and they shook hands.

'Do you drive an auto?' Abhishek asked.

'No-no.' The man was offended. 'I get the boys together.'

Abhishek was quickly pushed into line as one of the hired men ducked out. Third now in the row and having paid his first bribe, he was acutely conscious of the eyes on him.

He spent the next hour productively, speaking to the paid place-keepers; men who found themselves in the same queue every morning. He tried to memorize the details. Gautam and Gaurav, standing in front of him, were brothers who lived in a south Delhi government colony. Their father was a peon in the Central government.

'Doesn't matter which one, bhai,' Gaurav said, when Abhishek pushed gently for details. 'All same to same, these departments.'

They too were working, had day jobs, the brothers said, but did not say more. They earned 300 rupees each from their queuing duties.

'Not much,' Gautam reflected, 'but it pays for the cigarettes and beer.'

'And where do you come from, bhai? Dilli?' Gaurav asked.

Abhishek was beginning his prepared story when both the brothers and another paid queuer, who had been silently and sullenly chain-smoking behind him, were moved out. A couple and a single traveller took their places.

Fifty-year-old Hassan was from Amritsar. This was his eighth attempt to go to Pakistan to meet his grandparents, and it would be his final. 'If not this time, no more. They both are ninety and will not live much longer.' Every time he came for a visa, he said, the officers at the high commission created different demands. 'I was even ready to bribe them. I paid agents. Still, nothing. This is the last time, then bas, it's over.'

How could this happen in the middle of the city? How did the police get away with this? Right here, in one of the most protected parts of Delhi, the police illegally confined nearly two hundred people night after night. And no one knew about it? From the conversations around him, Abhishek figured that many applicants had travelled from outside the capital, and then come directly from railway and bus stations, having no money to spend on hotels or guest houses.

The cops started counting heads, working out their takings for the morning. It was time for Abhishek to leave. He told Hassan he had to pee. 'I will be back in a minute,' he said, and moved out before the man could reply.

At the end of the queue, he met the tout. 'Where are you going?'

'I have to pee. Can't hold it any longer,' Abhishek replied sheepishly.

The tout seemed annoyed. 'It is not allowed. The police get very angry. Be quick. Just go behind the lane.'

Abhishek walked around the corner. And out of the tout's line of vision, he broke into a run.

When Amir walked in a little after 8 a.m., earlier than usual, he was surprised to find Abhishek dozing in a chair. 'Hi. Good morning,' he said. 'You are early.'

'Good morning, sir.' Abhishek sat up. 'I came straight from the assignment.'

'Yes, of course.' It had slipped Amir's mind. 'Went well?'

'Very well, sir.'

'Give me two minutes,' Amir said, and went into his cabin.

When he had finished checking his emails, Amir asked Abhishek if he wanted to join him for breakfast.

'Yes, sir.' The boy's pleasure was evident.

'OK, let's go. On the way you can tell me what happened.' Amir grabbed his jacket and walked out.

'Let's go to the India Habitat Centre,' he suggested as they sat in the car. 'The American Diner there does a good breakfast. You must be hungry.'

Once past the busy ITO intersection, as the car turned right towards Mandi House, Amir asked, 'So tell me. How did it go?'

Abhishek was careful not to omit details. He told Amir of the high-handed policemen, the exhausted men and women, the touts, and the auto-rickshaws packed with young men. He also tried, as much as possible, to recreate for his boss the scene of the winter night, the people pleading with the unembarrassed money-snatchers in uniform, and his own moral outrage at the whole atrocity. 'It is a scandal, sir, that they get away with this. Something should be done.' Abhishek looked at Amir who hadn't spoken a word throughout.

'Indeed something must be done,' he finally said. 'To start with, you will get a huge breakfast. Then we will plan the story. And tomorrow those cops will be suspended. Come.'

'Remember one thing. Exclusives are fine,' Amir said to Abhishek as they tucked into their scrambled eggs. 'You get a story, like what you have today. No one else has it; so just by its exclusivity, it becomes noticed. But a good reporter is one who can stand out even with a routine story. Say a murder has taken place. Everyone goes; we all cover it. But only the *Statesman* reporter finds out that the victim made a final call at eight p.m. to so-and-so. That reporter and the report stand out from the rest. Do you understand?'

Abhishek nodded.

'Your fire story yesterday. I liked how you described the scene, the television lights blazing down on the burnt bodies. It transported the reader to the place. That's what you need to do; show them more than the camera can, through your words. Of the who, what, when and why, television has taken away the first three. All that remains is the why. And how,' Amir said, pouring himself some coffee. 'So keep asking yourself why. Why corruption, why murder, why theft – why, why, why, why? Make that the mantra.'

This time with Amir was an unexpected treat for Abhishek. The old reporter made up for his earlier aloofness with fabulous tales of his journalistic exploits. 'If you think I am a monster, you should have met my boss, T.R. Wig.' Amir smiled. 'I remember a policeman telling me, "Our deputy inspector generals – the DIGs – are pretty fearsome. Then there are their seniors, the inspector generals – the IGs – who scare the shit out of us. But Wig. No one is more terrifying than the WIG." Wig sahab knew the police beat extremely well. He was a tough taskmaster, but I learnt much from him. He taught me how to cover crime. The other beat I really liked was education.'

The stories poured forth. Amir had grown up in the north campus of Delhi University where both his parents were lecturers. 'The police lines were nearby. As a kid, I used to play basketball with the young officers. By the time I became a journalist, several of them occupied senior positions. That was a tremendous advantage. And I also knew the higher-ups in the university because of my parents.' He sipped his coffee thoughtfully. 'I was familiar with those beats because I spent years on them. I understood the nuances, the rhythms. I could almost predict the fallout of particular incidents. But today, because of television, the profession has completely changed.'

'You don't like television, sir?' Abhishek asked.

'It makes us, as some British journalist said, "an Alzheimer nation". We remember nothing of our past and we have no clue where we are going. Everything is now; you want everything immediately. Expertise is a dirty word today. I see youngsters' CVs which say they have done ten beats in one year. How is that possible? And at the end of it, a twenty-three-year-old, who has never experienced anything in her life, gets to tell my mother about the world. And you know the silliest thing – my mother believes it.' Amir shrugged and looked around for the waiter. 'Need another coffee. I have a long day ahead.'

In his few weeks at the *Express*, Abhishek had already heard the jokes about Amir's foray into television.

'He sounded like a cross between a pompous headmaster and a flailing child,' Divya Bhonsle, Amir's deputy, had cruelly remarked during an office lunch. From the way everyone present had joined in the laughter, Abhishek figured that his boss's misfortune in front of the camera provided an endless reservoir of amusement for the reporting team.

'Earlier,' Amir continued, once his mug had been refilled, 'it took years to become a senior reporter. A special correspondent meant that you had done the hard graft, put years in. The other day a television reporter came to me at the club and gave me his card. It said "Senior Special Correspondent". Never heard of a designation as fancy as that. And he was all of, thirty maybe? And these are the buggers who tell me about Delhi.' Amir shook his head, partly in disgust and partly in amusement.

'Do you like Delhi, sir?' Abhishek asked, refilling his plate. He was ravenous.

'I love Delhi. I could never live anywhere else. I love the winters of course, as everyone else does, but I even enjoy the summers. Hot summer afternoons here remind me of exotic places and stories, you know. I think it was your Bengali bard, Rabindranath Tagore, who said summer afternoons reminded him of Damascus and Samarkand. The thousand Arabian nights, he said, must have been conceived of in such baking afternoons. That's Delhi in the summer – shit hot poetry.'

Abhishek looked up at Amir, astonished.

The older reporter laughed. 'What, you think only Bengalis read poetry?'

'No-no, not that, sir. I mean ...'

'You people think Tagore and culture is your exclusive property, no? I have read more Bengali novels than most of you Bongs have. Sunil Ganguly is one of my favourite writers. I've read quite a few of the classics too. Saratchandra and Bankim. Anyway, what do you think of Delhi?'

'Delhi has no soul,' Abhishek began and immediately realized he had said the wrong thing.

'That is bullshit. It is only outsiders who say that. People who come to the city, but whose loyalties lie elsewhere,' Amir glowered.

Abhishek kept quiet. Growing up in Benares, he had become well used to this allegation that he did not belong. He was called gaddar, the traitor, in school because his grandfather, whom he had never met, was an Englishman. In Kolkata, where he was born and first went to school, Abhishek had been called Anglo; not necessarily a term of abuse in a city where the fascination for its colonial past still lingered. The lonely eleven-year-old, attempting to cash in on his novelty in a new town, discovered that Benares and its resurgent Hinduism did not deal kindly with deviations.

There is no place crueller than a children's playground. The older boys in school devised a torture for him: twenty questions, twenty rapid-fire questions. 'Who is the president of America? Who is the president of the USSR,' and then suddenly, 'Who is the president of your country?' If he paused, the chants would start: 'Gaddar, gaddar!'

Seeing Abhishek go quiet, Amir back-pedalled. 'Don't get me wrong,' he said. 'My ancestry is from Punjab. My parents came here as students. What I mean is, if you are a migratory bird, you don't really care about the place you stay. The Punjabis came here after the Partition, but they were forced to; they are not really migratory. They are not original Dilliwallahs, but they came here to settle. Whereas with, say, the Biharis or the labourers from Uttar Pradesh, their loyalties lie back home. They don't really care about Delhi like a person who is settled here. It's just a place to earn money which goes back to their village or town where, sooner or later, they will follow. They teach their children the same. They change Delhi for the worse.'

Amir thought for a while. 'Let me give you an example. Take your police friends for a moment. The commissioner comes from UP, and Uday is a Bihari. These people started coming in around the 1970s. And that's when Delhi changed. Before 1980, there were hardly any shoot-outs or police encounters. People like Uday brought what they had seen in their towns – they brought the gun culture here. In the 1990s, when there was a spate of robberies and murders, the police claimed they were committed by first-time criminals with no prior record and therefore harder to catch. The truth is that one lot knew the other. They had gone to the same schools; they were from the same bloody place.' Amir paused and took a sip of his coffee. 'I know I am being politically incorrect, but I am right. I know this city better than most. And now I need to pee.'

Abhishek ordered another round of coffee. He knew that he had just been bestowed a rare honour. Amir Akhtar, he was certain, did not regularly breakfast with a far junior colleague. The cold and discomfort of the previous night had been worth it.

'Just give me a first-person report,' Amir had instructed. 'Detail the scam in two paragraphs, and then give me your story – all the details, what you saw … This is front page. Two front pages in the first three weeks is very good, Abhishek.'

It was actually excellent, Amir was thinking as he looked in the bathroom mirror. What he liked most about Abhishek was that the boy kept quiet, observed and listened.

Amir hummed along with Elvis playing on the diner's jukebox as he made his way back to the table. He gulped his coffee without sitting down, and waved for the bill. 'Let's go,' he said.

He was looking forward to announcing Abhishek's latest story at the morning meeting. Some of his team were being nettled by this kid, he thought, a naughty grin spreading across his face.

Mayank was at his desk, staring at nothing in particular. He had a dilemma. Should he not talk to someone – a fellow officer perhaps, or someone senior – about Uday Kumar and the ongoing investigations? Last night he had finally understood why his boss was being so obstinately secretive with the Babloo Shankar investigations, and it put him in an awkward place.

Despite his meticulous research, it was only by chance that Mayank had made the discovery.

In a new development to his formal wooing of Ritika Tytler, he had been invited to a dinner at her house – her birthday dinner, his mother had informed him.

Dressed in a navy-blue blazer Mayank stood at the Tytlers' front door with a bouquet of roses, the eyes of every aged relative on him. Ritika's father immediately introduced him to his older brother, a former officer of Delhi Police. 'I don't know about birds of a feather, but I hear policemen like to flock together,' his prospective father-in-law had guffawed.

It was the kind of evening the young man dreaded. He never drank, and so could not fall back on alcohol to numb his brain against the awful inflictions the retired serviceman subjected it to: the unfailingly disappointing jokes, the bragging, the comparisons between the good old and the bad new days, and the worthlessness of the young.

Despite Ritika's floating presence, Mayank regretted coming. His eyes kept wandering over to the centre of the room where she and her friends had gathered. She, he felt, had barely acknowledged his presence, or his gift. The absence of any young male friend, however, gave him hope.

'I would have been made the commissioner,' Ritika's uncle was telling Mayank. 'Instead they got in Ravi Mishra. Mind you, he was a fine officer but he had never served in Delhi Police before. They got him because he was a Bihari. The home secretary too was a Bihari then; you see, the Maithili Brahmin lobby was very active. Punjabis were completely sidelined.'

Nodding his head, and sipping his third glass of Coke, Mayank wondered if he should try and talk to Ritika. Perhaps she was just being shy. But the rants of dissatisfied ambition next to him suddenly gave way to something more interesting.

'You work with Uday Kumar, young man?'

Mayank had not expected to be asked any questions about himself. 'Yes, sir,' he replied.

'Another Bihari. The chap was working under me. Was completely protected by the lobby. Botched up a major case because of his idiocy and lack of planning. But his clan protected him.'

The retired policeman had asked for another whisky and then told Mayank how Uday Kumar, without his boss's authorization or knowledge, had led a foolhardy operation to catch Babloo Shankar. The criminal had escaped, but with a bullet in his spine.

'He wanted to kill the man,' the ex-cop continued. 'There were no plans to take him alive. The team was a small one: Uday and four encounter specialists. That should have been the end of his career. The kidnapped girl belonged to a big business family, well connected in political circles. The father was willing to pay the ransom, but our hero stepped in. We never heard of the child again.'

Mayank was listening intently.

'But Uday's stars were aligned well. His role was hushed up and we as a department took the blame. I was in the south district then, posted as additional commissioner.'

'But surely Uday sir developed the intelligence with a team. People must have known about it ...' Mayank probed, hoping he sounded casual.

'Uday briefed his team at the very last minute. He said he had got an anonymous tip-off. Anonymous, my foot! He just wanted all the glory and when it went wrong, he ran to his political bosses to save his career ... Ah, the birthday cake. Come, let's eat.'

It had been an enlightening evening, Mayank thought, and now Uday had asked him to bring over the character profile he had made of Archana.

He walked slowly to his boss's office.

Uday was sitting with a slim gentleman in his early fifties, who was leaning back casually in his seat, his shiny leather brogues crossed in front of him, when Mayank entered the office.

'Come,' Uday said as he saluted. 'Meet Amir Akhtar of the *Express*. You must have heard of him.'

'Of course I have. Pleasure meeting you, sir. I know your reporter Abhishek Dutta quite well.'

'Yes, that boy of yours is well connected, Amir,' Uday added. 'Came with the commissioner's reference. But I am giving him a proper training. Sent him for a night patrol with Mayank and look, he has done a great story. I continue to be your regular supplier of news.'

'Yes. I wonder with you around why Delhi Police needs a press officer,' Amir replied, and Mayank stifled a smile. He had never witnessed a journalist being sardonic with his boss.

'Shall we start?' Uday reclaimed authority. 'Sit, Mayank. Amir has some information which he thinks is important to the Babloo case. You should hear this.'

Mayank kept his face impassive. Another player in Uday's game? What was going on?

'Before I do that, can I hear about Archana?' the journalist asked Mayank, who looked at Uday.

'Yes, go ahead. Even I want to hear it again,' Uday nodded.

Mayank was baffled. After all the secrecy, his boss was asking him to talk about the case and of its principal character before a journalist. His mind was frantically trying to make connections.

'Let me start with the physical characteristics,' Mayank said slowly. 'She is 5ft 3 inches. Oval face, dark eyes, small nose, medium build. Weighs just under fifty kilos. The problem with this description is that it applied to her when she was nineteen or twenty. We are not sure what she looks like now. I have three photographs sourced from Interpol taken in the last five years. As far as I can tell, they are of different women. I think in Archana's case,' he said, looking at Uday, 'it might be difficult to go by physical appearance.'

Mayank looked at his files and paused as the tea was served. He glanced at Uday for some clue. Till now he had kept his disclosures to a minimum; things that anyone with an Internet connection could discover. But his boss gave away nothing, so he continued.

'Archana, unlike Babloo, has no family history of crime. Her parents are from Indore where they still live. The father worked in a multinational pharmaceutical company, never changed jobs, and retired from the same place. Comfortable middle-class existence. She studied at St Mary's Convent and then came to Lady Shriram College in Delhi where she graduated with honours in history. Like Babloo, she chose to rebel against her family, only with more success. Indore Police confirm that her parents have cut all contact with her.'

'What you are saying,' Amir interrupted, 'is that you cannot find any explicable reason for her turning to crime. There is no childhood trauma, poverty, or anger that can explain it. Life is not a Hindi film where you can find reasons. Cause and effect doesn't always work, no?' Amir said, looking at Mayank wryly.

'Yes, but if you see patterns of the other female gangsters in Mumbai, they were all put in certain situations. Zenabai, for example. Or Mrs Paul or Jyoti.' Mayank did not like Amir's slightly patronizing tone.

'OK, let's do this crime psychology a bit later,' Uday muttered, suddenly impatient. 'Carry on with Archana, Mayank.'

'After graduation she goes off to Mumbai,' he resumed quickly. 'We do not know her exact connections there, whom she met, what she did in the early stages. But it seems very likely that her first film role came about because of her association with the top mafia bosses. *Mobster* was financed by Babloo; that we are certain of. She did a few music videos but nothing of note. The police hear of her first in 1991. She is twenty-one and masterminds the kidnapping of a prominent hotelier. Ransom paid, no case registered. There are five more kidnappings in the next one year: two film producers, two industrialists and the son of a banker. Then follows a period of relative calm before Babloo and Archana start operating here. By 1996, before Babloo escapes, Archana is being called Madame X, the most wanted female gangster in India.'

'Good. Now, can you tell Mayank what you know, Amir?' Uday stage-directed.

'I will, but just before that, what have you done to check on Archana's whereabouts? Your sources are telling you that she has vanished from Singapore and is headed here or is already here?'

Uday nodded.

Mayank was finding the scene increasingly surreal. Why on earth was his boss sharing all this with this man?

'This morning, it was just a hunch,' Amir said to them. 'But after hearing Uday and you, Mayank, I am pretty certain something is up.' He told them what Matera had witnessed.

'Two questions.' If he was to work like this, Mayank thought, so be it. 'First, can I meet your source? Second, why do you feel this is out of the ordinary? Salim Khan meets many people; some of them quite important, as we know. And is a Lexus car unusual in that neighbourhood?'

'I will tell my boy to come in,' Amir replied. 'In fact, I will bring him along. He can be a bit nervy. Answer to your second question is a bit more difficult. We know that if Babloo came here, he would most probably contact Salim. They have worked closely in the past, and Salim maintains links with the Mumbai underworld. I think that the possibility of Archana being in town and Babloo planning something here has a connection with what Matera saw. But fundamentally, Mayank, it's a hunch. And what I call a hunch is called intelligence in your circles.'

Mayank smiled. Amir's confidence was overpowering. Even his garrulous boss seemed careful. 'Thank you, sir,' he replied. 'I would like to follow this up immediately, if I may.'

'I will let you know. Uday, I have to leave now but we will be in touch. Pleasure meeting you, Mayank.'

As the reporter left the room, the young police officer turned to his boss. He needed some answers.

9

Standing in front of the mirror, Amit Mahajan frowned at his slouching reflection. 'Stand straight,' he barked, just as his father would, and pushed his chest out. He was not fat, but his mother's indulgence and a lack of exercise had produced the hint of a double chin and a readily available dimple. It made him look younger and, to his now critical gaze, childish. That morning he had shorn the few curls from just above his forehead. His mother would be infuriated, Amit knew. But for now there was another woman on his mind.

It was taking him an unusually long time to dress, the floor bearing witness to the decisions and revisions. Amit hoped it would be worth all the trouble. For the past six nights, his mission had failed repeatedly but that had hardly dented his sense of purpose. Each evening at the Sheraton club he felt certain that she would reappear, and her absence only renewed his hope. The morning after made him look forward to sunset.

Amit decided on a white shirt, an ash-coloured woollen jacket and Tommy Hilfiger jeans. No perfume; a dash of a mild aftershave would do. His least flamboyant watch, a brown-leather Swatch, found favour. He looked in the mirror again and was not entirely displeased with the effect.

At 10.15, he asked for the car to be brought to the main entrance. Amit had his own driving licence, acquired illegally, four years ago. But with the recent turmoil in their lives, his father now insisted on a chauffeur who, unknown to his young passenger, was always armed.

The Mahajan family proved what middle-class India could be with a bit of hard work and political dexterity, accompanied by an underdeveloped notion of morality. At this stage, however, calling the family middle class would be considered a serious calumny by Brigadier Devinder Mahajan (Retd). Part owner of Colorado Builders and Associates, Amit's father was a minor beneficiary of the government's Commonwealth Games munificence and had amassed a fortune. He, of course, would suggest that his economic achievements began long before pliable ministers and their bureaucrats, industrialists and their middlemen recognized the Games as a money-laundering opportunity on a scale unheard of even in a country riddled with corruption.

No, the Brigadier would say that his success owed as much to the risks he had taken in life, like renouncing his job in the army, where as an engineer with the Madras Sappers, institutionalized and risk-free corruption had been lucrative. Three years prior to retirement – possibly a few more, given the strong likelihood of his promotion to major general, he would add – Brig. Mahajan had resigned.

Along with his older brother who had settled in Colorado, USA, he had started a private venture, supplying spare motor vehicle parts to the Indian Army. His brother-in-law, a small-time industrialist and part-time hoodlum, had muscled his way to a seat in the Punjab Legislative Assembly. Suddenly there were more contracts than Brig. Mahajan could handle.

He branched off into real-estate development and Colorado Builders was born. They signed MoUs with partners in New

Zealand and Australia and started buying land in Ethiopia and Kenya, long before such a thing became fashionable among Indian businessmen. He felt justified in thinking of himself as a pioneer.

And then came the Commonwealth Games bonanza. Brigadier Mahajan and his associates acquired wealth beyond their wildest dreams. 'We are stinking-rich,' his wife Radha, who now took Dubai shopping vacations and scorned her army wives' friendship circles, liked to whisper to him in moments of rediscovered passion. Suddenly they needed tax lawyers and havens abroad; Swiss accounts had to be opened and security firms hired.

After the payouts came the payback. There were raids, questions and interrogations. Politician friends refused to take the Brigadier's calls. The press initially avoided the subject, busy as they were scavenging for their own scraps of this tempting new common wealth. But, once the story became too large to ignore, they turned into a pack of angry hounds. Journalists and their television cameras took up residence on the Mahajans' well-manicured lawns. Food waste, chocolate bar wrappers and chewing gum piled up under the shade of their imported palm trees. There were reports on Radha Mahajan's properties and of assets accumulated in the Brigadier's brother's name. Newspapers published hints of the foreign bank accounts, and the ex-serviceman's face began to appear on magazine covers.

The previous week, as their son was being mesmerized by an older woman, Brig. Mahajan and his wife decided to take a much-needed Nevada vacation – days before the investigative agencies and courts would freeze their passports.

If Babloo was upset, or his plans delayed by the Mahajans' departure, he did not convey it to Archana. 'Concentrate on the boy, but string the process out,' was the instruction.

Six nights after she had teased Amit with a first glimpse, Archana was also getting ready for her Friday evening. Even before the spotter called Imran to confirm that the boy was making his way to the club, Archana had laid out the dress she would wear. Amit had been to the club every night that week, a deviation from his usually quiet routine. Archana had little doubt that she was the reason for the change in lifestyle. It made Babloo's plans for an unsuspicious second meeting far easier than anticipated.

The red dress she had chosen hugged her body. It did not show off her cleavage, but he had seen enough of that already, she thought. Instead, it accentuated her breasts just enticingly enough. She had been working out in the gym these last four months, and it showed. Archana examined herself closely in the mirror. She would let her hair hang loose, she decided. She was pondering over footwear when Imran called. He was downstairs, waiting in the car.

'You are not coming to the club,' Archana told him as they drove. 'Remain within two miles, and I will call if you are needed.'

Imran remained silent. He was disappointed, but knew better than to argue. He had got a hard-on the moment he'd seen her coming out of the gate and all he wanted to do was to be slammed again on the car seat. He would grab her buttocks this time and lift her onto his cock.

'Is he alone?' Archana's voice cut through his thoughts. 'What did Usman say?'

'He reached the club alone but might be meeting friends

there,' Imran replied. 'In the last week, his friends have accompanied him twice.'

Archana lit a cigarette and studied herself in the rear-view mirror.

'I almost wish I was the boy,' Imran said, in spite of himself, and hesitantly smiled at her.

Archana looked at him, and without rancour, malice or flirtation, replied, 'No, you don't.'

There was a character she had planned for the boy, a certain persona, and everything needed to be consistent with it. She and Babloo had spent hours going over Amit Mahajan's details, and Archana had settled on the slightly hungry, horny older woman; just out of reach and something to be strived for. She had several other characters; the submissive girl-next-door being her mentor's favourite. For the boy, however, she had told Babloo, that wouldn't work.

A little past 11 p.m., Archana stepped out of the car and into her role. As she ascended the stairs to the club, Imran noticed that even the uniformly polite guards stole secretive glances at the retreating buttocks of Monika Mathur.

The models, fashionistas and beauty contestants were still at one another's houses, sipping whiskies and sniffing white lines. The Mexican DJ advertised on the door with his hair on fire, was yet to make an appearance. For now, canned music and disco lights stroked a vacant dance floor while moneyed men past their prime sat around in tight flashy clothes, pretending to lip sync, praying that for once they would not be paying cash for romance. What would they not give for an emotional upheaval of the sort that fill the young with despair.

The boy was sitting alone. Monika took a table where hungry eyes could feast on her and looked around for a waiter. She ordered a Margarita frozen. The fluorescent lights gave her dress a strange glow and she was unhappy with the effect. Men stared and she made eye contact engagingly. The drink came and she started playing with her mobile phone, sending imaginary and real texts including one to Imran that the target was here and he should call in forty-five minutes.

Monika knew that the boy was trying to summon up the courage to approach her. She refused to be less intimidating. He would have to work at it; must feel that he had achieved something. Let it take its time.

'Can I buy you a drink?' he asked, bending down close to her.

She looked up, startled, and then smiled. 'I am waiting for someone.' Seeing his slightly crestfallen face, she added, 'But I don't see why not. Have a seat.'

Amit Mahajan sat down quickly. His heart was pounding and his throat was parched. It had taken all his willpower, and then some more, to walk the few steps to her table. He waved at a waiter. 'What will you have?' he asked her. She ordered a second Margarita and he a Tom Collins. 'They make it well here,' he said as the waiter left. 'How is your drink?'

'Not the greatest I have had, nor the worst.'

He felt tongue-tied and looked down at the table.

'What is your name?'

'Amit Mahajan.'

'I am Monika Mathur,' she said, extending her hand. He shook it quickly.

'I am sorry if I have intruded,' Amit offered after a short silence.

'No ... I was getting a bit bored waiting. My fiancé should have been here half an hour back, but ...'

'Oh, OK.'

'So how old are you?' Monika asked Amit as the waiter set down their drinks.

'Twenty-five,' he replied.

'Yeah right, and I am eighteen.' Monika laughed. 'But I don't mind as long as it is not illegal to drink with you.'

'It's not,' Amit said, smiling shyly.

They clinked their glasses and Monika appraised the boy. He had worked hard at looking grown-up. Good; he had definitely taken the bait. When should he be allowed to bite?

'Is your drink OK?' Monika asked him.

'Yes, thank you. And yours?'

Monika nodded. The call came as instructed, and she spoke on her phone briefly before turning to him. 'Looks like it is your lucky night,' she said, her eyes twinkling. 'Dhruv just cancelled on me. He is stuck at the office. Can I buy you a drink? Or am I keeping you?'

'No-no, not at all. I mean it will be a pleasure.'

'Good,' she said, looking at him over the glass.

Amit admitted to Monika that he was actually twenty-one. He had graduated a year back from Delhi University and was going to the US in the autumn to study media management at Maryland. His two elder brothers were settled in the US and his father wanted him to join them. He had been helping out in the family business in Delhi and Punjab recently, but was not sure that he wanted to work in construction. He liked music. Rock was his favourite. He liked the older bands: Deep Purple and Dire Straits; also U2 and Bob Dylan. He hated hip hop. He was an avid reader – mostly fiction. He loved comics; *Calvin and Hobbes* and *Peanuts* were his favourites. He also liked *The Far Side*. She hadn't heard of it? Oh, but she must read them. Gary Larson, the cartoonist, had a great sense of humour. Maybe he could send a few to her. He had seen her last Friday actually. Did she come here regularly?

Just her second time, Monika told him. She had recently moved to Delhi from New Jersey where she had been working at IBM as a software developer. Her fiancé, Dhruv Chowdhury, was a banker in New York and they had been trying to get a posting back to India for a while now. They were planning marriage, kids and a future here. 'My playing days are coming to an end. Got to settle down and be an Indian wife – a desi bahu.' She giggled, and he laughed with her.

For Amit, the evening flew by. Monika was the easiest person to talk to. She laughed a lot, and loudly. Her conversation was interesting. And he could not keep his eyes off her. He wanted to see her again.

'I want to see you again,' Amit blurted.

'Why not?' Monika said after a moment's pause. 'I am not married yet, and nothing wrong with meeting a most interesting young man,' she added, touching his arm lightly. 'But tonight I have to rush, my dear. I have your number. Shall I call you?'

'Yes-yes.' Amit couldn't believe it. 'Will you really call?'

'Of course. Why wouldn't I?'

Giving Amit a light peck on the cheek, Monika swept away.

With a nominally six-day work week, frequently seven, most reporters tended to take it easy on Saturdays. Bosses were lenient on employees arriving after noon or leaving early for an evening show. The pages relied on features, long articles and stories held back from earlier in the week.

Public offices being closed, the reportage of public servants' shenanigans got a break.

Abhishek, not yet clued in to the languid pace of weekends, had arrived at his usual time of just a few minutes past 9 a.m. At the morning meeting, the editor Mihir Ghosh praised his story, 'Pakistani visas come at a high commission', and Amir announced that a departmental inquiry had been set up against the policemen. The general exuberance which met Abhishek's first story, however, was not repeated by his colleagues.

Abhishek had aligned himself to the younger lobby of reporters, and Rahul and Maya were protective of him. He had learnt very quickly that everything he said could be and would be misinterpreted: insignificant comments could lead to ferocious enmities. Having already stepped on a few toes and suddenly become Amir's blue-eyed boy, Abhishek attracted hostility, particularly from senior reporters.

Maya had tried to tell him that nothing was neutral in a reporting room, but it still took getting used to. Rahul, in his customarily blunt manner, counselled: 'They will bugger you anyway. If you bugger them back, they might do it cautiously next time.'

He may not have enjoyed newsroom politics, but Abhishek certainly liked the attention. He also admired the casual arrogance of his fraternity; their belief that they knew better. In the pressroom at the police headquarters, reporters dissected crime scenes and cases, made pronouncements against police officers, described their intimate relationships with gangsters, and how, at one time or other, their scoops had seen officers quaking in their boots. That two of his exclusives had actually created trouble was not lost on the young journalist. He was working on the arrogance.

Two nights ago he had called his mother to tell her that he wouldn't be joining the family on their annual visit to Kolkata this December. Holidays had always meant aunts, uncles, cousins, and their large family home in Jorasanko. His mother had never demanded anything else and his father, homesick even after sixteen years of living in Benares, never desired another destination.

'When will we see you?' his mother had asked, disappointed.

He wasn't sure, Abhishek had replied, but not before the probation period was over. That would be another five months. Yes, he liked the work and the salary was sufficient.

'We have been reading your stories,' his father had told him. 'Be careful of the police. They can be ruthless.'

'Yes, Baba,' Abhishek had replied politely.

It was almost 2 p.m. now and Abhishek felt hungry. He had done the routine checks and Delhi seemed to be enjoying the respite of the winter weekend. Rahul was the only reporter in the office.

'Boss, how about lunch?' Abhishek asked him.

Rahul looked at his watch. 'Wait another ten minutes. I know Shruti Sen, the features editor, has ordered food. It's her birthday today. I have told reception to let me know as soon as it comes. We can land up to wish her.'

Abhishek laughed. 'But I don't even know her.'

'You will get to when you wish her. Now let me finish this report.'

Abhishek's phone rang. It was the police press officer, Vikram Singh. The east district police was going to have a press conference at 4 p.m.; a murder had been solved. 'Do come,'

Vikram said. 'I have never heard of anything more gruesome in my thirty years of service.'

'Of course, sir. I will be there.'

'What?' Rahul asked as Abhishek disconnected.

'Some murder case that East Delhi police has solved.'

Now the phone on Rahul's desk rang. He grabbed the receiver. 'Birthday food is here,' he announced as he hung up.

The two reporters gleefully made their way, uninvited, to the features desk for their lunch.

Deputy commissioner of police, east district, Soumya Patnaik – call sign Echo 1 – was feeling good about the press conference. He had not allowed for any leaks and had told his junior officers that even a word to the press beforehand would be dealt with severely. The case was so horrifying and brutal that the news channels would have a field day. Prime-time coverage was assured.

By the time Soumya and his deputy entered the conference room, it was packed with chattering reporters. The red suitcase had been placed on a table, centre stage, as Soumya had instructed. He was relishing his impending moment of glory. After greeting a few familiar journalists he took a seat, indicating to his deputy to sit beside him. Vikram Singh had already parked himself in front of the cameras.

'Shall we start, friends?' Soumya began, and waited for the room to quieten down. 'East Delhi police this morning arrested a forty-three-year-old man from Seelampur in connection with a murder. Two weeks back a suitcase was found near Dilshad Garden.' The DCP paused dramatically and pointed at the red suitcase as cameras zoomed in on it. 'Upon opening it, the beat constable found a dismembered body of a child, a girl. We sent the body for immediate autopsy.'

Vikram had not exaggerated, Abhishek thought, as he took notes. He looked around. Even the older, hardened lot of crime reporters appeared squeamish and uncomfortable. The man arrested for the murder was the father of the eleven-year-old girl whose decomposing body was found chopped into bits. Soumya said that after strangling the child to death, the accused had masturbated on the body and then hacked it into several pieces.

'He had travelled with her from Allahabad, his home town, where his wife and two sons remain. We have sent a notice to the police there,' the officer said.

Baldev Pujara was a tailor who had been unemployed for nearly two years after the factory where he worked shut down. He told his wife that he had found employment in Delhi and would take their daughter with him, as managing three children would be difficult for her. In the city he had taken shelter in a slum, close to where the suitcase had been found.

'He paid for a room for a week. We found the owner of the place and questioned him, which gave us clues leading to the arrest,' Soumya added. Pujara, during interrogation, had confessed to the police that he had killed his daughter on his fourth night in Delhi. 'For three days, he aimlessly roamed the streets with the child. We are not yet sure why he waited or what he was intending. We hope to get custody of him from the magistrate tomorrow and continue the interrogation.'

After the press conference, the television reporters were the first to rush back to their offices to meet their prime-time deadlines. The newspaper reporters hung around a while, finishing their tea and snacks.

Abhishek approached the glowing DCP.

'Nice to meet you, Abhishek. I have been reading your stories and am told that you are the new kid on the block. Good, good,' Soumya said. 'If you have any questions on the case ...'

'Can I meet the accused, sir?' The reporter knew it was an unreasonable, almost impossible request.

'What? No, absolutely not. That is out of the question.' The policeman seemed taken aback.

'Why? He must still be in your lock-up, no?' Abhishek persisted.

'Yes. But I cannot give you permission. My boss will not allow it. I am sorry.' The boy was quite impertinent, Soumya thought.

Abhishek politely took his leave, retreated to a corner of the hall and dialled the commissioner's number. Delhi's topmost policeman came on the line immediately.

'I am very sorry to disturb you, sir,' Abhishek said.

'Not at all, Abhishek. It is a rare weekend off, actually. How are you doing?' Pratap said.

'I am well, sir, but I'm calling with an urgent request.'

'Yes, of course. Tell me.' The commissioner listened to Abhishek and decided to accede. 'Where are you now?' he asked.

'Still at the press conference venue and DCP Patnaik is here too.'

'OK, let me get back to you.'

Abhishek's heart pounded as he disconnected. There was no doubt that calling the police commissioner on his mobile phone on a Saturday was a breach of protocol, but it was done now.

Abhishek sat down and waited. He was not entirely sure why he wanted to meet this horrific murderer, but remembered what Amir had told him: 'Keep asking why.' Soumya Patnaik's statements gave no clue to the motive for such a morbid crime. And Abhishek knew it would be a terrific scoop if he did manage to meet the man. He was following Amir's other advice: go the extra distance in a routine story.

Across the room he saw Soumya take a call, and knew from the way the policeman came to attention that it must be from the commissioner.

As Soumya hung up, his eyes searched the room. He saw Abhishek and then turned towards his deputy. The two men had a quick chat and Soumya beckoned to the reporter.

'Hi ... the commissioner just called me.' The confusion and embarrassment in the officer's voice were apparent. There was no easy way to convey that what he had ruled out minutes ago, he would now have to arrange.

Abhishek tried to help. 'I am sorry, Mr Patnaik. I called the commissioner. I just thought it might be helpful for readers to understand, if possible, what this accused is like. But really, if you think ...'

'No-no ...' Soumya was intelligent enough to grab the olive branch of respect being offered. 'Let's do this. But I'm warning you; it will not be an easy assignment. I will keep a police constable in the room.'

Abhishek was taken to an adjoining building. On the first floor, along a bare corridor lit by a single low-wattage bulb, he was shown into a cell. The constable hit a switch and a light came on. There was a table, two chairs and a wooden bed without mattresses. In the corner, a dark-brown puddle gave off a putrid smell.

'Sit. I shall be back in a moment,' the constable told him as he went to bring the man Abhishek wanted to meet.

Abhishek shivered from the winter chill, accentuated by the fear that gripped him. The murderer sitting opposite him was not more than five feet tall. Everything about him appeared tiny – his head, his moustache, his eyes and face. Abhishek suddenly visualized the act: those small hands circling the neck of a terrified, uncomprehending child … The journalist kept his gaze on his notepad.

From the moment Baldev Pujara had entered the room, Abhishek had been off-footed. He had not known whether to greet the accused or stay silent. His middle-class, university upbringing had not prepared him for the nuances of starting a conversation with a man who had confessed to jerking off on his daughter's dead body. The constable who sat on the steel bed seemed tickled at Abhishek's discomfiture.

'Why did you do it?' It was the first question Abhishek could think of.

There was no response.

The constable, grinning, urged Baldev, 'Tell sir, go on.'

'What?' the accused asked, fixing his eyes on the nervous reporter.

Abhishek stumbled, unsure of what to say next. 'To your daughter … I mean …'

The man kept staring at him.

The policeman, almost friendly, prodded again: 'Sir is asking, why did you kill your daughter? Why did you put her in a suitcase?'

'I don't know. Just like that.'

If Abhishek had been expecting denials or reasoned explanations, he was to be disappointed. 'Did you plan this? When you came from Allahabad, did you know that you would do this?' he tried again.

'Yes,' Baldev said simply.

'You planned to put your daughter in a suitcase? Cut her up?' Abhishek asked, incredulity creeping into his question. He still couldn't bring himself to ask the man in front of him why he had masturbated on a dead child.

'No, I did not know that.'

'Then why … ?'

Baldev looked up at Abhishek and then at the constable. 'It happened.'

After ten minutes of similar responses, Abhishek decided to call it quits. He did not have the skills to extract or understand the motives behind the crime. He already had material for his exclusive: the atmosphere, his meeting with the accused – that was enough for six hundred words. He signalled to the constable and got up.

The policeman took Baldev back to his cell and Abhishek walked towards DCP Patnaik's office across the courtyard.

'How did you find him?' Soumya asked as he entered.

'Nothing to find,' Abhishek replied. 'He is quite repellant.'

'That he is. But enough material for your story?'

Abhishek noted the sarcasm in the voice. 'Yes, sir. Thanks to you. But I must leave now. Getting very late.'

'OK. But you know the amount of flak I will get from your colleagues for this? Everyone will want to know how you got to meet the accused and they did not.'

Abhishek smiled apologetically and hurried out.

He checked his phone. There were several missed calls from the office. He called his boss.

Amir was angry: 'Where are you? Every channel has the bloody story on air and you have vanished.'

Abhishek explained, not in an entirely modest voice, that he had got an exclusive interview with the killer. If he was expecting kudos, that did not come.

'That's fine,' Amir said. 'But it takes a minute to let the desk know so that the website can be updated. We have been running wire stories.'

A round the time Abhishek was sitting in the interrogation cell, Vikram had received a call from the commissioner's staff officer. 'Good evening, Shekhar-ji,' he said.

'Good evening, sir, good evening. Sorry to bother you on a weekend.'

'Arre, what weekend. Patnaik had a press conference. Just heading back.'

'Yes, I know,' Shekhar said. 'The commissioner just called me regarding this young reporter, Abhishek Dutta. I believe he was there.'

'Yes, I met him. Why, something wrong?'

'No, nothing much. The boss is impressed and wants to invite the boy for one of the year-end lunches. You decide when. Maybe coming week? But boss is wondering if he is getting a bit too good, no? Maybe you should check on him. He called the commissioner earlier to arrange for an interview with the accused. Boss had to agree.'

'Really?' Vikram was incensed. 'Let me see what I can do.'

Abhishek Dutta had grossly overstepped his mark, Vikram thought. He had bypassed the press office and gone straight to the very top. The commissioner was right; the bugger needed to be taught the rules.

10

❧

'**S**hall we go for a drink?' Rahul proposed and, before his wife could object, Maya answered for the group.

'Good idea. A drink after a movie is a must. Abhishek, do you know of any place around here?'

He shook his head. Abhishek liked the idea of spending time with Maya, but it was almost the end of the month and the bars in Saket, he had heard, were expensive.

Once a bustling, affordable neighbourhood on the outer circles of south Delhi, Saket, at the turn of the century, had attracted developers who were bent on turning it into another upmarket Defence Colony clone. Old houses and even older residents hesitantly exchanged their crumbling walls for brand-new apartments with modular kitchens. As an added incentive, there was cash; so much of it that the old-timers no longer had to suffer the indignity of their children's fluctuating generosity. The developers got flats, the owners got flats, and there were even a couple left over for renting. The slightly shabby houses in this large residential area were being quickly replaced by identical-looking apartments. The few original abodes that remained looked distinctive and unnatural. Their owners, conscious of their particularity, now pursued the builders. Everyone seemed to have won.

New tenants moved in, newer cars arrived. There was money

to be spent. The elderly wanted what television had for so long promised but impecuniousness denied, and the young tenants continued the lifestyles they'd adopted during their foreign degrees. Supermarkets stocked muesli, goat's cheese and rocket salad. Bars fashioned fresh names for jaded cocktails.

The four journalists were heading towards one such establishment. It was a Sunday evening. Abhishek's interview with Baldev Pujara had been carried as the second lead story. Amir had sat with him to write the article, drawing from the material a sense of atmosphere and drama. When Maya accused Amir of adding colour to a news story, he had promptly agreed. The story deserved it. Maya's stricken face had reaffirmed her earlier warning to Abhishek: in a newsroom nothing was neutral.

'What did you think of the film?' Abhishek asked as they took their seats at Ruby Tuesday.

'Oh, I loved it,' Madhumita, Rahul's wife, replied emphatically. 'For once, not usual Bollywood. Quite alternative and brave.'

Rahul nodded and Abhishek was just about to agree when Maya interjected: 'I think it was a clever film. It pretended to be alternative while pandering to our worst middle-class stereotypes.'

'Arre yaar, at least let me order a drink first,' Rahul pleaded with her in mock anguish, and winked at Abhishek. 'Madam did sociology in college. Now you will get an earful.'

Madhumita looked peeved. 'No, please. Do tell us your pronouncements.'

Maya, unmindful of the sarcasm, held forth. 'OK. Let's start with the film's premise,' she said. 'Young Indian-American banker comes back on a sabbatical to do some social research. Firmly rooted in our middle-class imagination of foreign-returned and yet slightly alternative, she, like many of us, is bored by the mainstream. Her relationship with Aamir Khan, the good-looking artist, follows set patterns. In India you need a local thing going. Artist equals alternative, therefore good choice during her research phase. There is some muddling with a washerman or washer-boy, if you prefer, to show that you are not really class conscious. The boy is poor, but his aspirations and ambitions are ours. We have carefully crafted this rags-to-riches story and his character fits right in. Poor boy wants to be rich and famous, and we will help him.'

'So what is wrong with that?' Madhumita asked with a look which suggested Rahul and Abhishek obviously shared her position.

'What is wrong is that if it caters to the status quo, as you just agreed, then don't call it alternative. And when have you seen a washer-boy with a six-pack and a stylish stubble?'

'Well, it wasn't a happy ending at least,' Rahul ventured to support his wife, fearing the night ahead.

'Agreed. It wasn't a formula film. All I objected to was calling it radical.' Maya spoke with the certainty of someone used to winning arguments.

There was an uncomfortable pause before Maya launched in again. 'Do you remember the films we used to admire as kids, the old ones, those blockbusters from the '60s and '70s? Rahul, you still sing those songs, no? They were mostly about the poor man, the poor family. They were the central characters, the heroes. Now the washerman is the outsider and wants to be like us. We are the protagonists now. Perhaps in a way you are right, Madhumita. It is radical. But that is not the sort of radicalism you espouse, do you?'

Their drinks arrived, interrupting Maya's flow. Rahul attempted various conversations but they petered out, as did the drinks, and he and Madhumita excused themselves early. 'Sorry guys. Staying with parents is difficult. It's a Sunday and they will be waiting for us for dinner.'

Abhishek and Maya nodded, relieved.

'Bad vibes between you and Madhumita?' Abhishek asked as soon as the couple left.

'We worked together once. I think the competitive edge remains and the fact that I am much smarter still rankles.'

Abhishek laughed. 'You were quite harsh.'

'About the movie? Absolutely not. It is just silly to give the label "radical" to anything you find remotely different from the formulaic. But listen, do you want to have dinner?' Maya saw the look of hesitation play on Abhishek's face, and added, 'It's on me, OK? Take me out when you get your salary.'

He smiled gratefully. 'Thanks, yes, I am a bit broke.'

They walked out of the bar and Maya recommended an Italian restaurant next door. 'The pizzas are very good and I love their salads. Do you like Italian?'

Abhishek chose not to admit that except for his mother's cooking and the vile university hostel fare, he knew nothing about food.

Inside, Maya ordered a bottle of red, a Pinot Noir, from the Burgundy region in France. 'I look at it this way,' she remarked. 'I just have to get used to being an ecological criminal.'

Abhishek hoped that silence would conceal his ignorance. Was she showing off, he wondered for a moment, and then let her expressive eyes convince him otherwise.

'So, tell me about yourself.' Maya leaned back.

'You'd be bored and out of here in a minute.'

'Look, if you are telling me that you are just a kid out of nowhere who comes in and does front-page reports with alarming regularity, becomes best mates with our crusty boss, and is generally the new hotshot of the reporting unit, then I am wasting money on expensive wine.'

'You mean you are getting me drunk to extract information?' Abhishek smiled at her.

'I am far more devious, my darling, and can stoop even lower, but yes, that is a possible reason,' Maya replied, with mischief in her eyes.

Abhishek shifted to safer terrain. 'I grew up in Benares and then came to Delhi for my graduation. I spent two years in Kolkata in between. My father teaches English at the Benares Hindu University. From graduation till now I sold washing machines for a year and then worked at a security magazine.'

Maya stared at him, and then heaved a dramatic sigh. 'Okay, I should cancel the wine.'

'Really, that is my life. Nothing remarkable. But tell me about yours.'

'I will tell you about mine, mister, when you buy the wine. This doesn't go on the expense account, you know. In fact, as you definitely know, we don't have an expense account. So let's start again. Where were you born?'

Abhishek was born in Kolkata. His father taught English at Ashutosh College, but got into a fight with the head of the department. 'You know how politicized the city is. The head was close to the ruling Communist Party and so was able to have my father transferred to Medinipur in south-western Bengal. He hated it. In fact, my father hates any place which is not Kolkata. After eight months there, he found this opening in Benares. Ma and two-year-old me followed a year later.'

The move was to be temporary, until this was patched and that was worked through, this political pressure applied and that party boss mollified. Abhishek was not sure when the sense of the transitory was given up for a compromised permanence.

'We still go to Kolkata every year, during the puja festivities, and then again in the December holidays,' Abhishek continued. 'The one thing drilled into me was that Benares was temporary; home was somewhere else. But my father has finally acknowledged that he will never teach in Kolkata and now talks about retirement housing rather than departmental politics.'

'What kind of a fight did he get into? Sounds quite serious if it was a life ban,' Maya asked, her usual loquacity mellowed by interest in her dinner companion and the quality of the wine.

'I am not sure of all the details. My father's family comes from a landowning class and I think we had already fallen foul of the government. In anyone else's case it might have been hushed over, but not in his.'

The Dutta family were not only landowners; his great-grandfather, Dev Shudhan Dutta, had been the city's most famous homeopath. 'I am told stories about him and about his daughter, my grandmother. She was quite a character in her younger days. Mohur Dutta – more of a whore Dutta.' Abhishek looked up and smiled at the shocked face across the table.

'Just for that one statement I will buy you drinks for a month, Abhi.' Maya looked like she was finally getting her money's worth. 'I knew there was more to you than your Bambi-eyed self.'

'Nothing to do with me.' He laughed. 'Didu died a month before I was born. My uncle doted on her and recreated a magical lady for me in his bedtime stories and afternoon yarns. Legend has it that she was quite a bold thing in the Kolkata of the '40s, just before Independence. She married an Englishman, John Goldwater. He was an itinerant traveller and theatre performer. They had two kids together, and then, as quietly as he had appeared, he vanished. Didu returned home, took back her space and her name, and carried right on as if nothing had happened. It was scandalous, but she didn't care.'

'Have you ever seen your grandfather's photo?'

'No, never. I asked, but no one seems to have any.'

'Oh, come on. There must be something.'

'To be honest, my father really blocked out his mother and there was barely any conversation about her at home. In fact, he should take the credit for "more of a whore", which came out when he and my uncle had some altercation over property matters. That's the strange thing in the family, you know. My father and my uncle are locked in this prolonged legal battle over our ancestral home. Baba has exhausted all his money and we are in quite a bad way. But every year we go and stay with my uncle in that disputed house, and you would never know that the two brothers have gone to court. The family dynamics, on the face of it, haven't changed.'

'You Bengalis are strange. This educated, gentlemanly veneer ...'

'Yes, that's our family.' Abhishek laughed.

'And your father – is he also a card-carrying Communist Party member like every good upper-class Kolkatan?'

'No; he hates them. He says the only achievement of the Left in West Bengal is the creation of the office-going clerk who consumes ten cups of tea a day and plays carom all afternoon.'

The food came and Abhishek concentrated on his pizza. Maya, nibbling on a caesar salad, remarked, 'It makes sense. The theatre movements dazzled Kolkata in the early '40s. The Indian People's Theatre Association had just been formed ... in 1942, I think. How old was your grandma then?'

'She was born in 1920. So she would have been in her early twenties at that point, and having a lot of fun. My great-grandfather was a big patron of theatre and there were always workshops happening at home. We still have this central courtyard where all sorts of stage personalities used to come. I have seen photos of Shombhu Mitra, Ritwik Ghatak and even Prithviraj Kapoor sipping chai there. Balraj Sahni, too, was a regular. My grandmother was involved with theatre from her childhood because of all this. And then my granddad came along.'

'Yes, of course.' Maya sipped her wine. 'There were all manner of foreign nationalities roaming around in Kolkata during the war years. So your granddad wouldn't have stuck out that much.'

'Did you do history as well as sociology?' Abhishek was impressed.

'Actually yes, I graduated in history and then did a master's in sociology.'

'Oh, I graduated in history too.'

Maya revealed little about herself. She was a Delhi girl, her father worked in the government; she did not specify where. She had been a journalist for three years now and quite liked it, but wouldn't continue for very long. It was time to get into more serious writing and research. 'What about you? Are you liking it?' she asked.

'Journalism? Yes, I love it. There is so much going on and so much energy,' Abhishek replied enthusiastically.

'Really?'

Abhishek had clearly said the wrong thing and paused to hear why.

'Energy? In sitting with those police morons and their supplicant reporters?'

'Well, I think there are some good journalists. They all seem to love anti-establishment stories,' Abhishek ventured.

'Anti-establishment, my ass. All they do is get gossip from one police officer and write about another. Then the other gets even. That's all. This friend of yours, Uday Kumar, he is a goon in police uniform. Do you know the number of people he has killed? If your reporters were honest, they would write about the fake encounters that he has staged. They know, but no one writes. There was a riot in north-east Delhi a few years back. I wasn't around then, but I have seen photos. In one, your man is lying on his back on the road and is shooting blindly over his head into the crowd, a cigarette dangling from his lips. Like he thought he was Dirty Harry or something. No one published those snaps.'

Maya signalled for the menu. 'Do you want dessert? I am going to have a coffee.'

'No; I am quite full, thank you. But can I ask something? If you know these things, why don't you write about them?'

'You are not getting my point, are you?' Maya shook her head, her face now serious. 'I am part of it. We all are. Every story has to conform to parameters. Break those and you are out. I didn't even try; I knew. But you will learn this when you get something that really hurts the order. For now, enjoy the adulation.'

'To be honest, I am petrified,' Abhishek confessed. 'What has happened to me in the last month is beyond my wildest dreams. Every day, I expect that the bubble will burst; somebody will expose me, my luck will run out. And then back to selling washing machines.'

'Endearing,' Maya said, smiling at him kindly. 'Don't worry; there are enough crooks around – and by crooks, I mean the police – for you to be in business for a long time. Moreover, you have Amir's backing. You are safe.'

'I am terrified of Amir. I never know where I am with him.'

'He is a difficult character for all of us. He has been around so long now that he has become part of the furniture. He likes the fact that he belongs, but he resents being taken for granted.'

Maya emptied three sachets of sugar into her coffee. 'I know, I know,' she said, putting her hands up. 'The only thing I share with you Bengalis is a sweet tooth.'

'Not me. I hate sweets,' Abhishek said, grimacing. 'Every time we went to Kolkata, I was force-fed. As a kid, I had a paranoia of those aunties. The moment I crossed the doorstep, they'd be stuffing me with rosogollas.'

'Yeah, actually you don't seem the sweet-eating type. You are quite lean and thin.'

Maya's remark caught Abhishek off guard and he blushed. Once again, he failed to respond the way he would have wanted to.

'You were telling me about Amir,' he said after an awkward pause.

'Not much to tell. He sold himself short. Stayed back in the comfort of city-reporting, doing what he knew well. His colleagues and juniors moved on. People with half his talent climbed the rungs much faster. Initially he was defiant, later he became disgruntled. We all know that, and so does he. That's what you see today – an excellent journalist who made his final move years ago. Now he just serves out time and tells newcomers like you stories of a glorious past.' Maya spoke without malice.

'But you are one of his favourites, aren't you?' Abhishek asked.

'Don't know about that, but yes, we get along. He misses Vivek. Can't imagine why. The man is such a snake.'

'Vivek really helped me, Maya.'

'Well, you better watch out. He is no one's friend,' Maya warned as she settled the bill.

'I know what you are scared of,' she said, once outside. 'You have had this sudden high. The fear of fall is natural.'

Maya was right, but it was more than that. Not only was he scared of falling short of the standards that he had inadvertently set himself, Abhishek was desperately struggling to act like he belonged. Mediocrity had always shielded him; in the throes of attention, he was both lustful and shy.

Maya linked her arm through his. Despite the layers of clothing, the proximity felt good. Abhishek did not have the audacity to think further; just the momentary closeness to this woman seemed enough.

'Sorry I went into that rant earlier. I do it every time I am drunk.' She laughed and pulled him closer. 'Let's hang out soon again.'

As they entered the car park, she asked him, 'Will you be able to ride back home? I live quite close by or would have given you a lift.'

'Yes-yes,' Abhishek said hurriedly. 'I need the scooter for the morning anyway.'

'OK then, goodnight.'

'Goodnight,' he replied and, kick-starting the scooter, began the cold ride home.

At the Crime Branch, the deputy commissioner and his assistant had reached an impasse. 'Yes, it is a gamble, Mayank. And I have been telling you this,' Uday tried to reason. 'I have just two options: I could tell the whole world about Babloo's possible plans; alert Interpol, the CBI and Mumbai Police and have him not turn up – and rest assured he would not – or I could play this absolutely quiet. Let him take the bait, do what he is planning, and then get him. Once he plays his hand, you can take all the bloody help you want, from whom you want. This is not about me arresting him,' the cop said, looking his younger counterpart in the eye. 'This is about Babloo Shankar being arrested.' Uday hoped he sounded convincing.

Mayank Sharma did not talk back to his seniors. If he had been a different sort of man, he might have enquired if his boss remembered that many years ago such an operation, shrouded in similar secrecy, had dramatically backfired. But Mayank's police training and upbringing restrained him. His dissent remained within accepted boundaries.

'Till now, sir, an attempt to narrow down a possible list of victims in just three of the districts has thrown up over five thousand names. It is impossible to even start monitoring this.'

'Yes,' Uday agreed. 'I think the only credible route left before us is to pursue Amir's. Meet that guy he told us about, and see what he says. Right now, I can't see any other way.'

Mayank remained silent. Uday knew this sharp young man – he would put his money on Mayank occupying the commissioner's chair someday – was thinking that he was being given pointless exercises to stay busy. And that was not far from the truth. But Uday also knew that one did not admit to such things. Apologizing to a junior was also a breach of protocol.

Mayank played along. 'Right, sir. I will contact Mr Akhtar and see when I can talk to his source. I'll make a full report. By the way, sir,' he added, as if as an afterthought, 'will I be included in this evening's operation?'

They both knew it would be hard for Uday to refuse. 'OK,'

said the officer, shortly. 'Rana Sen is in charge. Get a briefing from him at the afternoon team meeting.'

As Mayank saluted and left, Uday felt annoyed with himself. This was his first big case since he'd joined the Crime Branch, with a high probability of a shoot-out. He wanted to send only his toughest men; it was not a Mayank Sharma sort of job.

While the two policemen were locked in polite combat, Abhishek was having morning tea with Vikram in the press office downstairs. 'Boss, the commissioner has invited you for lunch next Wednesday,' Vikram told the young man, whose delight was evident. 'He is absolutely impressed with your work, Abhishek. Congratulations.'

It was a tradition, Vikram explained, for the commissioner of police to meet a few reporters individually at the end of each year. It gave him an opportunity to present his viewpoints and also listen to what journalists had to say about policing and its reportage.

'I must say, I was not expecting this,' the press officer admitted. 'I have never known any reporter to be invited so soon. Only the seniors are called, and only a select few at that.'

A cheerful face appeared around the door. 'Hi Vikram, how are things? Thought I might get a cup of tea with you. Haven't seen you in a while.'

Abhishek hadn't met the policeman before and Vikram did the introductions. 'Abhishek, meet Rohit Bansal, deputy commissioner of the Special Cell. Rohit, meet the new talent. Just got invited for lunch with the commissioner.'

'Really? That's quite something. I have read your stories.

Yesterday you interviewed that murderer, didn't you? And the sleeping cops story; that was excellent.'

Abhishek smiled, embarrassed and happy.

'Listen, I have a scoop for you,' Rohit said suddenly. 'Why don't you come with me for a minute, if you are not doing anything right now? Vikram, is that OK?'

In his office, Rohit explained that the Special Cell had registered a First Information Report against a company producing faulty transformers. 'This might not sound out of the ordinary, but the transformers are similar to the one which caused the Uphaar tragedy. Over fifty cinema halls and hotels now have them installed in their basements. So potentially there are many tragedies waiting to happen.'

Although he was barely in his teens at the time, Abhishek could remember the tragedy well. For months, it had been headline news. On 13 June 1997, fifty-nine people had been killed and more than a hundred injured when a fire had broken out during a film screening at Uphaar cinema in south Delhi. A faulty transformer in the basement had been identified as the cause. The incident had scarred the public psyche, sparking off a debate about health and safety standards across Indian cities. It did not take exceptional intelligence to recognize the newsworthiness of time bombs ticking away in the capital's public buildings.

Rohit was meticulous, showing Abhishek the report filed against the accused and making sure that he noted facts and figures correctly.

Abhishek, at the end of the meeting, thanked the policeman profusely.

'Always a delight to help someone Vikram recommends,' Rohit

said. 'I am sure we will work together in the future. One thing –
don't mention my name anywhere. Just quote me as a source.'

Vikram's office had filled up while Abhishek was away. He
cheerily called out to a few reporters as he walked in and took
a seat. The response was frosty.

A journalist from the Hindi newspaper *Sahara Samay* looked
at him accusingly, 'Boss, what you did yesterday was not right.'

'Why, what did I do?' Abhishek asked, as other reporters
turned to watch the exchange.

'That interview which you did with the murderer, Baldev
Pujara; any of us could have done that. But it is not right to give
a murderer's version of the events.'

'Why do you think we do not put a criminal's version?' another
senior reporter added, and then answered his own question
expansively: 'Public sympathy must not go out to them. Imagine
every criminal starts using the media as their mouthpiece. We
all can do such interviews, but we don't. Anyway,' he looked at
Vikram and shrugged dismissively, 'too many new kids with no
proper training, and this is what happens.'

Abhishek did not argue. These men were a bunch of lazy and
contented fools whom he had off-footed. He had turned a routine
story into a front-page exclusive. What they were claiming was
absolute rubbish. If getting interviews or meeting criminals
was that easy, they would all do it. Their asses must have been
thoroughly kicked by their bosses. Abhishek remembered what
Amir had told him during their breakfast chat: 'How successful
you are is reflected in how much your peers hate you. You should
only be bothered if they ignore you.'

'Well, fuck them,' Abhishek thought. 'I've got an exclusive,
and an invitation to lunch with the commissioner.'

'Singh sahab, I have to run,' he loudly interrupted a

conversation. 'What time should I be here on Wednesday for the commissioner's lunch?' The room went silent.

Vikram had seen a few journalistic ego clashes in his time, and he enjoyed the young man's guts. A fighter, Vikram smiled. Well, he would learn his lesson soon. 'At twelve thirty, Abhishek. Meet me here.'

'Thank you, sir.' Abhishek relished the dismayed expressions of the reporters as he all but skipped from the room. It was in this jubilant and defiant mood that the journalist thought of dropping in on Uday Kumar.

There was a time not so long ago when police shoot-outs were common, even encouraged, in Delhi. The press glorified the men in uniform as crusaders and the public seemed happy to see gangsters dead rather than wasting tax money in jails. But that time had passed.

In a case of mistaken identity, a team of cavalier policemen, greedy for out-of-turn promotions, had gunned down three innocent businessmen in one of the city's busiest markets. A lame attempt to plant weapons on the victims and claim that they belonged to some criminal gangs in Haryana was swiftly exposed. Delhi Police's reputation took a severe knock. In less than twenty-four hours, five policemen were arrested and the prevailing commissioner transferred. While appointing V.N. Pratap, the home ministry had warned him that they did not care for a repeat performance. Naturally, the commissioner was now cautious and absolutely adamant that he should be briefed on any operation that might involve a shoot-out.

Uday Kumar, for over three decades, had mastered the art of getting around bosses. The commissioner listened to his flawless presentation that minimized the risks and hinted at the glowing press tributes of the planned kidnapping bust. Despite being fully cognisant of his officer's guile, Pratap gave in.

That settled, Uday dropped in at the home ministry. He had been promised a new official residence for three years now, but something or the other always seemed to crop up. A new secretary in the personnel department, a Bihari whom he had once assisted on a minor matter, had promised to help.

Uday had only five years of service left; not much time, Alka often reminded him, if they were ever to live in an independent bungalow. She had gone to visit her parents a week back, and he was hoping that she would stay there all winter. He was enjoying the attentions of a busty woman provided by a Rolls Royce dealer whose showroom encroached on public space.

His morning errands over, Uday returned to his office and ordered lunch.

'Sir, Abhishek Dutta is here,' Mishra informed. 'Shall I tell him you are busy?'

Uday thought for a while. A bit of afternoon banter might help take his mind off things. 'No; send him in. And can you order a few more dosas from the canteen? He might want some food.'

Abhishek was having quite a day. Even though he had turned up unannounced, the senior policeman not only seemed pleased to see him but had also invited him to lunch.

Uday was in full flow, slurping sambar and delivering an unending stream of success stories when Abhishek decided to offer his opinion: 'It is a great story, sir, but doesn't it bother you that most of these shoot-outs are staged? I mean, everyone knows you stage encounters.'

The only compensation for what followed, Abhishek thought later, was that no one else had been there to witness it.

After the first moment of absolute incomprehension, Uday flew into a rage that turned into an almost physical assault. 'Bhenchod! You are telling Uday Kumar that he stages encounters? Do you know whom you are talking to? Who are you? How old are you? What have you seen?' Uday thumped the desk with every question.

Abhishek, struck dumb, wanted to curl up and make himself as small as possible.

'In every district where I worked, children in the streets knew my name. Every fucking resident knew me. And you come here, eat my food, and tell me that I fake encounters? You sons of bitches, you fucking journalists – you people should be lined up and shot!'

Abhishek did not know what to say, how to retract his question and defuse the anger.

Uday suddenly stopped and stared at him for what seemed like a long time. The corners of his mouth slowly twitched and a sly smile spread across his face.

Abhishek, extremely uncomfortable, looked away.

'Enough of this,' Uday said, lowering his voice. 'Let me show you how Uday Kumar works. We are sending a team to rescue a kidnapped boy this evening. And you, impudent fucker,' he said, pointing a fat finger at Abhishek, 'are going with them. See what happens, and then open your bloody mouth and tell me that I stage encounters.'

11

Abhishek was in the car with Ombir Rathi, a top Delhi Police shooter, his radio operator and the driver. They were following two other unmarked police vehicles heading towards a hotel in Meerut. A reconnaissance team led by Mayank had just informed them that a crowded evening market made the area unsuitable for shoot-outs.

It had taken Abhishek a while to piece together what was going on. The sixteen-year-old son of a well-to-do cloth merchant in west Delhi's Karol Bagh had disappeared three weeks ago. After all possible inquiries with friends and relatives had drawn a blank, the parents informed the police.

Four nights later, they received a telephone call on their landline. A man's voice informed the father that their son had been kidnapped, which both parents had suspected but refused to acknowledge. As an assurance of the boy's well-being, the kidnapper allowed the father to hear a hoarse whispery cry. The motive was money and the ransom demanded was five crore rupees. They would cut off the cry altogether if the police got involved.

The frightened mother forced her husband to cease conversations with the authorities. The district police apprised the Crime Branch, which discreetly took over the investigation.

They tapped the family's phones and recorded discussions of how and where the ransom was to be paid.

With the exchange imminent, Uday contacted the father and persuaded him that the Crime Branch would be able to pull off a rescue. Without his wife's knowledge, the man agreed.

'He's a fucking businessman. If he can help it, he won't pay,' Uday told his men.

The kidnappers had told the father to deliver the money at the hotel in Meerut where the police were now heading. The instructions had been clear: 'Bring the money in thousand-rupee notes. Give the suitcase to the hotel manager, then leave. The boy will be home the next day.' If the police or anyone else was informed, or the kidnappers were given any cause for suspicion, the parents would never see their son again.

The police had decided to stake out the hotel before the money was delivered. Three couples, police personnel under cover, had already checked in and would report on developments. Rana Sen, who was leading the operation, would decide with Uday the next course of action; most importantly, when, and if, they should attack.

Ombir was on the phone with Uday. 'Sir, do you know that it's the twenty-ninth of November today?'

'What about it?' Ombir's phone was on loudspeaker, and everyone in the car could hear the exchange.

'Three years ago today, sir … the Mehrauli shoot-out?'

'Arre, yes-yes. Make sure you take care of yourself. I don't want you shot again.'

'Ha, ha, yes sir, I will. The wife gets scared these days. We are becoming old.' Ombir put the phone down and looked at Abhishek. 'We should have got a bullet-proof vest for you,

Abhishek-ji,' he said, rubbing his chin thoughtfully, a glint of mischief in his eyes.

The reporter wondered if he should play along with Ombir's slightly morbid sense of humour or would it be interpreted as actual nerves? 'What was the Mehrauli case?' he deflected, allowing Ombir the opportunity for a bit of self-promotion. In his short stint as a journalist, Abhishek had quickly learnt that the best way to gain a policeman's confidence was to give ample space for stories.

'You have not heard of the Ramala case?' Ombir asked with mock incredulity.

'No. I just joined the profession.'

'But you must have watched the news, no? Every channel covered it. Ramala was the biggest gangster of Uttar Pradesh. Involved in over twenty murders. No one knows how many people he kidnapped and threatened. There were cases of robbery, armed intimidation, everything. We cornered him in Mehrauli. He was tough, I must admit. He didn't go down quietly or surrender. I was shot in the stomach.' Ombir looked at Abhishek, waiting for a reaction

'Really? How did it happen?' Abhishek offered.

'We stopped Ramala's car at a police checkpoint. He shot first. I went down but fired back. There were two others with me. Ramala opened the car door to get out. That was his mistake. We got clear shots at him. Spot dead.'

'Sir was in hospital for three months,' the driver contributed, his eyes wide in the rear-view mirror.

'Ah, no-no, it was nothing,' said Ombir, approving of the interruption. He looked at Abhishek. 'It could be an omen. The same date. Who knows?'

Hotel Moonlight stood at the very edge of Meerut, just

west of the Delhi highway. It was a pink two-storey building, surrounded by similarly unimaginative structures of varying shades. The evening bazaar was under way; in the cacophony of buying and selling, no one noticed the three cars pass by within minutes of each other and stop a few hundred metres from the hotel.

Abhishek and Ombir's vehicle was the last to arrive. They glided past the others and parked by a row of tin-roof tea shops that stood a little way from the main market.

'Chai, anybody? I need to stretch.' Ombir declared, jumping out rather nimbly, Abhishek thought, considering his size.

At the shop, they ordered cigarettes and four cups of tea. Ombir sat down next to Abhishek, bending the road-side bench with his bulk. While both the other cars were visible at some distance, Abhishek couldn't see the policemen. Mayank, he knew, would be somewhere in the crowd. A faint sense of dread started to trickle through him. The sight of the hotel, the marketplace teeming with people and deemed unsuitable for a shoot-out, and the sudden alacrity in Ombir's eyes. This was really happening – he was on a mission to rescue a kidnapped teenager.

'Our six have checked in.' Rana came up behind them. 'The father and uncle should be here any minute and once they deposit the money, we'll reassess the situation.'

Abhishek's hand shook as he sipped his tea.

'Meanwhile, Abhishek,' the cop turned to him and grinned, 'relax. You look like you are the one who's going to be shot.'

Abhishek smiled back weakly, his enthusiasm for bullet-related jokes fast waning.

'There they are,' Ombir said, nodding towards the hotel.

A grey Pajero stopped at the entrance, and from it emerged the two elderly gentlemen Abhishek had met that afternoon in

Uday's office. One of them carried a suitcase which must have contained the money. They entered the hotel and came out in less than a minute, without it. 'Good,' Rana muttered and, once the men began to drive away, called the father. 'Sir, Rana Sen here. Did everything go okay?' He listened for a moment. 'Just one man at the reception or was there anyone else? ... Okay, sir, I will be in touch. Please do not call me; if there is anything you need, call Uday sir.'

Rana turned to the others. 'Okay, baggage has been delivered. I expect to hear from our couples soon. Once we know the layout of the hotel and the number of people, we can plan further.'

Abhishek lit another cigarette and studied the man who was leading the operation. Rana Sen was of above-average height. His glasses and long, slightly unkempt hair made him look more like a college lecturer than a policeman. During the afternoon briefing, Abhishek had got the distinct impression that Uday was relying more on Ombir than on Rana, his senior.

'Sir, look!' Ombir leapt up suddenly, pointing towards the hotel. 'What the hell is this?'

Abhishek watched as two large police vans pulled up outside the hotel. Uniformed men leapt out and charged inside. Rana was already sprinting towards the building with Ombir behind him. Abhishek had to fight his way through the crowded street to keep up.

Just outside the hotel, Rana paused and turned to his junior officer: 'What should we do?'

'Go in and see,' Ombir replied and, without waiting for assent, led the way in.

'Stay here,' Rana commanded Abhishek over his shoulder.

Abhishek stood aside as the rest of the team, including Mayank, barged past; the door to the hotel lobby swung open and shut. He could hear Rana's shouts. Frightened, but overcome with curiosity, the reporter slipped in.

Ombir had a man pushed up against a wall, with a pistol stuck at the back of his neck, and Rana was screaming obscenities at the perplexed men.

Finally, Rana identified the group leader and advanced towards him, waving his ID in the man's face. 'Who the fuck are you? How did you get here? Who called you? Quickly, motherfucker, tell me quickly!'

The policeman, wrestling with the indignity of being abused in front of his team, said quietly, 'We were called in by the hotel staff.'

'What the fuck is going on?' Rana shouted, confusion getting the better of his anger. Pushing past the policemen, he sat down on the sofa. 'Ombir, get that manager here. I need to understand what just happened.'

Ombir released the man he had pinned against the wall, whose trousers bore the shameful piss-smelling evidence of his fear, and gestured for him to speak to Rana.

His name was Gaurav Kumar Chaturvedi. He had received a call a few days back from a man who had booked a room for tonight and tomorrow. The caller had said that he would arrive late, and a business associate would deliver his suitcase at some point during the evening. Chaturvedi had agreed to put it in the room the man had booked.

'This evening, sir,' the manager told Rana, 'three couples checked in, one after the other. I was surprised, as that hardly ever happens here. An hour later, the suitcase arrived. The men who delivered it seemed terrified and ran away before I could say anything. I was suspicious, so I forced it open. There are stacks of cash in it, sir. I immediately called the police. I did not want trouble.'

Rana beckoned to the police team leader. 'What is your name?'

'Inspector Rajiv Ranjan, sir.'

'Rajiv-ji,' Rana said, his voice now controlled, 'there has been a kidnapping. That was the ransom money this man found in the suitcase. The boy was kidnapped from Delhi and therefore in our jurisdiction. We are trying to get the kidnapper. All of you must leave right now and not show up again. It's possible that the kidnapper is somewhere around and if he has spotted you, the boy's life is in grave danger. I'll speak to your superiors later, but gather your men this instant and go away. Do you understand?'

'Yes, sir,' Ranjan replied and the chastened policemen left the reception, escorted by two of Rana's men.

The rest of the hotel employees were gathered in the reception. Abhishek felt sorry for the manager. Chaturvedi was embarrassed at having wet himself and still scared out of his wits. Ombir's insistent, almost violent, cross-examination was not helping. Chaturvedi's subordinates were relishing the spectacle. Every insult or hurt the man had ever dealt them was being deliciously avenged.

By now, Abhishek had deduced that the Crime Branch team had severely erred in its planning. The operation had been built around the premise that the hotel staff were involved, either directly or otherwise, in the kidnapping. In any case, checking three couples, almost simultaneously, into the Moonlight was not a subtle move.

Rana was in damage-control mode. 'From now on, no one leaves the hotel without my permission,' he told the hotel employees. 'Call home and say a wedding party has arrived suddenly. Mayank, can you see that these calls are supervised, and then take away the mobile phones.' He then instructed the manager to put up a 'No Vacancy' board at the entrance.

'We don't have one, sir,' the manager mumbled.

'Then make one,' the officer snapped. 'And go and change your clothes ... Ombir,' he said, turning towards his colleague, 'everyone stays in tonight. And we'll put a couple of men at the reception with the manager. We have to be very careful.'

Since no other rooms were occupied, things moved quickly. The suitcase was placed in a corner room on the first floor, with Mayank and Abhishek opposite and Ombir and Rana next door. Four policemen designated for night duty occupied the ground floor.

It was a little past 9 p.m. by the time all the arrangements were completed. The manager, humiliated and shaken, was put to work. He had to procure several bottles of whisky and some tandoori chicken. 'Get mutton kebabs too,' Ombir called after him.

The bathroom tiles were cracked and, to Abhishek's bare feet, felt like slippery ice. The cold water came down in a gush, the hot water in a trickle, and the two wouldn't mix. After standing naked for a while, shivering beside the shower, he gave up. He dressed hurriedly and washed his face at the dirty sink; the water, muddy at first, stinging his face and eyes. He wet his hair and armpits. Mayank had taken a shower and Abhishek wanted to at least pretend he had done the same.

When he tip-toed out, his friend was already dressed. The room was tiny and miserable, its wretchedness accentuated by the chill. By way of furniture, there was a double bed with a dirty blanket on it, a sofa fraying at the edges, two chairs and a table. A framed picture of mountains, a river and a quaint old cottage only served to emphasize the joylessness of the present surroundings. A cupboard stood in the corner, useless to the two men. None of the team had brought luggage, not even those who had checked in.

After a half-hour break, the men were to reconvene on the ground floor. Rana had told the manager to serve the women constables their dinner separately. They had been dismissed for the night and, Abhishek presumed, from the operation. Their role had backfired and now they were a liability.

'Major mistake.' Mayank frowned. 'We should have staggered the check-in of the couples. This area doesn't look like a place where people come for a quickie, does it?'

He began lacing his shoes. 'Plus, we had kind of assumed that the hotel guys were in on the whole thing. That blew up in our faces.' He checked his pistol and put it into his pocket. 'Let's go. I want to get this drinking business done with.'

As the two young men joined the gathering, a constable pulled up chairs for them.

'Sit, sit.' Rana waved them in. 'Whisky and soda?'

Abhishek nodded, reaching for the fried chicken on the table.

'Mayank, Coke again?' Rana asked his junior officer, smiling.

'Yes, sir,' Mayank replied, embarrassed. 'Don't worry; I'll help myself. Thank you.'

Rana gulped down two shots. Pouring his third, he asked Ombir, 'So, what do you think?'

'Can't say, sir. Depends. If someone was watching, this operation is over.'

'What will happen to the boy?'

Ombir remained silent.

'Very wrong planning,' Rana muttered, to no one in particular. His phone rang and he stepped out to take the call.

'Everyone,' Rana said, re-entering the room. 'We seem okay. The kidnappers called the boy's father. He has confirmed the delivery, and they don't seem to have noticed anything.'

Abhishek sensed the collective sigh of relief. A kidnapping rescue gone wrong usually meant death for the victim, and second chances were rare. Glasses were refilled. Ombir and his fellow policeman Surinder were remarkable raconteurs and, as quickly as the whisky dried up, the anecdotes flowed.

Ombir had married a girl from a lower caste and his family had disowned him. His three brothers had stripped him of the family property. 'I had no option but to join the police to get my land back. I could have become a gangster, I guess, but then one of you might have arrested me.'

Amid the laughter, Ombir turned to Rana and added, 'I know what these men do to keep themselves amused in the lock-up, sir. I prefer not be face down on the floor every time one of them gets drunk and starts missing his sister-in-law.'

Rana let out a loud snort, slamming his glass down on the table and slapping his thigh. The Central services officer had allowed himself to join in the bawdy banter. Abhishek noted the beaming policemen. The barriers that class erected, whisky battered down.

'Get some more drinks, someone,' Ombir told his constables. The hotel manager whom Mayank had invited to join the group had been sitting in a corner, sipping from his glass, a look of terrified gratitude on his face. He jumped up to fetch more whisky.

A little past 1 a.m., Rana pushed back his chair with an air of finality. The party was over.

Abhishek went to his room and got into bed, fully clothed. He was exhausted. Just as he was dropping off, Mayank walked in, dragging the suitcase with him.

'For tonight, you and I are the caretakers of fifty million rupees. Rana sir did not want to risk keeping so much money in that room. If the kidnappers show up, they can be stalled downstairs and we'll put the suitcase back,' Mayank said, pushing it under the bed.

Abhishek sat up. 'That will really help me sleep.'

'It's intended to keep you awake.' Mayank laughed. 'Uday sir was right, you know,' he added. 'The father is one of those really rich stingy types. If he had put the money into a decent suitcase, the lock wouldn't have broken so easily. All this might have been avoided if the manager hadn't seen the money. It's such terrible quality, the wheels just came off. Fifty million in a five-hundred-rupee suitcase.' He cursed under his breath, checked his pistol again, and put it under the pillow.

'So what do you think will happen?' Abhishek had come along to witness an Uday Kumar success story, but so far the operation had proved disastrous.

'Can't say. We only stand a chance if the kidnappers show up. But even then, we won't know whether to attack or not. It might put the boy's life in danger. That will be the thing to decide: to go for it, or wait.'

Mayank got under the covers and shivered. 'Hey, have you told your parents that you won't be home tonight?'

'I stay alone. They are in Benares, remember? But I should have called the office. No one knows why I have vanished.'

'You're smiling,' Mayank remarked, as he stretched to turn the lights off.

'Yes. I was just imagining what my parents would say if they knew. For them, this is absolutely unthinkable. I was not even allowed to get into playground scuffles. And rescuing kidnapped children … I think my mother would have a heart attack.' Abhishek chuckled in the dark.

'I know what you mean.' Mayank laughed. 'My parents talk of the police as if it's all promotions and parties. That pistols are involved, and lock-up beatings and mild torture, doesn't cross their minds.' He paused. 'I really didn't think I would ever join the police.'

'Oh? You said you were always obsessed with the civil services?'

'Yes, but not necessarily the police. In fact, when I first took the exams, I could only get into Customs. I quit in the third week of training. Anyway, that's an altogether different story.'

'Go on, tell me. I don't think we are getting much sleep tonight anyway. Let me turn on the bedside lamp.' Abhishek fiddled with the switch for some time and then gave up. 'Not working.'

'The dark tale of Customs must be told in darkness.'

'That bad?' Abhishek laughed.

'Depends. For some, it's a windfall. You see, in the police you can survive if you are honest; in Customs you cannot. The police have a workable model. An honest cop will not leave you; a corrupt one will negotiate. Customs is different. It's impossible not to be part of the system.'

'Even you?'

'At the end of my first day of training, at the Chennai port, I was offered a brown envelope. I refused and it didn't come back. The first two days, my seniors paid for lunch. On the third day I told the orderly, I would pay and ordered a soft drink. It cost seven hundred rupees. I was shocked. In the next few days,

I came to learn that the orderly got a massive cut every time something was ordered. So six hundred and fifty went to him for the soft drink.'

'Why is that?'

'He was part of Customs. He got a cut like everyone else and this was the way to pay him. My colleagues used to collect together all the bribe money they'd taken over the last twenty-four hours and put it in a kitty. After they paid for their extortionate lunch they split the remaining cash between them, each taking away a fat envelope. I didn't want to eat lunch with the bribe money nor could I afford those rates on my stipend. On the fourth day, I brought my own sandwiches. I was ostracized, of course. Beginning of the third week, I went to the Customs commissioner and handed in my resignation.'

'Now I understand what my father always said about this cousin of his,' Abhishek mulled aloud. 'Baba told Ma that he never came for family lunches because he would lose his day's cut. But I am sure there are a hundred more ways for a policeman to make money, no?'

'There are more ways but also more risks. The difference is a policeman forces someone to pay; in Customs, people want to pay, especially at ports.'

'Why would people want to pay?'

'Convenience, boss. Bypassing demurrage, for example.' Mayank paused to drink from a bottle of water. 'Demurrage basically means holding charges. The longer a consignment is held in port, the more an importer has to pay. So he pays speed money to the Customs officials to clear his consignment. The bribe is always less than demurrage charges, so the importer is more than happy to pay. And there are millions of consignments.

The money is unimaginable … Damn, I am going to have to brave it and go to the loo.' Mayank rushed out from under the covers.

Abhishek checked his phone. It was nearly 2 a.m. There were several missed calls from the office and a text from Amir asking about his whereabouts. He replied: 'All okay. Will explain.'

Mayank came out of the bathroom, checked under the bed and smiled at Abhishek. He switched off the bathroom light and slipped back under the covers.

'Besides this demurrage, what other ways?' Abhishek was enjoying Mayank's casual exposé.

'Well, Customs guys like certain kinds of consignments. Benzene, for example, has a very high import duty. Toulene, with almost the same chemical component, is far cheaper to import. Passing off Benzene as Toulene is a major earner. Importers pay handsomely and it's difficult to detect.'

Both men fell silent. The windows rattled as a truck rumbled past. The resident hotel dog barked somewhere in the corridors. In response, an unending echo was taken up by every street cur in the vicinity. Another truck followed, continuing the cycle of rattles and shakes, barks and yelps.

'You know, I've never met a man like Ombir,' Abhishek said.

'I hope you understand that he is the real team leader. Not Rana Sen. Rana and I are both senior to Ombir, but we don't have his street credentials or knowledge.'

'Yes, that's quite clear.'

'Men like Ombir and Surinder are a strange breed. They can buy Rana and me ten times over. You think they do our dirty work for the measly amount the government pays them? They wouldn't put their lives at risk for peanuts. When they are not working for the force, they are hired goons for the biggest property developers, the top industrialists. The police job provides them with immunity.'

'Why are you telling me all this?' Abhishek asked suddenly. 'I am a journalist.'

'Because I'll set Ombir on you if you write a word about this.' Both men chuckled and the bed creaked. 'But really,' Mayank said, 'this is common knowledge. It's hardly newsworthy.'

'What you mean is, everyone else knows the boundaries.' Abhishek was still smarting from Uday's earlier attack.

'Let's not get into that now,' Mayank replied.

'Tired?' Abhishek asked.

'Yes, suddenly. Whatever happens, tomorrow is going to be a long day. Try to sleep.'

A bhishek woke with a start. He had slumbered fitfully for most of the night but just as the dark winter sky had started to brighten, he had fallen into a deep comatose sleep. The first thing he saw was Mayank sitting at the foot of the bed, loading his pistol. It was 7 a.m.

'They didn't come?' Abhishek sat up, instantly awake.

'We have to plan as if they will. Get ready quickly. Breakfast in ten minutes.'

They ate in the room while Rana, who had joined them, gave a quick update. 'We are taking up positions in the hotel and outside. We'll replace the suitcase in the room opposite. Abhishek, you stay here and keep a watch on the door through this keyhole. If someone comes up, don't do anything. Do not go out, do not call anyone. Come, Mayank.'

For the next hour, Abhishek kept his eye to the keyhole. The question resurfaced: What would happen if he were to remove a bundle or two of the cash? No one would know. It was a passing thought, a momentary deviation, quashed immediately.

Soon his eyes started to wander from the keyhole. If the kidnappers came, there were others positioned downstairs who would take action. Rana might as well have asked him to go back to bed.

The telephone rang, piercing the stillness of the room and startling Abhishek. It was past 9 a.m. Abhishek had dozed off for more than an hour, and his neck hurt. He sped across the room to pick up the receiver. It was Rana, his voice a low urgent whisper laced with panic: 'A guy is coming up. We think he is the driver, so don't stop him.' The cop must have been really tense if he had imagined even for a moment that Abhishek would go anywhere near him.

He resumed his position at the keyhole just as the man came up the stairs and entered the room, closing the door behind him. He emerged a few minutes later and Abhishek could hear the sound of the wheel-less suitcase scraping across the hall and bumping down the stairs.

After ten pensive minutes, the phone rang again. 'Come down,' Rana said. Relieved at the prospect of joining the others, Abhishek rushed out. There were only five policemen at the reception. The rest, Rana explained, were tailing the man's car.

Abhishek suddenly found that his knees were shaking. He sat down on the sofa and Rana crouched next to him. 'The man is probably just a taxi driver, sent to do the pick-up and settle bills. Ombir posed as the manager but couldn't get anything out of him. He had to be careful not to make him suspicious, just in case.'

The officer's phone rang. 'Yes, Ombir?' He listened for a few moments. 'Okay, I am on my way.' He turned to Abhishek. 'The driver has stopped the car a few kilometres away, in the middle of a market. You stay here. I'll let you know what happens.'

For the next four hours Abhishek sat alone at the reception, empty now except for one constable and the exhausted manager, neither of whom seemed keen on a conversation. Abhishek consumed three cups of tea and finished an entire packet of cigarettes before Surinder dashed up to him. 'Come quickly. Sir is calling you.'

They drove to the marketplace. It wasn't overly crowded, though it bore signs that a great wave of buyers had recently passed through. Stray dogs fought in clusters over discarded food scraps, tired shopkeepers and their attendants had ceased to bother with the afternoon hagglers and an army of ragpickers systematically combed the dusty roads for what could be scavenged and perhaps salvaged.

Surinder looked out of the window for a moment and pointed towards a lane of pottery shops. Up ahead, hands linked behind him, Rana was chatting with a shopkeeper.

As instructed, Abhishek walked up the lane and passed Rana. He continued slowly, stopping at shops and looking at flower vases. He paused to watch a potter at his wheel.

'Abhishek,' he heard Rana beside him. 'I am a bit worried. Listen carefully. The driver has been waiting in this market and no one has turned up. Ombir thinks that someone might have been watching the car and seen us lurking. So I'm pulling the team off the streets. All of us look like fucking policemen. You don't. I'm going to ask you to keep an eye on that car. Stay close and if someone comes and talks to the driver or the car leaves, all you have to do is call me. We'll be nearby, so don't worry.'

Abhishek was seriously worried. He knew it showed on his

face and he made no attempt to hide it. This was no time for machismo.

Rana saw his expression but ignored it. He had a kidnapped boy to think about. 'You'll be fine,' he said, and was off.

Abhishek looked around. There was no sign of any other policemen. He scouted for a tea stall from where he could watch the car. He could see the driver, stretched out on the front seat, his feet sticking out of the window. The man could not possibly know what was in the suitcase. No way would he sleep like that if he knew, Abhishek thought.

An hour passed. He had finished three packets of Britannia biscuits when a man finally approached the vehicle. Abhishek froze. He watched as the man woke the driver, spoke with him briefly and, after scanning the market, got into the front seat. Abhishek pulled out his mobile. 'Fuck!' he swore aloud. No signal.

He ran towards a phone booth and woke the man at the counter.

'What do you want?'

'I have to make a local call.'

'No local call. Only long distance,' the man said irritably, upset at having been roused from his afternoon nap.

'This is urgent,' Abhishek pleaded. His one fucking task, and he was floundering like an imbecile. Anger, quite rare in Abhishek, took over. 'Listen to me,' he said in a different tone. 'Delhi Police. Now give me the bloody phone.' He grabbed the receiver and called Rana who took it on the first ring. 'Someone just came. They have left in the car,' he blurted.

'Yes, we've seen him, and I can see you. Mayank is following the car. Ombir is coming to pick you up.'

Abhishek threw down a ten-rupee note and rushed out. A

Maruti van drew up and Ombir, sliding the door open, almost dragged him in.

There were four policemen inside. Abhishek squeezed into the back seat between Ombir and Surinder. Not a word was exchanged as they drove through the narrow street until Mayank called to report that the car they were tailing had suddenly taken a U-turn. It would be crossing them any minute.

'Bhenchod, what is he doing?' Ombir punched the seat in front as the car went past. It re-entered the market and stopped at a fruit-juice stall. They followed and parked a hundred metres ahead.

All five heads in the van turned to observe the two men who had wandered over to the juicewallah. 'They are drinking fruit juice!' Ombir was incredulous. 'Motherfucker, I haven't eaten the whole fucking day and this bastard is drinking juice. Fuck it, we are taking him. Turn around.' He checked his pistol. Surinder grasped what looked like a sub-machine gun.

A few metres before they reached the car, the driver switched off the engine and the van glided forward noiselessly. At the same time, Ombir slid open the passenger door.

Both men had their backs to the street when the unmarked police van came up behind them. Abhishek saw Ombir reaching for the suspected kidnapper. One hand grabbed his belt from below, the other his jacket collar. The officer almost lifted the man off the ground, the juice glass flying in the air, and the next moment he was on the floor of the van. Surinder, meanwhile, had jumped out and bundled the driver into the back of the van.

It was over in less than a minute and, before the astonished bystanders could react, the motley group was speeding away. The radio operator held the man down, while Ombir dealt quick, sharp blows to the man's stomach and ribs. For a few moments, the only audible sounds were the man's grunts and gasps, until Ombir hissed into his ear: 'Tell me where the boy is or I'll kill you.' Abhishek absolutely believed that he would. So did the man, who croaked, 'In Ghaziabad. He's in Ghaziabad.'

'Stop the car,' Ombir commanded. 'Abhishek, tell Rana sir we are heading to Ghaziabad. Bring him and Mayank sir there.'

Once again, the reporter found himself alone on the street. He began to walk towards the market, trying to connect to Rana's mobile. Suddenly he heard his name being shouted.

'What the hell happened?' Rana asked, running to meet him. Abhishek explained quickly.

'Oh fuck. They took him in without asking me. Okay, get in.'

'Ghaziabad,' the anxious policeman told the driver, climbing in the front seat. He turned to look at Abhishek. 'Explain to me again what happened. No rush. Tell me in detail.'

As he explained how they had followed the car, Mayank's phone call to Ombir and the sudden decision to take the men, Abhishek felt sorry for Rana. Even he knew more than the team leader, who had simply been abandoned. Ombir had taken over and made the vital decisions.

When Abhishek finished, a sardonic, angry smile spread over the policeman's face. 'So Ombir decided to attack because the man was drinking juice while he was hungry. Great. That's fucking great.'

Rana called Mayank and updated him. 'Bring the rest of the team to Ghaziabad.' As soon as he hung up, his phone rang. 'Yes, Ombir?' He listened for a while. 'Make sure the boy is safe. Else both of us are against the wall.' Cutting the line, he lit a cigarette. 'The man's confessed he has an accomplice, his older brother. Apparently he is not with the boy right now. If that's true, the boy should be fine.'

For the next half-hour, as twilight set in, they drove in silence, each lost in his own thoughts: Rana in helpless fury at being undermined again, Abhishek replaying the methodical ferocity of the violence he had just witnessed.

As the car entered Ghaziabad, the police officer's phone rang again. He listened for a moment and then let out a relieved, 'Thank God. Shabash, Ombir, well done. Give me the exact address ... okay.' He hung up, and shouted, 'Yes, yes, yes,' thumping the driver on the back and turning back to shake Abhishek's hand. 'The boy is safe.' He called Uday.

When Abhishek entered the darkened room, the boy was lying buried under a mass of blankets. He looked up fearfully, and sank his head back in the pillow. 'Please don't hurt me, uncle.' The whisper was barely audible.

Abhishek went and sat beside him. 'I'm not going to hurt you at all,' he said gently. 'I'm part of the police team, Rudra. I'll turn on the table lamp here so you can see me clearly.'

The boy was sixteen, Abhishek had been told, but looked older now. Three weeks of captivity had left him with uneven facial hair and sunken desperate eyes, adding years to his face.

He grasped the hand offered to him. 'I can't believe you've come for me. I never thought I would see my parents again. I really did not. I was so scared, so scared. They beat me every day.'

Rudra had been locked up in the kidnappers' family home, which had been empty for a few months while their parents were away visiting a relative. Ombir had discovered the boy, bound hand and foot, inside a tiny room under the staircase which served as the household shrine. 'I used to look at Lakshmiji and pray to be rescued,' Rudra told Abhishek listlessly. 'They did not take me to the toilet. I was forced to do it there, in front of the gods.'

He was fed once a day. They used to remove his gag but didn't free his hands. 'I ate like a dog. I felt like throwing up. They wouldn't even wash my face.'

Abhishek felt a pang of guilt. Should he let the boy be? Should he take him to the bathroom, get him to shower? He shouldn't be the one hearing this; he wasn't trained. But the interview with Rudra, moments after a police team rescued him, would complete the scoop.

Rana and Abhishek had arrived ten minutes after the boy had been found. Ombir and Surinder had greeted them at the entrance, touching Rana's feet as a mark of deference. Abhishek saw how quickly the officer forgot, or at least pretended to, their gross transgressions.

Everyone had gathered in the living room: Rana, Ombir and Mayank on a sofa, Abhishek and the constables standing, and the kidnapper sitting crossed-legged on the floor, a pistol casually trained on his drooping head.

Ombir updated the others on what he had learnt. 'They are brothers, sir, Sandeep and Shekhar Chauhan,' he said, addressing Rana. 'Got the idea from the newspapers. First attempt; complete amateurs. The plan was hilarious. This fucker,' Ombir slapped the man across the face, 'pretended to be a girl when calling that idiot – arre, what's his name … yes, Rudra. Poor fucker got conned. Ai, show how you did the girl's voice.' Another slap.

Sandeep spoke in a nasal croak: 'Hello. How are you?'

'We'll see how good a girl you are when you dance for us tonight,' a constable sniggered.

'Why did they target this kid?' Rana asked Ombir.

'This one's son went to the same school as Rudra,' he answered, knocking Sandeep on the head. 'They heard of the fancy cars and clothes and birthday parties. First they scoped out the father's shop and then got the boy's number. Did you take it from your son's phone?'

Sandeep remained quiet and then as Ombir's giant hand came towards him, said, 'Yes. But I swear, he did not know.'

'How long did you do this for?' Rana asked.

'He told me that he kept calling for over two weeks,' Ombir replied. 'The boy finally agreed to meet and they invited him to the All India Institute of Medical Sciences. They got him to come one evening when it was dark and busy. He approached the car as instructed, expecting a pretty face. Instead, these two jumped out.'

The reporter posed his final question to Rudra. 'Did you really believe it was a girl on the phone?'

'It was. It was a girl. I am sure,' the boy replied, sobbing.

Enough, Abhishek thought. He had more than sufficient material in any case. Outside, he could hear joyous cheers. Uday Kumar must have arrived.

'Come, Abhishek, get into the car,' Uday said, before issuing his final instructions. He ordered two policemen to remain at the house in case the brother returned. 'Rana, Mayank, come to the office. Ombir, you too. Surinder, take that motherfucker to the Darya Ganj lock-up. And the driver too, but make sure he's treated well. We'll need him as a witness. I'll see you all at the office.'

Uday joined Abhishek in the back seat of the car. 'So what do you think, Mr Dutta? I hope your opinion about Uday Kumar has changed now.'

Abhishek looked at Uday's smug face and smiled. 'Great operation, sir. Congratulations.'

'Thank you. Where shall I drop you?'

'I'll go to the *Express* office, sir. I can get off at the police headquarters. It's just past ten. Enough time to file the story tonight.'

'Story? What story? I have to write the arrest report first. You can't file anything before that.'

Abhishek was stunned. 'But tomorrow everyone will know.'

'Yes, there will be a press conference. No exclusives on this one.'

'My boss will be upset,' Abhishek tried a weak, final plea. 'He doesn't even know where I've been.'

'Don't worry about Amir. I'll talk to him. You stay in Mayur Vihar, don't you? I'll drop you there. Go and rest. I'll see you tomorrow.'

12

Hi. Havent forgotten u. Coffee tomorrow? Monika xxx

In the early hours of 30 November 2011, three days and three agonizing nights after meeting Monika Mathur, Amit Mahajan received a text from her.

He had been close to despair, and had willed himself the previous evening not to go looking for her at the Sheraton. Instead, he had invited two friends home and, over violent computer games, had dismissed her face; shot and lacerated it on screen.

Late in the night, when Amit was alone in bed, she had come back to smile at him, unblemished, promising him unthinkable pleasures, her bosom heaving and comforting. He had sunk his head in, breathing the rich chocolate aroma of her skin, begging forgiveness for his earlier cruelty.

As with everything that had happened between Archana, alias Monika, and Amit, the text message had been thought through carefully. The spotter outside the Mahajans' house informed Imran that the boy had chosen to stay indoors. After a brief chat with Babloo, Archana had decided that her target's misery should not be allowed to transform into something beyond her control.

The absence of the boy's parents had complicated the situation. Now everything had to be planned meticulously to coincide with their return to India. Babloo's man at the Central Bureau of Investigation had informed him that the government would force the Mahajans to come back within a month. Until then, Archana's game with their son had to be played out with care.

She had wanted to understand the layout of the house, map the getaway, construct in elaborate detail, as she always did, every step of the operation. But Babloo had been adamant that she visit the house only once, on the day of the kidnapping. He did not want regular sightings of her by the house staff. By bribing a New Delhi Municipal Corporation clerk, he had instead procured for her the floor plans of the opulent two-storey house. He was also using his local contacts to plant men in the family's security and chauffeur services, and hoped that the groundwork would be completed within a month. Until then, Amit Mahajan had to be kept interested and restrained. Archana knew of the dangers with the young ones: give in too easily and they lose interest; keep away for too long and offended pride finds succour in other distractions. The middle-aged were easier; they could not, for a long time, believe their luck.

'You just don't want me to fuck him, no?' Archana had teased her mentor when refused permission to visit the house.

But Babloo was in no mood for flirtatiousness. 'You'll fuck him when and if there is a need. In fact, if required, you will fuck the whole city. But for now keep your mouth shut.'

Babloo was always under-confident and therefore thorough, but Archana had rarely seen him so edgy. More must be riding on this kidnapping than he was letting on, she thought. But she didn't doubt his loyalty – if she was not being told something, there must be a good reason.

Archana first met Babloo as a nineteen-year-old in Mumbai where she was bedding third-rate directors and a few first-rate ones too, hoping to land a role. Babloo quickly showed her how equations could change. 'If you had a dick,' he told her, 'they would all be sucking on it now.' Archana had laughed, delirious to be on the other side of power.

Mobster flopped despite all Babloo's interventions. He had ensured that no other releases took place the week her film hit the cinemas, that every big-billed actor turned up for the launch party, that only friendly reviews made it to print. The only thing Babloo couldn't guarantee was public appreciation. Archana decided to move on.

When she first came to Babloo, he was living in an apartment near Colaba, not very far from the Mumbai Police headquarters. Archana had been surprised at his willingness to take her on and become her mentor.

On their first night together, Babloo had explained his life and its rules: 'You think everyone is afraid of me, don't you? You are wrong. I am afraid of everyone, everything – the man guarding the door, the maid who comes each morning, the newspaper boy … even you. The thing I won't be afraid of – that will be the thing which will kill me.' He told her about his fearless brother. 'He had his eyes gouged out. Hands chopped off. I think of him when I get brave.'

Babloo showed Archana two large suitcases filled with five-hundred-rupee notes. 'Real ones,' he affirmed. 'What do I do with this money? How much can one spend? Can't keep it in the bank. Can't do anything.'

Archana was astonished. She could count a hundred ways to spend it.

Over the years, Babloo taught her discretion and fear.

In return, she provided companionship and a fiercely loyal friendship that quickly spiralled into love.

Archana came out of the shower, wrapped in a towel, and checked her phone. There were two missed calls from Amit. No doubt he wanted to know the time and place. For that he would have to wait a little longer.

Archana's daytime wardrobe was designed not to attract attention. She dressed quickly, without fretting over details. Every weekday she left the house by 9 a.m. and returned just after 6 p.m., establishing a work routine. She was reacquainting herself with Delhi, visiting places she knew during her college years and discovering the recent changes. She went to markets, visited cinemas, checked out restaurants, museums and galleries. Sometimes, like today, she would spend time in one of the larger public parks, but she never went to the same place twice. She tipped reasonably at restaurants and was careful not to draw attention. Babloo had to struggle over this: her proclivity to flirtation had to be almost surgically removed.

Archana went into the kitchen to prepare a light breakfast. Imran would wake up in a while. He left the house an hour after her, once the maid had come and gone. They had insisted she come no earlier, as their separate sleeping arrangements would have invited suspicion. Archana did not mind Imran. He had proven to be unobtrusive. She was not disinclined, she thought smiling, to another fuck.

'Where are all the bloody tea stalls?' Amir muttered, scanning the strip of smart new shops that had replaced his favourite gossip centres. 'I don't want fucking Uncle Chipps in the morning.'

The Inter State Bus Terminus was unrecognizable. Like the railway stations and airports, it had been given a facelift. The filth and grime, low-end drugs, cheap food and book stalls that sold paperback porn along with newspapers had been ousted in favour of coffee chains and sandwich outlets.

It was eight o'clock on a December morning and already the place seemed close to bursting. Rows of empty buses stood with their engines running, belching out fumes. People rushed to and from ticket counters and crammed into disorderly queues. Drivers and conductors shouted for passengers to clamber on board. And vehicles rolled in from provincial hinterlands, disgorging bleary-eyed workers ready to begin their day's mission to keep the capital functioning.

Amir had little patience or curiosity for the human drama that was unfolding around him. It was bitterly cold and foggy, his head hurt, and Mihir Ghosh was quitting. And it was his birthday.

'Bloody hell,' Amir shouted, finding the toilet doors locked. He accosted a man who was sweeping the floor. 'Why are these closed?'

'New toilets. The people dirty them. So the manager keeps them locked.'

'Where the fuck do I piss then?'

'Go around the back,' the man said nonchalantly. 'Against the wall there.'

Amir stomped off. He finally found everything he needed: the designated pissing wall and, next to it, a man with a stove burner selling tea.

'I don't want a plastic cup,' he told the chaiwallah.

The man nodded, producing a glass from under his seat and filling it from the bubbling saucepan on the stove.

'No, no, make a fresh one. Put more leaves and just one spoon of sugar. Very little milk,' Amir ordered.

The chaiwallah looked up at him, thought of saying something, and then decided against it. He took out a new pot, poured some water from a jerry can, and put it over the flame.

Too much fucking rum last night, Amir groaned inwardly, as he sat on a bench. He had not intended to get drunk; no, it was to be a regular night like any other, and then Shobha had called. She always did this; call the day before his birthday. 'I want to be the first,' she used to say in happier times. These days he wished she wouldn't bother at all.

So, Mihir-da was leaving. Amir had seen it coming. The management had been after him for a while now, and the issue of annual increments had been used to accelerate the showdown. Mihir-da's recommendations were in most cases rejected, and his journalists would not see any substantial pay hikes. The paper's declining fortune and the financial crisis were the stated reasons, but the hefty raises for corporate employees over the journalists told Mihir Ghosh that he was being snubbed and his authority undermined.

'The stand-off is between the management and me. The journalists will suffer if I don't go,' he informed Amir during an afternoon chat in his office. 'Just giving you an early heads-up. You must do what is right for you.'

Amir had nodded dejectedly. Mihir-da was thinking of moving back to his sphere of specialization, economic reporting, and joining a business paper. Senior editors, when changing jobs, usually brought their own core team with them; loyal journalists whom they could trust. But there would not be place for a city reporter in this move. Mihir Ghosh was telling Amir that they were parting ways.

Amir did not expect anything from the annual increment. The money did not bother him. His needs were few. He stayed in his mother's house, had no dependants and hated travel. The club bills would not break the bank. Publishers sent him the books he wanted and his nieces sent him compilation CDs, which was the only music he listened to.

No, money was not the issue. It was the ignominy that bothered him. The CEO knew that, unlike other journalists, Amir Akhtar had no place left to run. He had worked in almost every mainstream newspaper in the city and while a few might still take him back, there would be no improvement in his salary or position.

Amir rarely indulged in regret or self-pity. There were very few things he would have done differently in his career, except perhaps that disastrous dalliance with television. He had no illusions about his own talent. In fact, as he constantly reminded his colleagues, journalism required little, and most journalists had none. 'Engineers need expertise, doctors need to know their craft, even plumbers. We just need a fucking social science degree and it's licence to throw muck at anyone,' he used to say.

Amir had defied this lack of talent through doggedness. He did not understand news convergence, could not design a page to save his life, and felt no empathy for youngsters whose CVs boasted an ability to produce a paper from scratch. He was a reporter first and today, he was being told, he was a reporter lost. He could leave; the paper would not care.

The tea came. Amir gratefully took the first sip. 'Ah, excellent,' he complimented the chaiwallah. It was almost half past eight now. Where was that idiot Matera? He thought of calling and then decided to give it another few minutes.

Finishing the tea in two long slurps, and getting up to stretch,

Amir asked for another. No, this moping would not do, he told himself. There was work to be done. It did not matter how his job was going, who got what increments; he was still the chief reporter of a newspaper. And he had Babloo Shankar to contend with.

Amir thought about Abhishek. The boy had simply vanished yesterday. Repeated phone calls had gone unanswered and apart from that one text, he had heard nothing. Mihir-da had wanted to inform the police but Amir had resisted, though he had asked the night reporter to check for accidents and casualties. Reporters, the good ones, should disappear once in a while.

The sun broke through the fog and Amir could make out the city's skyline. The three new flyovers, now roaring overhead, had done nothing to ease the traffic. Several buses, each unrelenting, blocked the entrance to the terminus. The conductors jumped out of their vehicles and traded insults as they tried to guide their drivers.

Amir recalled Samuel Pereira, the deputy commissioner for traffic, telling him that every day one thousand new private cars joined the seventy varieties of vehicles choking Delhi. 'Buses, cars, two-wheelers, auto-rickshaws, cycle rickshaws, bullock carts and push carts. You want to make this city a Shanghai or a Hong Kong? It's a joke,' Samuel had ranted. 'Every bullock cart comes with its own fucking union and a politician to defend it. You need a firing squad, not traffic minders.'

Matera crept up beside Amir, startling him. 'Sorry sir, my bike had a puncture.'

'Stop lying.' Amir laughed, feeling better after the tea. 'You are behaving like my reporters. Except they come up with better excuses.'

Matera grinned.

'Listen,' Amir said, making space on the bench, 'you have to come with me to meet a few policemen.' Seeing Matera's dismayed look, he added reassuringly, 'Don't worry. I will be there with you. This might even help you to get to know some of the big bosses, after all those two-bit constables you spend your time with.'

The young man didn't complain. Amir had kept the police off him on several occasions over the years and if he was needed now, he did not have much choice. 'Whom will we meet?' he enquired.

'Uday Kumar.'

'Really?' Matera brightened visibly, imagining the stories he would have for his colleagues.

'What's happening with your boss? Any news?' Amir changed the subject.

'Not much. I haven't seen that car or the woman again. Only news is, Salim Bhai has asked Dilshan – he works with me – to join some security agency for a while. Bhai said he is arranging everything.'

'Do you know which agency?'

'I can't remember the name but I can find out.'

'Do that. It's very important,' Amir said, getting up. 'Now let's go. We'll talk more on the way. Come in my car. You can pick up your bike later.' He could barely contain his excitement.

'How can you hold this newspaper to your personal embargo? What gives you the right to go for a story and then not write it?' Mihir Ghosh was livid.

Abhishek, as requested by Uday, had withheld the police-rescue story. The *Asian Metro* had published it, though with few operational details. Earlier this morning at the meeting, when the editor asked how the story had been missed, Abhishek had proudly announced that he had been part of the police team and the story lacked meat.

'I can't believe this,' Mihir continued, shaking his head. 'You go for a story, you get it and then because a policeman asks, you don't do it? Whom do you work for? Delhi Police or the *Express*?'

Abhishek could sense the silent euphoria of the other reporters in the room. 'I am sorry, sir,' he said as contritely as possible.

'Sorry doesn't help, Abhishek. And remember this: You are only as good as your last story.'

Amir said nothing throughout the exchange. Normally he defended his reporters in front of the bosses or took the blame, but today his feelings were ambivalent. Part of him wanted Abhishek to get a dressing-down. But he couldn't quite dismiss the thought that he would have done exactly the same as the boy had. Protecting sources and respecting confidence were paramount. He knew that Mihir-da as a journalist thought the same, but as an editor, the newspaper was his priority.

He decided that he would have a chat with Abhishek later, but right now, let him face the music. Amir wanted to see if he handled criticism as well as he soaked up appreciation. He noticed the smirks on the faces of his reporters. At least some people were enjoying themselves.

'Abhishek, can you come into my office for a moment?' Amir said as they filed out of the morning meeting.

The reporter, looking a bit dazed, said, 'I have a lunch with the police commissioner, sir.'

'At the police headquarters? I have a meeting there as well. Give me five minutes and we'll talk on the way.'

As they descended the stairs of the office building, Amir asked Abhishek, 'Why did you not tell me where you were?'

'Uday Kumar told me not to.'

'You must work out your loyalties, Abhishek. Neither Uday Kumar nor any of your other policemen will give you the time of day if you weren't a journalist. Your new friends will vanish overnight. They are friends with the correspondent of the *Express* – not you.'

Abhishek quelled a sense of self-righteous anger. The morning scolding had come as a shock. He had been disappointed to see the story in another newspaper, but he had done his best given the circumstances. He had expected something of a hero's welcome. After all, a boy's life had been saved and he had played a major part in it. Instead, he found that no one, not even Maya and Rahul, gave a damn. 'They are behaving as if they go up Mount Everest to shit each morning,' he had thought, looking at the almost bored faces of his colleagues as he had related his experiences.

'So how can we retrieve this story?' Amir asked as they stepped onto the street.

Abhishek thought for a moment. 'Today they'll have the press conference, and most newspapers will focus on the police operation. I have an interview with the victim which we could carry as an exclusive. And I think we should present the story in the context of kidnappings in India. It has become a very lucrative business, and this one was a copycat crime. I did some research last night after getting home. This year there have been three thousand kidnappings in Delhi – more than double last year's figures. I was planning to ask the commissioner some questions during lunch.'

Amir had to stop himself from slapping Abhishek on the

back with delight. Instead, he said, 'Fine. I'll ask someone from the business desk to provide inputs on Delhi's economic growth, and we can link that to the rise in kidnappings. Why didn't you tell Mihir-da about the exclusive with the boy?'

'I was wishing I hadn't opened my mouth at all, sir. Landed me in enough trouble.'

'You'll get used to it. Can't expect to be praised all the time.'

They grinned at each other and walked in silence for a moment until Abhishek spoke again: 'I've got another story, Amir sir.'

He told Amir about the faulty transformers which threatened sites all over the city. He did not reveal his source nor did his boss ask.

'I think this is front-page. Scandalous,' Amir shook his head in astonishment. 'So the kidnap interview can go as the headline on the city page and this story on the front. Fuck me, this is big. I will tell Mihir-da as soon as I get back. What time do you return?'

'As soon as the press conference finishes, sir, at about five o'clock.'

A few reporters were already present at the PRO office when the two men entered. Vikram jumped out of his chair and rushed across the table to shake Amir's hand. 'Good fortune on my office, Amir sahab, you are here.'

Amir, bowed slightly, amused. 'Singh sahab, how are you? Yes, it has been a while.'

'Please come, sit, sit.' The policeman ushered him to the sofa.

Abhishek noted that the other crime reporters stood up to greet his boss. This was only the second time that he had witnessed Amir in a situation outside the office. Vikram was loudly introducing his 'great friend Amir Akhtar' to two newcomers.

'Shakti Bhai!' Amir grabbed the hand of the journalist who had admonished Abhishek the other day. 'How are you? I hear you've been giving my reporter a hard time about news ethics? You don't think an interview with a deranged murderer is a scoop?'

Abhishek was shocked at how Amir could have known; he certainly hadn't mentioned it. Shakti squirmed, his usual bravado gone.

'Cigarette?' Vikram plonked himself beside Amir on the sofa.

'Isn't smoking banned in government buildings?' Amir raised an eyebrow at the eager-to-please policeman.

'Absolutely. But those are new rules. For old-timers, old rules.'

'I have to reinvent myself to the new times or I'll become obsolete. Given up smoking.'

'Amir, okay, I will have to take your boy to the commissioner's office,' Vikram said, getting up. 'Do you want to join him? I'm sure boss will be delighted.'

'No, no. You go ahead. I have another meeting.'

As they climbed the stairs to the first floor, Vikram probed Abhishek, 'So, did you get a good story from Rohit Bansal the other day? I don't think I saw anything ...'

'Yes, it's probably scheduled for tomorrow,' Abhishek replied evasively.

A mir had not been to the Delhi Police press office for a while. Almost three years, he thought to himself, as he settled back in the sofa and listened to the conversations around him. Despite the new faces, the stories remained the same. A young man was relating how an inspector had come to his residence, pleading with him not to do a particular report. 'I took pity on him when he said he had three daughters to marry off,' the journalist bragged.

When Amir Akhtar had been a regular at the police headquarters, the press office had felt different. There were fewer newspapers then and the single government-aided news channel rarely bothered to send reporters. Competition between newspapers had been gentler, even gentlemanly, in those days. Amir, even now, refused to put women on the crime beat; the rest of the beats had plenty.

Amir knew that he'd covered crime for longer than he should have. Most of his peer group had moved on but he had always been averse to change. Once, during a late-night shift, he had ignored a tip-off about a 'fight between two gangs in Old Delhi', preferring, instead, a chat in the smoke-filled darkroom with a photographer. The fight had turned out to be a full-blown communal riot that raged on for weeks. He could not answer his editor when asked how a reporter with his experience could have disregarded the information coming from a communally sensitive area. Amir realized that there was a thin line between knowing a beat so well that you understood every nuance, and getting so comfortable that you became cynical towards news. He'd requested a move to cover education.

'Which crook are you off to meet today?' Vikram was back at his side.

'Uday Kumar.' Amir knew lying was pointless. Little happened in this building that passed Vikram by. 'Haven't seen him in ages. Thought we should do lunch. In fact,' he said, making to leave, 'I should be on my way.'

'Uday is becoming a favourite of your paper. What's going on?' Vikram asked with a smile.

'Isn't Uday everyone's favourite?' Amir retorted lightly, waving goodbye and stepping out.

In the corridor he met Mayank, hurrying towards him. 'Afternoon, sir,' he said.

'Mayank, good afternoon. We meet again.' Amir shook his hand warmly. 'We're both headed to the same office, I suppose?'

'Yes, sir.'

Before the editorial meeting that morning, Amir had introduced Matera and Mayank to each other, leaving only when he had been sure his ward was comfortable. He had appreciated the immediate kindness the young policeman had shown to Matera, sensing the man's vulnerability. He had offered him a cup of tea, sat with him and asked friendly questions. These were courtesies he rarely found in the ruffians in uniform today.

Amir had few illusions about men in power, especially civil servants whom he rated lower than politicians. 'At least politicians have to go back to the electorate,' the journalist argued. 'They have to seek a mandate. The bureaucrats have to pass one bloody exam and that's it – they can lord over our lives forever.' This one's a rare gem among the assorted assholes, Amir thought as he climbed the staircase with Mayank.

'So, Mayank, what has Matera told you?' Uday came straight to the point as soon as they were seated.

'Salim Khan seems keen to put a mole into a security agency in Delhi, sir. The name of the agency is …' Mayank referred to his files ' … A to Z Security Solutions.'

'I know its owner – Mukund Deswal,' Uday offered. 'He's part of central Delhi's land mafia. The security business is all cash; the perfect place for that bastard's black money. I can lean on him to give Salim's man the job. No problem.'

Amir objected. 'That might not be the best way to go. Salim entertains a lot of people at his dens. You know the variety – politicians, businessmen, even a couple of your colleagues. Your man Deswal and Salim might already know each other. If you intervene and Salim gets to know, this lead is over. Better to let Matera inform us.'

'Yes, you're right,' Uday conceded quickly.

'I've done some research on this security agency, sir,' Mayank said, his head still bent over his notes. 'Right now, they are the most successful in north India. In Delhi alone they have almost twenty thousand clients. This includes not only personal family-based security, but also some of the top industrial units.'

'Ah, Deswal has become big in recent times,' Uday smirked. 'You know, Amir, security is the business to get into. Big money, they say. Can't fucking fail. Everyone is afraid for their lives or for their cash. Maybe I should retire now and open an agency.'

'Perhaps you should,' Amir retorted, suddenly impatient, 'if you can't let somebody finish what he is saying.'

Mayank's usually indomitable boss looked chastened. There was an equation between these two men that the young officer failed to grasp. 'Given the sheer number of clients at A to Z,' he continued, looking from one to the other, 'this information still leaves us with an impossibly high number of potential victims. What we need to watch for closely is the particular posting Salim's man goes for. If we can discover this, and if it is indeed Babloo's doing, we have a very strong lead.'

'Excellent,' said Amir, nodding at Mayank. 'What do you think, Uday?'

'Yes, but you'll still need inside information. Mayank, are you proposing we find someone at the agency?'

'Yes, sir. And I might have just the person. I'll confirm it in a day or two.'

'Okay, good,' Uday said. 'So here we are now: I am almost sure Archana is in town and that seems corroborated by what Matera told you the other day, Amir. But my sources can't confirm Babloo's whereabouts. I've requested the airports to watch out for a man in a wheelchair. Unless he has suddenly managed to walk, Babloo hasn't entered the country through the usual route. We know he's been in Singapore till recently. So the land route option is not feasible, unless he flies to Nepal or Bangladesh and comes in from there.'

'And what if he does?' Amir asked.

'Nothing that we can do,' Uday replied. 'Too many corridors. Also, Babloo has very good local operators there.'

The meeting ended soon with responsibilities set: Amir would keep in close contact with Matera, Mayank would build on his contacts at A to Z Security, while Uday would quiz his sources for clues on Babloo. Even as they tried to give each other tasks and set deadlines, all three men knew that what they were doing was waiting for Babloo Shankar to make the next move.

'We must ask ourselves what kind of society we are policing, mustn't we?' Commissioner Pratap said to Abhishek, who nodded between mouthfuls of chicken biryani.

'Let me tell you what happened the other day, which really made me wonder if I am the right person to head this force.' Pratap helped himself to some soup. 'Gruesome incident in Mayur Vihar. You stay there, don't you? This man, posing as a courier, rings the doorbell of a third-floor apartment. It's midafternoon. The husband has left for work, the maid has come and gone. Mother is giving her nine-month-old daughter a bath. She opens the door to a man who shoves her inside. He has a knife with him. He ties the woman to a chair, then takes his time going through the cupboards, the safe. He takes the jewellery, takes the cash, and after about half an hour he is ready to leave. Suddenly the infant starts to cry and he notices her. She's still in the tub. Maybe the water's got cold. She's wearing these thin gold earrings. He tries to rip them off her ears. The baby screams and the man drowns her in the tub of water. Right there, in front of her mother. For a pair of earrings, he takes a life.' Pratap paused and looked at his lunch companion, who had stopped eating. 'Now tell me, how do I police this society? What kind of a man is this? I police human beings. Is he human? If we are to police animals, do I have to become an animal too?'

Abhishek reached for his notepad.

'No, no. This is not for a story. I am asking your opinion. Tell me what you think.'

Abhishek answered slowly. 'I don't know, sir. I wish I did. In the last one month, I have seen more things than in my entire life. I have no opinion. Right now, I think I am just observing.'

'Yes,' the commissioner said kindly. 'It must have been quite a month for you. I'm glad that you say you are observing. When you start having opinions, you can write editorials.' He chuckled. 'You know, editors and senior police officers are much the same. We have opinions. We don't go out on the streets any more. It's you guys – reporters, the younger policemen, my constables – who are our eyes and ears. We need your curiosity.'

Abhishek was enjoying the lunch but did not forget work. He asked the commissioner to explain the rise in kidnappings in Delhi.

'I don't know. Perhaps it's the influx of migrants,' Pratap said after a thoughtful pause. 'People come here from all over the country in search of a better life. In the villages, in the small towns, everyone knew each other. They had an identity, right? You were the tailor's son; somebody was the cobbler, barber ... whatever. Here, who knows you? No one. There's a feeling of having been set loose. People can do anything. And they do. They kidnap, kill, rape.'

'Are you saying rising migration to the cities is a problem?'

'No, I'm not saying that,' the cop replied quickly. 'The home minister would kill me if I said that, given his plans for a fifty per cent urban India. I know that's the worldwide trend, but here it will wreak havoc, Abhishek. The entire social fabric of this country is being changed. Suddenly some people have got very rich. Others want it too and will stop at nothing to get it.' He paused. 'Look, I can't give you a quote on this. Ask Uday. He has all the quotes in the world.'

Pratap poured himself a glass of water and then sat back on the sofa. 'The other day you met that man who butchered his daughter. Uff, horrific. Why do you think he did it in Delhi and not in his home town? One word: anonymity.'

The commissioner suddenly looked tired, and for a moment Abhishek felt he had been offered a rare glimpse inside the mind of one of Delhi's most powerful men.

Over coffee, Pratap told him, 'I've followed your reports with much appreciation. You've done very good and impartial work, and you have rightfully taken the police to task. As I've offered before, we should work together. I've given you my personal number. You can come to me for anything you feel like. I mean it.'

Abhishek was ecstatic. 'Sir, I couldn't have done anything

without your help. I appreciate it and will respond in any way I can.'

By the time he took his leave, the morning's scolding had faded to nothing. Abhishek felt on top of the world. A month ago, he was just another college graduate looking for a job. Now he took part in thrilling police operations, wrote front-page news stories and lunched with Delhi's topmost policeman. Had Abhishek been given to emotional displays, he would have punched the air. Instead, he kept walking, head down, hands in his jacket pockets.

His host was also satisfied with how the lunch meeting had gone. It had been calculated to do one thing: make the young journalist toe the line, and the commissioner was fairly sure that Abhishek had been bought. In his many years of service, he had never met a journalist who could not be wooed by power. They might scoff at money – in any case, blatant bribery wasn't his style – but power was always an effective, and cleaner seducer. A little homework on Abhishek had revealed his small-town middle-class upbringing. In years to come, Pratap knew, the gifts offered would have to be upped. But for now, words of praise and understanding from the establishment were enough.

There was one other matter. Pratap rang his staff officer. 'Have you heard from Vikram on the Abhishek Dutta issue? Is something being done?' A little destabilization would be useful.

13

Abhishek, buried under four blankets, was waiting to hear the thud against his front door. The December weather was mercilessly cold and the single window of his one-room quarters, bloated during the monsoon to a size slightly bigger than the frame, wouldn't shut properly. The blow heater he had bought with his first pay cheque had given up after three days of relentless work. On most mornings Abhishek took his time, steeling himself before his toes would make their first tentative flirtation with the world beyond the covers. But today would be different. Today he had a headline scoop.

The moment he heard the thump of the papers falling in the corridor, he rushed outside. With a triumphant glance at the front pages, he jumped back into bed with the newspaper, intending to savour every word.

He read it luxuriously, delighting at the accompanying archive shot of the blazing Uphaar cinema. This would cause a stir, he smiled, before finally turning back to his P.D. James murder mystery. He had been reading *The Lighthouse* for over a month now and was keen to get it over with. During his school and college years, Abhishek could get Adam Dalgliesh to wrap up most investigations in a day or two but these days he was dragging his feet. The detective had just taken ill with a deadly virus when Abhishek's phone rang.

'Good morning. This is Nayyar here.'

He couldn't immediately place the name. Ah yes, the editor's PA. They had been introduced briefly once and though Abhishek passed the man's cubicle every day, there had never been any further interaction.

'Good morning, Mr Nayyar,' he said, puzzled by the call.

'Can you come to the office immediately? The editor wants to meet you.'

'Why, what has happened?'

'I don't know. But Mr Ghosh says it's very urgent.'

'Okay. I will get there as soon as possible.'

Abhishek's scooter refused to budge and no amount of furious kick-starting would make it relent. He tried to stem the rising panic as he woke up a reluctant and cold-numbed auto driver.

The morning rush was grinding into motion. Plunging through the thick fog that still enveloped the city, the population made its resigned way along repeated routes towards known chores. As his auto rattled and wove its precarious way towards the offices of the *Express*, Abhishek tried to imagine what might have provoked this early morning summons. Could Uday Kumar have complained about the interview with the kidnapped boy? Had he missed something major?

Mihir Ghosh was restlessly pacing the floor of his office when Abhishek was shown in. 'Sit,' he told the nervous-looking boy. 'Now, who gave you the story?'

'Which one, sir?' Abhishek asked.

'Today's front page,' Mihir snapped.

Abhishek hesitated, and then said, 'A source, sir.'

'Which source? In the police?'

'Yes.' He nodded.

'Well, your source is trying to get you thrown out of your job and me out of mine.'

There was a knock on the door and Amir walked in. He nodded at Abhishek and took a chair. 'What's going on, Mihir-da?' he asked. Abhishek could sense from his tone that his boss was on his side.

'You know what's going on. Your reporter has been made a fool of, and I am up shit creek without a paddle.'

Amir smiled at the image. 'Well, we all cleared the story, including you. If he has been a fool, he has an excuse – he's just one month into the profession. What about us?'

In the moment of quiet that ensued, Abhishek ventured, 'May I ask what has happened?'

'The company that is producing those faulty transformers belongs to the Thapars, the family that owns this paper,' Amir told him. 'Effectively, we've used the front page of the newspaper to screw its owners.'

There was a brief silence and then, to Abhishek's astonishment, the two senior newsmen began to laugh. Mihir was bent over his desk, shaking with mirth. Amir turned to Abhishek: 'You do realize that you've been had? And you've fucked us over too. Now get out and wait for me in my cabin.'

'I am sorry. I really shouldn't have asked.' Amit was horrified. He could not believe his own audacity.

'No … that's fine,' Monika said quietly, her eyes still on him. 'I have asked myself the same question several times. You must be very perceptive if you caught on. It's something I don't speak of to anyone.' She took a sip of her coffee. 'I've been with him for two years now and both our parents wanted it, I guess. He is a successful banker, has roots in the same community as mine. So it just made sense. I know, to you lovelorn youngsters that might sound like a compromise, a cop-out, but …' Her voice trailed off, and Amit could almost reach out and touch her sadness.

They had been sitting at the Café Coffee Day outlet for more than an hour, and were on their second round of cappuccinos. Monika had come late, just at the moment when Amit had decided she wasn't going to show up.

He'd seen her through the glass façade of the cafe, waiting on the other side of the road for a lull in the traffic. Amit felt a gushing sense of relief, followed by panic. How should he appear? Nonchalant? As if he hadn't seen her crossing the street, busy as he was on his mobile? Should he get up to kiss her? Or just keep sitting and extend a hand when she reached him?

Monika had waved cheerily as she entered, and Amit had jumped up from his chair, nearly knocking over his cup. She'd smiled and kissed him on the cheek, tossing her bag beside her as she sat. 'Ooofff, what a day! Sorry I'm late, but terrible bloody time at office. I need a coffee. You well? You're looking good.'

Now he was feeling calmer and confident.

'Why did you come back to India? You wouldn't have had to marry in the US, no? You could have just lived with him as you were before,' Amit probed gently.

'My parents are here in Chandigarh and I have been away for … what …' she thought a while, 'thirteen years. They're getting old. From Delhi, I can go and visit them on weekends. But to answer your question: Do I love him? I don't know. It works for both of us. But convenience,' Monika said, almost to herself, 'must not be mistaken for love.'

Since yesterday morning, when he'd first got her text, Amit had been preparing his stories – facts with dabs of fiction that would make his mostly unremarkable life seem interesting. He was desperate to sound interesting, look interesting. But the evening found him floating effortlessly in the magic world of Monika's words. He was surprised at how easily she confided in him and to discover that under the strong, almost unapproachable exterior, there was a vulnerable core.

Monika's self-effacing humour put him at ease, especially her fresh-off-the-boat America stories. She had gone to the US on a scholarship in the fall of 1997 for a master's in software development. 'I had the unfortunate experience of landing in Houston. My uncle lives there with his wife. On my second day there he had to go to office, so to keep me entertained he dropped me off at one of those gigantic malls. I spent a whole day there gazing at the stores: Saks Fifth Avenue, Gap, Tommy Hilfiger. I got hungry and there were so many food places, but I couldn't go in. I was terrified of their accent and embarrassed at mine.' Monika gestured at the interiors of the shiny cafe they were sitting in now. 'In the 1990s, there was nothing like this. The only coffee we got was that foamy milky coffee made in huge machines with steam coming out of them. We called it expresso coffee. Do you know the type I mean?'

Amit nodded. It was his favourite, actually.

'So there I was in this massive mall, tired and jet-lagged, and in front of me loomed Starbucks. I stood outside for twenty minutes before daring to go in. A girl at the counter asked me what I wanted. There were a hundred varieties of coffee and they all sounded Greek to me.'

Amit burst out laughing, unable to visualize this confident woman struggling to order a coffee.

'I was terrified. Anyway, so I saw the magic word "espresso" with an S. I know that, I thought, and asked for it. When it came,

I was shocked by the black liquid at the bottom of the cup. The girl saw my confused look and asked, "Were you expecting something else?" Timidly I said, "Some milk and sugar, I guess." She took the cup away from me and brought me a larger one. "Here you go. Next time it will be Café Latte for you."' Monika mimicked the American drawl remarkably well. 'I didn't even know how the fuck to spell that,' she said, making a face.

Amit shook his head. 'If that could happen to you, I am not even going to make it off the plane.'

'Oh no, you'll be fine,' Monika assured him. 'America is not new to you.'

'I haven't been there before.'

'I mean that you know America. What you get there, you get here now. You see the same movies, go to the same malls, the same food, the same clothes. When I went, it was all very different.'

They left the cafe an hour later. Amit wanted to go to a club, but Monika pleaded a rain check. 'I'm very tired, Amit, and have work tomorrow. Perhaps next week? I really had fun though.'

On his way home, Amit thought of the hundred things he had meant to tell her and now, after the evening was over, a hundred more came to mind. She was so different from what he'd thought. She was lovely. He prayed that she would want to meet him again.

Amir looked up irritably at Shankar Lal, the head receptionist-cum-dogsbody of the Press Club. Lal was a bit too servile for Amir's liking and interrupting him, when his rook was being threatened from the right and a bishop lay immobile, was foolhardy. 'What is it, Shankar?' he asked impatiently.

'Sir-ji, your reporter Abhishek sir is here. He wants to meet you. Shall I let him in on your number?'

Amir was surprised; he was not expecting Abhishek here tonight. 'He wants to meet me?'

Lal nodded.

Amir thought for a while before saying, 'Okay, ask him to wait in the bar. I'll come after the game. See that he gets a drink.'

Amir apologized to his partner Ganesh, who seemed oblivious to the interruption. There was something unnerving about playing chess with Ganesh Ranganathan when he was drunk. The man's eyes never wavered from the board, as though scared that a pawn might accidentally wander off.

Amir and Ganesh were of the same age and for many years had worked together as reporters at *The Morning Herald*. Six months back Ganesh had decided that he did not have it in him any more, and quit. He needed to devote more time to his family, he said, and proceeded to spend all of it at the club. Both men knew each other well, so much so that the first sixteen moves of their game never varied.

'I've been reading this boy's reports ... Abhishek Dutta. Is he good?' Ganesh asked, his eyes still fixed on one square.

'Yes. Very.' Amir was trying to concentrate, but Abhishek's unannounced arrival had disturbed him. What was he doing here? He was supposed to be with his college friends at the university.

Amir had granted him the day off to meet friends, provided he still did the routine checks and would work the following Sunday. A kidnapping and a malicious plant in one week would stagger even the most hardened hack. But before letting him go, Amir had interrogated the boy. 'Stop this source confidentiality crap. You think I don't know where you get your stories? You think I believe you just happened to pass by the Pakistan High Commission at four a.m. without any help from a certain Mayank Sharma?'

Amir knew he had made an unfair move, but it had got the desired result. Abhishek told him about the so-called chance meeting with DCP Rohit Bansal in Vikram Singh's office.

'I'll do my best to defend you, Abhishek. Look, it's a valid story and we all know it, including Mihir-da and the proprietors. But the situation is tricky. Let's see what happens. No point worrying about it right now.'

After Abhishek left, Amir had called the police PRO. 'Singh sahab, why are you after our reporters?'

'Arre, Amir,' Vikram had replied, 'what are you saying? What has happened?'

'Let's not play games. I'll make sure Abhishek gets your message. But no more of this, okay?' Amir heard the subdued chuckle.

'I don't know what you are talking about, Amir, but I agree as always. It was good to see you the other day. Come again soon.'

Then it was damage control. Amir had called the police commissioner and arranged an immediate meeting with Romesh Thapar. It went well, he was told. No cases would be registered, at least for the moment.

'Three moves and it's over,' Ganesh said.

'Yes, I know.'

Amir brooded for a quarter of an hour more before giving up. 'Fuck. Okay, I am off. How about Saturday?'

Ganesh nodded, his eyes still on the board.

It was nearly closing time at the club when Amir finally joined Abhishek. 'Sit, sit. What are you having? Rum?'

Abhishek nodded.

'Good, let's order a few quickly. Where is Shankar when he's needed? Damn, once again I haven't eaten anything. I need food.'

Despite the kitchen having closed, Shankar managed to provide Amir with some mutton korma and naan.

'Was everything okay at the office?' Abhishek asked.

'Yes, for now,' Amir slurred between mouthfuls. 'But were you not supposed to be meeting friends at the university?'

'Yes, sir. I met a former classmate who is doing a PhD. Stays on campus. He told me something that I think would make for a great story.'

'Fuck, man, you are back to discuss a story now? Couldn't it have waited till morning?'

'Sir, it's a very good story. I think you might like to hear it.'

'Okay, go on.'

'My friend, sir, recently got his driver's licence. He just paid a bribe to the touts at the licensing agency on Rajpur Road and then, within an hour, he got a licence. So I am thinking, I should do what we did for the visa story. Go get a licence made and detail how the process works. What do you think?'

Amir's reaction was disappointing. 'What's the story here? We all know, everyone knows, that you can pay money and get a licence. You can get anything for money – ration cards, gas cylinders, out-of-turn petrol pump allocations. God knows the many miracles of this city. So where's the story?'

'Well, maybe I can show how it's done.' Abhishek's confidence was deflating rapidly.

'That will only encourage more people and benefit the touts. Nothing else.'

Lal took his time cleaning the table and Amir took the hint.

'Oh, okay, bill.' He looked at his crestfallen reporter, and said, 'Come, let's have tea. I need to sober up.'

Just outside the Press Club, beyond the parking lot, was a row of brightly lit dhabas that remained open till early in the morning, despite pressure from the police. When respectable establishments closed their doors in deference to licensing laws, much of the city's respected stopped here before heading homewards, gluttony satisfied and chai-craving quenched. Amir's affection for these late-night luxuries went further than most, and he lobbied actively for their survival. There was no shop owner on this stretch, not even among the scores of helpers, waiters, cleaners and cooks, who did not know Amir sahab and crave his patronage. He enjoyed their attention almost as much as their bread pakore.

'Sir, to mine today. You promised the last time.' A young boy sprinted up to them and grabbed Amir's hand.

'Ai, Chhotu, how are you?' Amir smiled. 'Come, we'll sit here,' he told Abhishek. 'Chhotu, chai.'

The boy ran off to get the tea.

'The police did a good job on you with that plant today.' Amir's grizzled face broke into a youthful grin.

'Yes, can you please tell me what happened there?'

'They were trying to tell you who the boss is. Put you in your place, I guess. In a way, it's a good thing. You've forced them to take notice of you.'

'You mean that Rohit Bansal gave me the story just to land me in trouble?'

'Not necessarily him; higher-ups most probably. But don't let that bother you. Just be very fucking careful and cross-check stories in the future.'

'With whom?'

'Well, I guess you could have checked with the company that was producing the transformers.'

'Wouldn't the story then immediately be blocked? I mean, if the company ...'

'To be honest, it was a damn good story to run and most reporters would have done exactly what you did. I certainly would have. So I am not blaming you.'

Abhishek considered this for a while. 'That just can't be it. I should understand how to avoid plants like this, no?'

'Look, all investigative agencies – and the police are just one of them – have always used journalists to plant stories. We know that. But if the story is good – and yours was – we go ahead. No one gives a story for free.'

'You mean every story is a plant?'

'Most exclusives are. Let me give you an example. Do you remember the ISRO spy scandal? 1994? No, of course you don't. Case in Kerala involving a Maldivian woman, Indian scientists, senior policemen. After the case breaks, I get this call from an officer from the Intelligence Bureau. He takes me out for lunch and gives me a thick dossier that totally indicts a very senior police official. A cracker of a story, I thought. Then I get another call. This guy is from Research and Analysis Wing.'

Amir paused to signal for a bottle of mineral water. 'You know RAW, right? International espionage; cousins of the fucking FBI and the KGB. So he too takes me out for lunch and gives me another fat dossier on the case. This one totally exonerates the policeman. I go back to both of them, hand them their bogus papers and tell them to find someone bloody else to plant their bullshit on. Turned out, the whole thing had been a set-up by the Indian intelligence agencies from the start.'

Amir drank thirstily from the bottle. 'The thing to remember is that you are dealing with lives. One story can finish off an innocent person. A man I knew, a mid-level bureaucrat; someone planted a corruption case against him in one of the papers. He committed suicide. Later, the sons of bitches retracted their case. But the story had been done – the man was dead.'

Abhishek had been meaning to ask Amir something. 'You remember I had lunch with the commissioner the other day?'

'Yes.'

'We were discussing things like morality and accountability, and he told me about this man who was shot dead in the Press Club a couple of years back. He said there were more than two hundred members present, yet no one came forward as a witness. Is that true?'

'Yes, it is. I was there too, if you are asking. I was the club president, and in my office at the time of the shooting. That is what I told the police.' Amir waved at Chhotu for the bill. 'Enough for one night. Come, let's go.'

As they walked towards Amir's car, he asked Abhishek, 'So, how's it going between you and our lady?'

'Which lady, sir?'

'Maya Srivastava, you fucker. I hear you're watching movies together.'

'Oh, that. Rahul and his wife were there too.'

'Yes, but they didn't stay for dinner, did they?'

Abhishek smiled. 'Rahul has got a big mouth.'

'Don't try and second-guess my sources, young man,' his boss replied. 'But never mind that. What's going on?'

Abhishek was amused by Amir's curiosity. 'Well, I like her. She is very idealistic and strong.'

'Ha, has she been giving you her crap? Don't get taken in by everything she says. You know her family, right? The epitome of establishment. She is no left-wing liberal.'

'I have no idea about her background,' Abhishek said. The conversation would be about her only when the wine was on him, he remembered.

'Then you should find out. You are a reporter, no?' Amir raised his eyebrows at him. 'By the way, I've been thinking of your story idea. I think there is a way to make this story huge. But we have to be inventive.'

R ajni Bhatia, transport commissioner of Delhi, was enjoying a lie-in. Half awake in bed, she relished the thought of not having to see her tiresome PA and that absolute disaster of a minister for two whole weeks. From under the duvet, she could hear Bruno's bark and her husband Chandan's muted conversation with the gardener. Gently assured that all was well with the world, she went back to sleep.

'Rajni, get up please. Quickly.'

She heard the urgency in her husband's voice and knew that her holiday was over. He was standing next to the bed, a newspaper in his hand. 'What is it?' Rajni asked.

He placed the paper in front of her along with her reading glasses, and then retreated to the window.

GET A DRIVING LICENCE IN THE
VICE-PRESIDENT'S NAME

'Good lord, what is this?' Rajni shrieked, scanning the paper and struggling to sit up. Her mobile rang. It was the chief minister's residence. 'Oh great,' she muttered, and let it ring.

Covering the entire top half of the newspaper's front page were copies of two driving licences. The mugshot on both belonged to the same person – the reporter. One licence was in the name of the vice-president, M. Narayan Murthy; the other, Delhi's lieutenant governor S.N. Krishna.

The implications of the forgeries dawned on the transport commissioner as she read the report. The journalist had visited two licensing centres – Rajpur Road and Ashok Vihar – and procured a permanent driving licence through touts at each. There had been no identity checks. The authorities had accepted the official address of the state dignitaries without question.

At Rajpur Road, despite asking for a two-wheeler licence, the reporter had been asked to drive a car, there being no two-wheelers available. When he said that he did not know how, he was asked to get into a vehicle with another man already at the wheel. Sitting in the passenger seat, one hand on the steering wheel, he was taken on a few laps of an empty field. Somewhere, he was told, there was an instructor watching who had just passed his driving test. Once he got out of the car, another hopeful applicant got in.

At the second licence centre, there was not even the pretence of a test, the report stated. From behind his desk, an official waved three fingers at the journalist and asked, 'How many?' The man seemed satisfied with the reporter's answer and cleared the file.

Within a few hours at each place, the reporter had obtained two genuine driving licences with fake names and addresses. That these details were of the vice-president and lieutenant governor of Delhi meant that heads would now roll.

'He even managed to use their official addresses,' Rajni's

husband remarked as she finished the article. 'How could that happen?'

'Oh, stop being so fucking sanctimonious. Run a government department like mine and you'll know. Well,' she said, throwing off the covers, 'that was a short holiday.'

She put on her dressing gown and, picking up the newspaper and mobile, headed for the bathroom. At the door, she turned and said to her husband, 'Sorry, Chandan, but the shit is just about to hit the fan. The phones will start to ring. Don't even bother answering ... and switch on the television, will you, darling, to see what the news channels are saying.'

'How is it not a valid news story?' Mihir Ghosh asked Divya Bhonsle, more surprised than sarcastic.

'Well, it doesn't say anything new, does it? It's the same old "corruption in public office" shit. I mean, so bloody what? We all know that. Old wine in new bottle.' Amir's deputy was being ridiculously mean.

Abhishek looked at Amir, who winked. He smiled back. 'Go ahead, Divya,' he thought, 'make yourself look small.'

'I agree,' said Mihir coolly. 'But please show me a news story that says anything new? The sports pages have the same sports stories; the features pages, the same gossip about the same film stars; the national pages; the city pages – the same stories. Just because a story on corruption has been done before ...' The phone on the editor's desk rang loudly, cutting him off. 'Excuse me,' he said.

'Hello. Oh hi, Frances.' He listened for a while. 'Yes, that's okay. Why don't you call him in ... say twenty minutes? I'll let him know. Thanks very much.'

Turning towards the reporting unit gathered for their morning meeting, Mihir announced, 'That was Frances Baker of the *New York Times*. Wants to have a chat with you, Abhishek, about today's story. Speak to her but do be sure to say that despite the corruption, it is Indian democracy that allows the press to do such exposés. Don't let her make this an anti-India rant. So, Divya, I've had at least ten news channels calling me for interviews. There will be inquiries, suspensions and dismissals. The government is in a tizzy. Tomorrow there will be follow-ups in every national newspaper. To answer your question – yes, I think it's a valid news story.'

14

Abhishek was in an underground parking lot filled with cars, trying to find a place for his scooter. Unlike the car park at the *Express*, where scores of two-wheelers lined in rows kept each other company, here his second-hand Bajaj was an anomaly.

He took the lift to the ground level, emerging in the afternoon sunlight at the foot of an impressive, shiny new complex. This was his first visit to Gurgaon, a suburb which in the past decade had come of age. Delhi was choked for places of leisure and its cultural capital still managed to stand in the way of a club membership or a desired table for the newly moneyed. In quest of golf courses and Olympic-size swimming pools, these new gods of India created Gurgaon.

After an hour's struggle against four-wheel drives and their bullying honks on the road, for a moment, Abhishek was disorientated by the quiet polish of the air-conditioned interior. His own office building involuntarily sprang to mind: its entrance regularly picketed by workers protesting the closing of an Urdu newspaper, the red stains of betel-nut juice on the walls marking a losing battle. Here, instead of annoying parking attendants clogging the staircase, a receptionist smartly directed him to the News Today offices on the third floor, checking his name against a list of expected visitors. Could he please pin this pass on so that it was clearly visible? A uniformed security guard accompanied him to the lift.

'Can I get you something?' a young woman asked as she seated Abhishek in the lobby.

'A glass of water, please,' he said, sinking into the plush leather sofa.

A flat-screen television was showing the news and Abhishek glowed inwardly as he saw the headlines flashing the licensing story and the upcoming inquiry. Tepid coffee in a plastic cup and a few cookies were graciously offered to him with a glass of water.

Several of the faces around him were recognizable from television. People moved about quickly. Even the receptionist, though glued to a chair beside a large computer screen, seemed to convey alacrity. At this hour, back at the *Express*, a few subeditors would be lounging on worn sofas, detaining whoever passed with lazy sociability. Gossip would permeate the room, slowing even the most urgent tasks.

Abhishek kept his eyes fixed on the television screen as he noticed Sandeep Bhushan, News Today's crime reporter, entering the lobby. This was one encounter Abhishek had hoped to avoid.

'Boss, what are you doing here?'

'Hi, Sandeep. How are you?'

'You here for a job? Whom are you meeting?' Sandeep asked.

'No, no. Was just passing through,' Abhishek floundered. 'Vivek Sethi, my former colleague, is here now. I dropped by to meet him.'

'Passing through Gurgaon? Anyway, good story yesterday. I'm doing a follow-up. Guess I'll be seeing more of you around.'

Abhishek was still recovering from the awkward encounter when an impeccably dressed man of about his age approached.

'Abhishek Dutta? My name is Neeraj Mishra. I'm the human resources manager here. Please do come.'

He had purchased that voice in a foreign university, Abhishek thought. Something about the man immediately made him feel inadequate.

Neeraj seated Abhishek in a small conference room one floor above.

'Right. Let me have a look at your CV,' he began.

'I haven't got a CV. I mean, I wasn't told to bring anything.'

Neeraj frowned. 'You have come here for a job, haven't you?'

The voice was impossibly supercilious and it grated.

'Well, I don't know. I was told to meet Samir Saxena this evening and that's why I came.'

'Yes, but all appointments must go through us. That's how we operate here. Who called you?'

'Vivek Sethi.'

Neeraj excused himself and returned ten minutes later, slightly deflated. 'Mr Saxena is indeed waiting for you. If you will follow me, please.'

After Vivek's call last night, Abhishek had phoned to tell his mother he would be meeting Samir Saxena. She had been rendered speechless, he could tell. For a moment he thought she had fainted. He asked her if she had been following his licence story in Benares.

'Yes, yes. It's on television here. But tell me, what will you wear? And make sure you take a shower. Will you go to the temple first?'

Abhishek had smiled. Religion and hygiene – Ma managed to bring them into everything. But he knew she was proud. By tomorrow their entire colony would know.

Samir Saxena's face invaded bedrooms and living rooms

all over India. It contorted itself earnestly in hotel lobbies and restaurants, and bore down smilingly from billboards on highways from Mumbai to the Bay of Bengal. Samir was India's first news celebrity and, for two decades, its most respected icon. Abhishek had seen the man reporting on wars in the Middle East, and earthquakes in Pakistan, conversing with heads of state in New York and Beijing, and dining with the Clintons. Bollywood mughals begged his presence at their movie premieres.

Abhishek was about to meet a childhood hero.

Neeraj led him to a newsroom which covered an entire floor and buzzed with activity. Someone was recording a piece to camera in one corner and dozens of television screens flashed overhead. People were clustered around computers, speaking impenetrable jargon on phones and to each other. Abhishek tried, for a fleeting moment, to picture Amir here but it was too incongruous, almost cruel.

There were glass cabins in each corner and Abhishek followed Neeraj towards the largest. He could see Samir Saxena sitting with his back to the newsroom, staring out of a window. He was the only one who seemed to be without a job, Abhishek thought, as he was shown in.

Samir swivelled around in his chair and stood up smiling, hand outstretched. He was taller than he appeared on TV and the curly hair had streaks of grey, but the grin was as infectious in person as it was on screen. Abhishek was a bit taken aback by the clothes – a smart jacket and tie with trackpants and sports shoes. He kept his eyes on Samir's face, not letting the surprise show.

'Abhishek, come, come. I've been waiting for you. You're late. No matter. Sit, sit.'

'I am sorry, sir. I was here in time but had to wait downstairs, and then Neeraj Mishra had a meeting with me.'

'Neeraj who?' Samir asked.

'The human resources gentleman who just showed me up – Neeraj Mishra.'

'Ah, these management idiots. Don't worry about them. Tell me, how are you?'

The words came out in a rush. Abhishek tried to say how honoured he was to meet Samir, how his work life was taking off; his new experiences, and the terrific feeling of being a journalist. Samir kept smiling indulgently, nodding.

'My parents are big fans of yours,' the young man ended.

'Thank you, Abhishek, thank you. But it's not all glamour, my friend. Have you seen my trousers?'

'Yes, I did, actually,' Abhishek said hesitantly.

'I was playing soccer with my son and was suddenly called in to anchor. Thankfully there are always a few shirts and jackets lying around in the studio. They promised that there would be no long shots.' Samir flashed his trademark, toothy grin. 'But enough of me. Until now, my friend, you've been playing Twenty20 games. That's not really cricket, is it? Tell me, are you ready to play Test matches?'

Before Abhishek could think of a suitable response, Samir continued, 'That's an unfair question. Vivek, good man that he is, has not told you what this is about, has he? I've been following your stories and we could do with a person like you. We want young fresh faces with a commitment to journalism. Everyone here is a star but I want reporters. So come, join my team.'

Abhishek had not expected things to happen so easily, and certainly not that Samir Saxena would be courting him. He groped for an appropriate reaction.

'Look, go take a tour of the premises and think about it,'

Samir said kindly. 'Let's get that idiot – what was his name – Neeraj Mishra to show you around. What do you say?'

News Today occupied four floors of a nine-storey building in one of Gurgaon's biggest commercial sectors. Sitting in the canteen having a coffee, Abhishek stared at this new India being constructed in front of his eyes; high-rise buildings climbing higher as cement mixers whirred and cranes slung more and more metal onto the horizon. IBM, Microsoft and Intel rubbed shoulders with the home-grown multinationals, Reliance and Wipro. L'Oréal and Lakmé jostled for attention beside an immense cut-out of Shah Rukh Khan telling everyone to 'Get Fairer in Four Weeks'.

The reporter was being offered a choice between the chaos of central Delhi and the sleekness of this office; the pizza- and hot-dog-serving cafeteria and the oily dosas of the airless dhaba at ITO, forever crowded with newspaper vendors and press boys in grimy clothes.

'You have a gym?' Abhishek asked in awe as Neeraj showed off the facilities.

'Yes, of course. A trainer comes twice a week. You can make an appointment.'

Abhishek had a sudden vision of Vivek Sethi panting away on the treadmill.

'It's very important for us that our employees look after their health,' Neeraj explained. 'We encourage everyone to be regulars here. Also, and this we will discuss in detail later, we'll be offering you comprehensive health insurance.'

Back in the newsroom, Samir was standing with two journalists, watching a television screen. Neeraj left Abhishek to wait in the boss's cabin.

After an incredible hour, he was suddenly alone. He made a

few calls – routine checks – and was relieved to learn there had been no major incidents. He wondered what he was going to tell Amir.

'All okay?' Maya asked worriedly as Abhishek joined his colleagues in a cafe.

He nodded. 'Guys, I need your advice. Something has come up. News Today has offered me a position in their investigative bureau. They want me to join immediately.'

'Wow,' Rahul exclaimed. 'Congratulations, boss. This is good news. What's the package?'

Rahul always came to the point, Abhishek thought. Yes, the package was good. Brilliant, in fact. During the ride back, his mind had vacillated uneasily between thoughts of betrayal and the promise of creature comforts. Besides a salary of 50,000 rupees, the company would help him relocate to an apartment in Gurgaon. They would even give him a car loan. 'I'll need to learn driving,' he had told Samir.

'After what you've done,' his prospective boss had laughed, 'I doubt anyone would give you a licence.'

'Why did you call us?' Maya asked sharply.

'To discuss this with you.' Abhishek was surprised at the question and the tone.

'Discuss or gloat? You've already made up your mind, haven't you? You are just telling us how great everybody finds you and that we should share the same feeling. You're great. We agree. How many more times do you want us to say it?'

'Hey, take it easy, Maya.' Rahul looked from one to the other.

'What do you mean, take it easy, Rahul?' She turned on him. 'He sends us this worrying text to meet him urgently. I come rushing from an assignment, and all he has to say is that he has been offered fuckloads of money for a new job. I mean, what the hell? If he wants to fish for compliments, can't he at least wait?'

'Maya, I really wanted your opinion on this,' Abhishek said indignantly, stunned at her aggression.

'Really? You really want my opinion? Then I think you should think things through much more before you say yes. You have barely understood journalism. You have got a few lucky stories with help from the bosses; nothing more. So, calm down and maybe you'll learn something.'

Abhishek felt angry and humiliated. Maya was so rude to him these days. When Mihir had rebuked him, she had not offered a word of support or commiseration. She never mentioned his stories. And now, here she was, once again revealing a mean, selfish streak. All because he had asked for advice on a job offer he had got. And she hadn't.

'You are right, Maya, I shouldn't have come to you for advice. Sorry for wasting your time. But since you have come, at least hear me out.'

Rahul was looking increasingly uncomfortable.

'I don't know much about journalism perhaps,' Abhishek continued, 'but I have come to know something about journalists. None of you are happy when a colleague does well. Tell me, how many stories have you done in the past month that have hit the front page?'

'Okay, Abhishek, stop,' Rahul interrupted. 'Let's go, guys.'

'No, no, let him finish,' Maya said quietly. 'I want to hear this.'

'I don't have much to say. Just that you wouldn't really know the value of money, would you? Your father runs the intelligence services in this country. How would you know what it is to live on a meagre salary like mine when you go for assignments in a chauffeur-driven government car?'

'That's it. Stop right there,' Maya exploded, pointing a finger at him. 'You burn your bridges too easily, Abhishek Dutta. I pray you never have to turn back. Bye.' She stormed out.

'What the fuck was that?' Rahul asked. 'Have you gone mad?'

'Sorry, boss,' Abhishek said, embarrassed and defensive. 'But tell me, did I say anything that's incorrect?'

'That family shit was way out of line,' Rahul said, shaking his head. 'Who told you that anyway?'

'Just got to know. Her father heads RAW and she tells me about morality!'

'Okay, let's go now,' Rahul said, getting up. 'I've got work to do. Coffee is on you today. Congratulations again.'

Abhishek decided to walk the half-kilometre to the office. He had checked the police bulletin. The three road accidents, the chain-snatching case and minor burglary could all go in the daily crime brief.

Despite the anger he was feeling, some of Maya's venom had stuck. As his work was praised and his stories repeatedly hit the front pages, he had often wondered how it was all possible. She was right. What did he know about investigative journalism? But with the money offered by the channel, there was really no choice. When he'd called his parents to give them the news, his father had simply said, 'After thirty years of service I don't earn that much. Take it.'

Abhishek dragged his feet as he climbed the steps to his office. How would he explain this? Television … What would his caustic old boss say?

Amir was the first person he saw as he entered.

'Will you quickly finish the crime diary? Is there anything else?' Amir asked.

'No, nothing special today. I wanted to have a word with you at some point.'

'Yes, I know. The evening meeting is in ten minutes. So after that?'

Abhishek headed towards the reporting unit. What did he mean he knew? Who had told him? Divya and Kavita looked up from their work as he came in. The glances they exchanged told Abhishek that he need not bother making any announcements. The unofficial wire agency had done the job.

He sat down at his desk and switched on the computer.

'So, I hear congratulations are in order.' Kavita's sarcasm was palpable.

Abhishek looked up inquiringly.

'Oh, come off it,' she said, exasperated. 'When are you leaving?'

'It's just an offer. I haven't decided anything.'

'For God's sake, Abhishek, at least tell the truth sometimes,' Divya joined in. 'You've decided and you're joining. Why can't you just say that? What's the big deal? You think we will be begging you to stay?' She snorted and turned back to the screen.

What the hell was the matter with all of them? Why were they so vicious? Abhishek was livid but said nothing. Rahul and Maya sat at their desks quietly, avoiding eye contact.

'Seems like a graveyard in here. What's up?' Amir came in from the evening meeting in unusually high spirits. 'I wish I got this silence every time I wanted it. Abhishek, shall we?'

Once inside his cabin, Amir said, 'Tell me?'

'You know, right?' Abhishek hesitated.

'No, I don't. Please tell me what you want to say.'

'Okay, sorry. I thought you knew. Thing is I've just been offered a job at News Today as a senior investigative reporter. It happened this afternoon.'

'Okay, good,' Amir said without a trace of emotion. 'When do you want to join?'

'Well, Samir Saxena said Monday but that's too soon, of course, and I will stay as long as you need me.'

'No, don't worry about that. You put in your papers right now and I will hand it to the editor.'

'Right now?' Abhishek was stunned.

'Yes. You don't have a notice period. You are on probation. So just write the letter.' Amir handed him a pen and paper and turned to the computer screen.

How does one write a resignation letter? What do you say? Do you just write that you've been offered a better job and therefore need to leave? Do you say you are grateful for opportunities given; no hard feelings, assuming there will be some, and you hope to stay in touch? How do you write contradictions into an official goodbye – the turmoil of not wanting to leave and the lure of what awaits?

Abhishek sat, pen in hand, wondering how his world had become this unpredictable.

'Look, go to your desk. Write it there,' Amir relented.

Abhishek, nearing tears, hurriedly left the cabin.

That same December weekend, a man on a stretcher, accompanied by a doctor and nurse, landed at Kolkata International Airport. From there they immediately proceeded towards Delhi where, as the paperwork produced by the doctor suggested, the patient was scheduled to have open-heart surgery.

To Babloo Shankar, the timing and choice of the port of entry had been obvious. Kolkata airport employed the laziest bunch of officials in the country and, on a weekend, they begrudged every minute spent behind the airless booths. In the unlikely event of any vigilance among the staff, Babloo had also ensured that two compromised senior intelligence officers were placed on standby.

That Sunday afternoon, just before he headed out to meet Abhishek Dutta for coffee, ACP Mayank Sharma was informed that Salim Khan's man had secured a place in A to Z Security Solutions.

On the same evening, Monika and Amit watched a movie together. Babloo was yet to meet her. First, he wanted to be absolutely certain his entry into Delhi had gone unnoticed. Monika had arranged the last-minute date with the boy almost in retaliation. Amit did not notice any difference though, and throughout the film their shoulders touched.

That night, Imran got lucky.

15

'I grew up all over the world. My father was in the foreign services. Spent my childhood in North Africa and the US. Went to school in Europe and then for a bit in Latin America.' Rajiv Bose's impeccable accent and modulated diction had made him a star among television anchors. To Abhishek, it made him sound incredibly conceited.

It was Abhishek's second day of training and he was shadowing Rajiv on an assignment: 'a baptism by fire', Samir Saxena had told him. 'If you can endure Rajiv,' he'd said, 'you'll be able to tolerate anybody.'

The two young men were on their way to a judicial hearing that had dragged on for three years. The central Delhi slum clearances of the late 1990s had displaced thousands, giving the government the not disagreeable task of doling out housing contracts to building companies. The government, satisfied with the takings, sat back; so did the contractors. The few buildings that did come up were of substandard quality, uninhabitable by even the dregs they were meant for. But unlike their would-be inhabitants, the buildings refused to go away, standing unfinished at the limits of the city, paint peeling, walls crumbling. A few NGOs picked up the matter. The corruption was so blatant that the government was forced to acknowledge accountability and, to forestall any further consequences, set up a judicial inquiry.

The very judges who had first authorized the demolition of the slums, now retired, extended their stay in their official residences with their official perks to preside over the inquiry. As far as they were concerned, it could go on for ever.

'What a waste of time,' Rajiv complained loudly as they emerged from the two-hour hearing. 'No bloody progress.'

Minutes later, he gave a live update from the channel's OB van, the outdoor broadcasting facilities which were stationed close by. Rajiv spoke excitedly to the camera, saying how crucially important the session had been in uncovering the rot of corruption in high places.

Unclipping his lapel mike, Rajiv suggested lunch. 'I'm hungry. No point in hurrying back to the office. What do you think?' he asked Santosh Jain, the cameraman.

'Good idea. If I go back to office now, they'll put me on another assignment,' Santosh replied.

'Shall we go to the Press Club? We're very close …' Abhishek trailed off, seeing Rajiv's expression.

'You're not serious, are you? We'll go to Pandara Road. Gulatis does good kebabs.'

In the car, unable to contain himself, Abhishek asked, 'Rajiv, you said that nothing happened at the inquiry commission today. But you reported it very differently.'

'I know, I know,' he replied dismissively. 'I had to give it a spin. If I'd said, "Look, nothing happened," they wouldn't put me on air, would they? We've spent almost four hours on this and I must at least get something out of it and so should the channel. They, after all, pay for this car and our salaries. And they're about to buy us lunch.'

Rajiv paused to take a call and then continued, 'You are new, so you don't know this yet: It's all about getting your face on television; no one cares about what you're saying. Who knows anything anyway about this inquiry? At the end of the day, the more stories you get your mug on, the better for you.'

The initiation carried on over lunch. 'In the past two years, the entire fucking place has turned into a bloody ghetto. The earlier journalists who joined News Today were all like me, with parents in the services; quite a few in the foreign and administrative. But things are changing so quickly.'

Santosh smiled, shaking his head.

Rajiv looked at him. 'Ai, bastard, now don't go and rat to your friends in the fucking Hindi unit,' he said, and turned back to Abhishek. 'You missed our golden period. From 2000, when I joined, until 2006, this was the best place to work. We were like a family. All of us came from similar backgrounds, and we produced quality work. We were the best English channel in the country.'

'It still is, no?'

'Yes, but being the best English channel doesn't matter any more. We started the Hindi broadcast in 2006 and now all the money is spent on those motherfuckers. These Hindi reporters, a few years back, wouldn't dare talk to us. Today they get higher salaries and bigger studios; the whole focus of the organization has shifted. They rule the fucking place. It's the same shit everywhere. There's money in vernacular. And money always wins.'

Abhishek knew very little about news television and its politics. Along with the hundreds of changes in the universe of his childhood and youth – mobile phones, Internet, MP3s, DVDs – he had taken for granted the transition from state television to private ownership, the sudden appearance of cable television and twenty-four-hour news, and the launch of a hundred regional and local channels. His mother, deprived of her friends and relatives in Benares, took to the nationally available Bengali channels with a passion. His father, grudging of their lowbrow entertainment and politics at first, got used to them and later became addicted.

'Whatever you say, Rajiv, the Hindi reporters work very hard,' Santosh ventured tentatively.

'And we don't, motherfucker? That's the problem; we are seen as privileged and therefore you think we don't have to work hard. You think my father gets stories and reads the news for me?'

The manager approached, stemming the flow of Rajiv's indignation. 'Mr Bose, is everything all right?' he asked politely.

Rajiv quelled his surprise at being recognized. 'Yes, we ordered quite a while back and have to return to the office. If you could kindly see to our order.'

The man trudged off to make inquiries.

'Are you a regular here?' Abhishek asked.

'No, not at all.'

'Arre, everyone knows the boss. He's the next Samir Saxena,' Santosh said hastily, trying to make up for his earlier gaffe.

'Yes, it does happen,' Rajiv said, attempting modesty. 'It will happen to you very soon, Mr Dutta. But at times it can be embarrassing.'

Abhishek couldn't imagine his colleague being put off by any sort of attention.

'I was driving one day near India Gate with an ex-girlfriend. We were at the traffic light and this guy tapped on the window. I rolled down the glass thinking, oh another one who wants to get my autograph. I put on my fake smile and extended my hand. The fucker was asking for directions.'

Santosh and Abhishek burst out laughing.

'I never heard the end of it from the girl I was with.'

The waiter brought in the starters and Rajiv suggested beer.

'I shouldn't,' Abhishek replied, though tempted. 'I have a meeting with the marketing head.'

'Oh, Rajan. He's a good chap – a dopehead. Don't worry about him. Santosh?'

The cameraman nodded between mouthfuls of kebab.

On their way back to the office, Rajiv rounded up the act. 'Perhaps I was being too negative,' he told Abhishek. 'News Today is still the best place to work and they really look after you well. As an anchor, I get a wardrobe allowance. They have the best canteen that I know of and if you work after eight, dinner is free. And our salaries are better than most.' He looked at his junior colleague. 'Did you get a decent deal?'

'Yes.'

'Good. Welcome to the big league. You don't have to go to the Press Club any more.'

Abhishek smiled.

'Listen,' Rajiv added. 'Every Friday we go to this club in Sector 21, Airwaves. We are such regulars that we call it the mosque. Why don't you come along? I'll tell the gang and you can get introduced properly. Okay?'

Abhishek nodded, grateful to be accepted while conscious that the cameraman sitting in front was not invited.

U day looked at the traffic in irritation. 'Put the red light on,' he told the radio operator.

Half an hour later, light flashing and siren screaming urgency, the DCP reached the India International Centre.

'Late again,' Amir remarked as they shook hands.

'Sorry, boss, last-minute meeting. How are you?'

Amir had taken a table on the lawns, and was drinking coffee.
'I'm well. But you are the one with the stories. So tell me.'

'Can't I ask you out for lunch without a reason any more?'
Uday asked, signalling towards a waiter. Amir smiled a
meaningful smile and the policeman shrugged his shoulders.
'Well, yes, I am a bit worried and need to talk to you. But let
me order a beer first.'

On this winter afternoon, with the mild, comforting sunshine
bathing the green courtyards of this elite Delhi establishment,
no one observing the two men would have noticed anything
amiss. They were, like the other diners here, powerful citizens
who ruled and shaped the city. At wine-laden tables, in corridors
and lobbies, outside the library, influential people discussed
matters of national and international significance: Chinese
goods swamping Indian markets, the US's tunnel vision on
all matters Pakistani, the deplorable corruption and greed of
African governments. A conversation about a kidnapper, his
links to international terrorists and the consequences of his
possible return to Delhi would not be considered extraordinary;
if anything, it might seem trivial. Among the crème de la crème
of the capital's elite, Uday Kumar and Amir Akhtar risked being
dismissed as men of no real importance.

The city and the safety of its inhabitants had never been a
personal priority for Uday. Rather, it was the need to maintain
a certain self-image that motivated him to work. That he loved
a good fight was a bonus – he enjoyed what he was doing.
That these qualities had led him to knock off a dozen dreaded
criminals, track down robbers, terrorists and on occasion even
politicians, was to him coincidental, though he was pleased that
it usually worked out that way.

But this afternoon, the decorated police officer was worried that he might have got things wrong.

Amir heard Uday out without interrupting.

'What do you think? I really have fucked up, haven't I?'

'I don't think so,' Amir said slowly. 'Not if what you wanted to achieve in the first place is anything to go by. You,' he said with a sudden vehemence, pointing a finger, 'wanted Babloo back. Now that you know he is, you're scared. Uday Kumar, your balls have shrunk. Are you getting old?'

'Yes, I am and so are you. This time, the consequences of a mess-up are not worth considering. In this media market, I won't be able to hush it up.'

'Or you might finally become a hero,' Amir said and then urgently added, 'Uday, listen, don't waste any more time. Get the machinery moving. Put the men out. Put the word out. If Babloo is here, the time for silence is over.'

Driving back to office, Amir allowed the concerns he had hidden from his friend to surface. He asked himself the question that had been bothering him for weeks: Why had he not insisted Uday call in surveillance, ask for help, alert the border agencies? The answer was always the same: Amir too wanted, almost needed, Babloo back in Delhi. He knew that all he had to do was break the story in the newspaper and every police department in the country would be alerted. But what an uninspiring story that would be.

He went over what he had just heard, not without some admiration for his old ally. Salim Khan's man had got the job in the security agency, which told him that things would now move quickly, Uday had said. The plan had become too elaborate for remote control. If Babloo had anything to do with all this, he would want to be here, managing movements, giving instructions.

'I reviewed the log entries for every Singapore flight that has landed in the past two weeks,' Uday had told him. 'In Kolkata, I discover, a man arrives on a stretcher. Same age as Babloo. Comes with a doctor and a nurse. I get the passport details of all three and ask my contacts in Downtown Core to check them out. Everything is fine except that the owners of these passports are still in Singapore. Next I obtained the video logs from the airport. Although the image is not clear, I am more than certain it's our man. I am sending it to the labs but, prima facie, I am convinced.'

From Kolkata, Uday traced the trio's arrival in Delhi. He checked the Apollo Hospital where the man should have been admitted. He checked every other major and then minor hospital. The three had vanished.

At the traffic light, Amir rolled up the car window and put on a CD; one of his niece's compilations of Hindi hits. He was impressed by how Uday, with barely any resources, had managed to zero in on Babloo's entry into the city. Amir had, over the years, met and known enough policemen, detectives, spies and so-called intelligence officers to acknowledge Uday's unmatched acumen.

And loyalty, thought Amir. That was the quality he valued most. Fifteen years ago, in the fiasco with Babloo, Uday hadn't mentioned Amir's role to anyone. He had taken the heat, played cover-up and managed, with a politician's dexterity, to bounce back. 'I took the call, not you,' he'd said when Amir had offered to stand up.

In the last ten years, Amir had seen far less of Uday than he would have liked. Immediately after the incident, the two had clung to each other. They met regularly, went drinking together and, on a few occasions, went away on holiday. Amir was privy to Uday's marital problems and his fondness for fair, buxom women. Then Uday was posted to the Nicobar Islands for three years. On his return they met enthusiastically, but the need and the necessity, their shared shameful secret, had been dissipated by other distractions.

At the office car park, Chhote Lal approached Amir. 'Sir, Abhishek-da has left, I hear.'

'Yes.' he nodded. 'Why? What is it to you?'

Chhote Lal looked a little embarrassed and then said, 'Sorry sir, small man, big talk maybe, but my younger brother has just finished a diploma in journalism. Maybe you can call him for an interview?'

A bhishek was sitting alone in a large conference room, waiting for his five o'clock briefing with Rajan Chachra, head of the marketing division. It was nearly six now, but given the frenetic activity of the past two days, Abhishek didn't mind the wait.

His throat ached and the Strepsils were not helping. Since the lunch with Rajiv, Abhishek had been made to work on his diction with a tall thin girl called Roopleena Bhattacharya. She'd told him that the channel preferred a BBC accent and, though never exactly rude, she smiled condescendingly every time he tripped over his vowels. 'Bengalis have this problem,' she said as he faltered over 'hurt' and 'heart'; 'slip', 'sleep' and 'slippers'.

Abhishek's voice, played back to him, had sounded terribly immature, lacking the conviction and surety his new colleagues could so effortlessly summon. After an hour and a half of modulation exercises and earnest readings of past voice-over scripts – from gong healers in the Himalayas to a prosthetic-limb project in Jaipur – Roopleena had dismissed him with a printout of *Bell's Elocution Manual*. 'Practise your pronunciation at home, especially the vowel sounds.'

'Sorry I'm late.' The man plonked down an armload of papers. He was short and plump, and his eyes twinkled with merriment. 'I am Rajan.'

Abhishek warmed to him immediately.

'So, let me see … what are we doing today? You know, normally these inductions take place in larger groups with all sorts of pie charts and diagrams. Boring shit. Let's make it quick. If you have questions later, you can always come back to me. Okay?'

'Yes, absolutely,' Abhishek replied.

'Do you have any idea what marketing slash branding is all about?'

'Only the basic facts,' Abhishek replied, not wanting to appear a total novice.

'Okay. Briefly, television marketing is all about standing out from the clutter of other channels. So that when a viewer reaches for his remote, wanting to know what is going on in the world, he comes to us.' Rajan paused for a moment and then said, 'Let me give you an example. Think early '90s. What did we have? One lone government-run channel, Doordarshan. You thought television, you thought Doordarshan – news, sports, drama; it was all there. Today any cable connection gives you two hundred channels. But just saying you are a news channel doesn't help; there are over sixty news channels alone. You need to get more specific. Is it Hindi or English? Or Malayalam or Assamese and all the rest? And then finally, and most importantly, what sort of a news channel are you? When you think News Today, what is the first thing that comes to mind?'

Abhishek waited, but the question was not rhetorical. 'Well, as you guys say, "For You, 24x7."'

'Correct. You mentioned our tag line. "For you",' Rajan said, using his forefingers as inverted commas, 'tells you that we come from a viewer-centric position. There are news channels that say, "We are the quickest." Others say, "We are the most truthful." Our marketing strategy is, "It's all about you, the viewer."'

'Look sharp.' Rajan grinned at Abhishek. 'I will now tell you why you journalists need to know all this. Once we've decided the positioning of the channel, it needs to be reinforced constantly – hoardings, posters, public-relations exercises. But most of all, if we say we are for the audience, it must jolly well reflect in our programming. And that is where you come in. At News Today, editorial works very closely with marketing. We have joint exercises, drives, we plan promotions together.'

Abhishek slipped out his notepad.

'For example, last month we did a half-hour special on corruption and the Commonwealth Games scandal. We had viewers call in with their thoughts. It empowers them. We not only hear their concerns, we *air* them. See what I mean? We were the ones who started citizen journalism in India and now everyone has jumped on the bandwagon.'

Rajan looked at his watch.

'Are you getting late?' Abhishek asked.

'No, brother. In our business, you don't get late – you are always late. I have a meeting with the boss. But our conversation isn't over. Let's meet soon.'

The villages of Mehrauli sat for decades, unnoticed, on the edges of south Delhi's affluence. They were sprawling agricultural lands, scattered with mud huts and shanties where old men, sporting white turbans, kurtas and dhotis, smoked hookahs on scorching summer afternoons in the dappled shade of some aged tree that once did a good job of providing relief, but now was just disease-ridden and tired.

Via Mehrauli's pock-marked tarmac, as Delhi's old money started travelling towards the up and coming Gurgaon, such sights were a piquant distraction, a sort of Disney Land version of an Indian village for city kids and their indulgent parents to gawp at.

In the final decade of the twentieth century, as the economy was being liberalized, these agricultural lands were set free. There was a price to be paid, of course. Indian expats sent the money, and their parents, remembering those suburban dream homes they had so ardently admired on that visit to the US, bought up acres of farmland. Or perhaps the money came from Canada, Australia or New Zealand, the nationalities of currency being irrelevant once exchanged for this soil. The rates were good and everyone benefited; poor farmers learnt about tax evasion, and in foreign lands, sons and daughters could sleep with less guilt about their desertion.

Mehrauli quickly transformed into a fenced-off network of farmhouses animated by the antics of Bollywood stars at the weddings of the fortunate five hundred. But it remained disfigured by a few village hamlets, where old men unrepentantly gurgled at their hookahs and goggled at the fancy women in their fancy cars. From the safety of their vehicles, the women giggled and goggled back.

These were the pockets of resistance. Some villages and

their communities refused to give up their lands, preferring the security of tradition to the lure of cash. Others held on for the more lucrative deal they heard had been offered to their distant cousins; astronomical sums that would release them forever from the bondage of farming and its miserly rewards.

It was in one such neighbourhood that Babloo Shankar had taken up residence. Although his men in Delhi had secured a year's lease on a farmhouse barely three kilometres away, he preferred the crowded obscurity of the village. It was a stronghold of the local Gujjar community and three of its elders had once worked with his brother. In such places old loyalties were gilded protection, particularly when backed up with hard cash. Babloo employed both to secure listening outposts, figure out police networks and ensure a blanket of invisibility.

That morning he had made his second run to the farmhouse and his first extended visit. Archana arrived late in the afternoon and by nightfall they were sitting together on the sofa, slightly inebriated, satiated, plotting the next few months.

A kidnapping that was not for ransom – the concept was alien to Archana. But Babloo explained that if it went the way he wanted, money would flow. The perception of threat, dehshat, was their retirement plan, their ticket to stardom, politics.

'One kidnapping that stuns the world and then you are made; the media will make you. Think of Dawood bhai. He hasn't done a thing in twenty years. The Mumbai blasts were enough. Think of Charles Sobhraj. Nothing to him, but he is a star. He gets book contracts, film deals. What do I get? Who remembers me but for some old, one-foot-in-the-grave gangsters and retired policemen.'

To Archana, this was a surprising change in her cautious mentor, who since 9/11 had refused to engage in anything remotely risky, preferring to work on his front as a diamond merchant in Singapore.

Now finally she was being allowed to put her talents back to use, but she wanted the basics clear. 'How will the money come, Babloo?'

'After the attacks on Parliament, India has gone in for US-style data sharing. Twenty-one different agencies, including police, income tax, banks, the various intelligence agencies and border security forces – all of them have access to the country's secrets. It's called NATGRID. All the information in one place. In a country as corrupt as ours, that is never a good idea.' Babloo smiled. 'Too many officials know too much. One greased palm and you have all the data.'

From here, the plan was dazzlingly simple. A kidnapping which hits the headlines, lets people know Babloo Shankar is back, and then simply a few phone calls to the millionaires and billionaires whose details are stored in NATGRID. Babloo showed Archana the income-tax returns of India's top seventy industrialists. They laughed at the treasure trove of phone numbers and personal details.

'The only thing they need to know is fear – fear of Babloo Shankar. The rest is easy.'

'Why didn't you tell me this before? Didn't you trust me?' Archana asked.

'If I didn't, I would not tell you even now,' he replied. 'I just wanted you to focus on the boy, get his attention. That's done; now you need to know more.'

'And what happens to me?' she asked, staring out into the darkness beyond the balcony.

'Not much will change on the ground. You'll continue to control the Singapore business along with Rohit. I've eliminated two of your Nepali threats since you left. Verma will make a hit on the last one any day now. All you have to do is make sure the cash flows through the usual channels into India. Rohit will iron out any other wrinkles.'

'How long have you been planning this?' Archana asked after a long silence.

'Since the day I was forced to leave, darling,' Babloo said before raising himself to get back into the wheelchair. Archana made to help but he waved her away. He wheeled himself towards the toilet, then paused at the door. 'If the plan works, in five years you will be back too. Think about that.'

She thought about it, looking for a loophole, a flaw.

'What follows from the act is much more difficult to control,' Babloo had explained to her several years ago, when an operation had gone wrong. 'Until the kidnapping, everything is in your hands. After that, you scramble to control the situation while everyone will work to take it away from you. The thing you have got in your favour is preparation. Remember, they are unprepared, while you have planned everything.'

Babloo came back into the room, 'It will take two months before we can act,' he warned her, gently. The Mahajans will be back in January, but he still needed to finalize the end game.

'Are you sure this will work?' Archana asked.

'The only thing I am sure of is that another bullet will kill me. I have to remove that possibility and then yes, it will work.'

16

Karuna Joseph was already at her desk at 7 a.m., the sole person on the entire corporate floor. She grimaced at Abhishek as he walked in. 'I'm just going through the numbers. Afraid it's going to be one of those really, really bad days. There is a dip in our ratings this week.'

It was Friday, and Abhishek had been instructed to spend the morning understanding the complex science of television ratings; the most crucial training session yet, he'd been told. His eyes itched with tiredness. He had passed an uncomfortable night on the office couch, having thought it preferable to the forty-kilometre commute through the paralysing morning fog.

'Shall I get coffee,' he offered.

'Yes, please. And would you order breakfast too?'

The canteen, to Abhishek's surprise, was already bustling with activity. He recognized several people from the news desk as he joined the queue to the food counter. Two girls, the interns he'd met yesterday, waved at him. He asked for Karuna's food to be sent to her desk, deciding to have his up here, amid the morning buzz.

The room was broad and spacious with a high ceiling. Sunlight streamed in through a large glass façade, lending it a cheery brightness. Abhishek took a table in the corner, the Gurgaon skyline before him. Below, despite the early hour, labourers were already at work in the construction sites, clearing roads, laying cables, bringing in bricks while two monstrous excavators disembowelled the earth. Other workers sat in a row, drinking tea and feeding their babies.

'Mind if I join you?' It was Dilip, the night editor who had just finished his shift. 'It's ratings for you this morning, isn't it?'

Abhishek nodded.

'Very important. In fact it's the most important thing in our whole goddamned universe. You'll soon realize that good stories, bad stories don't matter as long as ratings are high. But they mean nothing. We all know that. It's completely compromised, the entire system.'

'How is it compromised?' Abhishek let the man talk as he tucked into his breakfast.

'You know Reeta Kapoor, right? Big Bollywood player, owns Desraj Films, one of India's largest production companies. They produce perhaps the highest number of television serials. Recently, we learnt that Kapoor's company was paying off every surveyed household in south Mumbai. The whole bloody thing was doctored. It went on for a year and no one said a word.'

'Why?'

'What do you mean why?' Dilip was impatient. 'Because the entire system rests on credibility. Billions are involved. If we expose the fraud, the advertising industry which is based on this rating bullshit collapses like a pack of cards. That's why.'

Abhishek wanted to ask more but Dilip had noticed the interns. He beckoned to them to join their table. 'Fresh meat,' he said, winking at Abhishek, who left quickly, leaving him to entertain his new breakfast companions.

At the lifts, he met Sandeep Ghoshal, the head of the sales

division, whose presentation the previous day had lasted over an hour.

'Good morning, er ...'

'Abhishek. Good morning.'

'Yes, of course. How are you? Ratings morning for you, isn't it? I hear the news is not the best. Rajan and I have a crisis meeting upstairs with the CEO. See you later,' Sandeep said, hurrying off.

Yesterday's session had been taxing. Unlike easy-going Rajan, the sales head had been stiff and officious and came prepared with the dreaded slide show and presentation. 'Please do take notes. Nothing your editors tell you will be as important,' he'd said seriously, smothering the new recruit's attempt at a smile. Amir would have taken this guy to pieces, Abhishek had thought.

'You need to know this. The more effectively a journalist can match the needs of a client, the happier we all are. I'll give you an example,' Sandeep had lectured. 'If one of our year-round partners, say ICICI bank, is planning a surge in ad spend, our sales team will have to offer them incentives.' He'd paused to check if Abhishek was writing this down. 'Incentives could be regular stories on credit cards, reports on housing or car loans, or advice on the best fixed-deposit returns. We inform the editorial bosses of these drives, and reporters like you are instructed accordingly.' The sales head had kept on tirelessly ... 'The principle of selling remains the same for our seasonal clients. We offer a woollen-garment manufacturer stories on how cold it will be this season; or we'll offer a story on the dangers of old-style air conditioners to a supplier of a new model. Legitimate stories. So we get their money, you guys go do the stories.'

Karuna's breakfast tray was still untouched when Abhishek joined her.

'Alarm bells are going off. We've dipped in almost every analysis,' she said, looking weary. 'I mean, a year back, no one would have bothered with a less than one-point dip, but now ... Ah, look who is here. Hello, Lata.'

Abhishek looked up to see an anxious-looking middle-aged lady approach the desk. 'Tell me,' she said, gripping the edge of the table as Karuna squinted at the screen.

'15.1,' Karuna said, and Lata dramatically slumped to the floor.

'Oh, hell,' she wailed, staring at the carpet.

Karuna caught Abhishek's eye and suppressed a giggle.

A reed-thin young man about Abhishek's age sloped into the office. 'Lata,' he laughed. 'Fucked again? You should look for another job. Karuna, hit me darling.'

'You're the one who is fucked, Gopal Manwani. Two-point dip in your show.' Karuna was evidently delighted at the man's arrival.

'And who might you be?' Gopal asked, flopping down beside Abhishek.

Karuna did the introductions.

'Welcome, welcome; more the merrier. Now, Karuna, tell me about the other programmes. Are we on a collective decline, which will spare my individual ass, or is it just me and dear old Lata here? Lata-ji, get your bum off the floor.'

'It's not funny, Gopal.' Lata said, winching herself up.

'Right, get out, both of you. I have to finish this,' Karuna told them.

'You kill me, darling, but all right. I must take Lata for coffee. She's getting a bit skinny without nourishment.'

He put an arm around her and they walked off.

'That guy is our most talented producer,' Karuna told

Abhishek. 'Quite a riot too,' she added, grinning at the computer screen. 'Listen, this report is going to take forever. Can I meet you some other time to explain what these guys are getting so worked up about?'

Abhishek walked downstairs to the newsroom and sat down on a sofa by the wall. He felt exhausted and lonely. No one knew him here. In the midst of this hectic activity – reporters and input editors, producers, 'weather girls', cameramen dashing about, librarians, assistants – Abhishek was struggling to find his place.

Maya had been right – he had no special talent. The quite extraordinary happenings of the recent months had been a combination of luck and help from the people he had come to depend on and think of as friends. He hadn't met Vivek ever since joining News Today. His predecessor at the *Express* had contracted dengue fever while on a story in rural Bihar and was in hospital, though he was expected back next week. It would be nice to see a familiar face.

'Did you see that arse!' Rajiv spoke phlegmatically into Abhishek's ear over the blare of the music.

'She reads the weather, doesn't she?' Abhishek flinched.

'Yeah.' Rajiv grinned. 'Boy, inside those pants, it must be as warm and wet as Kerala in August.'

Abhishek smiled weakly. It was not that he was unfamiliar with sexual jokes. Yet, Rajiv's blatant leeriness made him uncomfortable.

Abhishek's only experience of romance had been a lingering affair that had lasted two summers. He had fallen in love with a classmate during rehearsals for a school play and then, for six months, had spoken his heart out to her on a mobile phone plan that allowed cheap calls after 11 p.m. A year passed before he'd dared to hold her hand in a restaurant where he courageously consumed beer while she drank hot chocolate. That's how far his hands ever got. She broke up with him soon after, telling him he had 'no future'.

'You have a girlfriend?' Rajiv asked.

Abhishek shook his head.

'Don't worry. Our office is the most promiscuous place you will ever find. Everyone fucks everyone. The bosses encourage it, I think. No need to go anywhere – eat, shit and fuck in office. Want another drink?'

Their whiskies were served, and Rajiv went on. 'Journalism as a whole is a slutty profession.'

'Yes, I have heard that but,' Abhishek smiled at his mildly drunk new friend, 'no experience.'

'That's because you hang out at the Press Club. Who will you bang there? Those old geezers? Do you see that guy?' Rajiv pointed at a fastidious-looking man drinking by himself. 'Gautam. He's in the production team. That fucker has slept with more women in the office than he can count on both hands. By the time he leaves here tonight, he'll have two babes begging to suck him off. Fuck, here comes the party spoiler.'

'What are you guys celebrating? Don't you know the ratings are down,' Gopal said, sliding his skinny frame onto their sofa.

'Not my show ratings,' Rajiv said promptly. 'I've got better ratings than even Samir.'

'You are God, Rajiv,' Gopal said, his face solemn. 'Now if only God would buy this poor disciple a drink ...'

'Fuck off. I'm going to grab some of that booty.' Rajiv advanced towards the dance floor.

'What are you having? Whisky?' Gopal asked Abhishek, who nodded.

'Too manly for me. I need a pink drink with loads of ice cream.'

It was midnight and Airwaves was filled to capacity. The DJ had ceased his attempts to get people on the dance floor with house and grunge and reverted to Bollywood remixes. Abhishek was enjoying the spectacle of swaying hips and short clothes. His brushes with this buzzing and busty India were rare. He smiled at the prospect of things to come.

'I'm glad to see you're enjoying yourself,' Gopal remarked.

'This is new for me,' he muttered, acutely embarrassed for some reason. 'My usual haunt was the Press Club and before that, drinking out of stainless-steel glasses in friends' houses.'

'Ah, rags-to-riches story.' Gopal laughed. 'Are you not somebody's son? Did you not go to St Stephen's?'

'No. Hindu College, actually. But I am somebody's son.' Abhishek grinned. 'My father teaches at the Benares Hindu University.'

Gopal looked surprised. 'Ah, you are from the reserved quota. Here that means being exceptionally talented. Are you?'

Before Abhishek could reply, Rajiv rushed over. 'News break,' he told Gopal, who nodded. 'Come,' he said to Abhishek and the two pushed their way out of the club, reaching the car park at a run.

'Get in,' Rajiv said as he opened the car door. 'A plane has crashed; an MiG 21 or something. Not quite sure. I'm getting into office to go on air. We have to start live broadcast and I'm the only anchor around. Do you want to go to the spot?'

'Yes, of course.'

'Okay. Let me call the input desk.'

Rajiv dialled the number. 'Hi, Dilip, I'm coming in. I have Abhishek with me. We can send him to the spot.'

There was a pause and Abhishek was not sure of the reaction.

'Well, who else? Sonal has gone to cover the hospital fire in Malka Ganj and it will take too long to get her back. I am sure Abhishek can do OBs. He watched me this morning. Keep the car out. We'll be there in two minutes.' Rajiv hung up and said, 'You owe me big-time, Mr Dutta. This is your big break.'

Safdarjung Airport in south Delhi was not a regular commercial airport and was mostly used in flight training. It also functioned as a hangar for small private aircrafts. By the time Abhishek got there, several television teams had already gathered.

The moment he stepped out of the car, a cameraman he did not recognize rushed up to him. 'Boss, shall we go on air? The link is ready. I've taken some shots of the aircraft from the bridge. Nothing remarkable though; the fire was already doused,' he said.

'Hi, I am Abhishek,' said the new reporter, trying to buy a moment in which to figure out what was going on.

'Yes, Rajiv told me. I am Rupesh. Three other news channels have started their live updates and I am ready to roll.'

Abhishek's mobile started to ring. It was Rajiv. 'Have you reached? I need some information for my voice-over.'

'Give me five minutes, Rajiv. I've just arrived.'

Except for one harried-looking airport official, Abhishek could only see journalists. Despite the cold of the December night, the short, balding man was perspiring under a barrage of lights and questions. Mikes were being thrust into his face as journalists demanded answers in Hindi and English.

Amid the confusion and shouting, Abhishek gathered that an MiG 24 – the latest version of the Russian combat aircraft that India had been buying for decades, and which crashed with disturbing regularity every three months or so – had failed to take off and had collided with a boundary wall. Seconds before the collision, the pilot had managed to bail out and, though injured, was in no grave danger. The incident had occurred just after 10 p.m. during a routine night exercise.

The OB van was waiting nearby and a few shots had already been uplinked. Rupesh told Abhishek, 'Boss, you'd better start now. They're all waiting. We are behind the other channels.'

The cameraman and the driver quickly wired him up with an earpiece and lapel mike. Within seconds, and before he could have a chat with Rajiv, Abhishek heard a voice in his earpiece saying they were going live in thirty. Another voice started the countdown: twenty-nine, twenty-eight, twenty-seven …

Twenty seconds later, he could hear Rajiv's voice stating that an MiG 21 had crashed at Safdarjung Airport and they were going live to their reporter at the spot, Abhishek Dutta, for further updates. 'Not MiG 21 – 24,' Abhishek thought, his knees shaking as he tried to keep his gaze on the camera lens as instructed. Then he was on air and Rajiv was talking to him. 'Abhishek, tell us what is going on at the scene. What do you see in front of you?'

'Well, there is not really much going on right now,' he said nervously. There was a pause and he thought he had been cut off. 'Hello?'

'Abhishek, yes, we are here.' Rajiv's voice came to him again. 'Can you tell us what happened?'

'Yes,' Abhishek replied. 'First I must tell you that it was an MiG 24 and not an MiG 21, as you just said, that has crashed. It happened around ten p.m. when the plane … it was on a night practice flight … failed to take off from the runway. It crashed into the boundary wall but the pilot managed to eject just before contact.'

'Right. Could you tell us how many people were there in the plane? Were cabin crew and other members inside the aircraft?'

Abhishek was a bit puzzled by the question. 'Rajiv, this is a fighter aircraft so there is space only for two people. There were no co-pilots as far as I know and certainly no cabin crew.'

'So there were no casualties?'

'The pilot, I have been told, has suffered some injuries but is in no serious danger.'

Rajiv signed off.

It was nearly three in the morning when they were finally allowed onto the airstrip. Orange floodlights cut through the fog, eerily illuminating the damaged plane and the lone fire engine standing empty beside it. The cameramen rushed towards the wall. In the initial excitement Abhishek had forgotten about the chill, but now in the vast empty field his hands felt frozen as he carried the tripod and battery kit.

Somebody from the input desk called him to ask if there were any developments and Abhishek said no. The person asked him to take a few vox pops. Abhishek, not knowing what that meant, said he would and, hanging up, asked his cameraman.

'Oh, that means getting interviews of eyewitnesses. I don't think anyone will be around at this time of the night though. It's freezing and anyway, this is no spectacle.'

'So what do we do?'

'I think you should call Rajiv and figure it out. Can I borrow a cigarette?'

Abhishek handed him the packet and, taking shelter under a hangar, called Rajiv.

'Good job,' the anchor said, coming on the line immediately. 'Are there any updates or should we keep rolling with the same?'

Abhishek said that there was not much else to report and no eyewitnesses that he could find.

Rajiv was kind and gently told him to go home. 'Look, I know it has been a long day for you; all that boring ratings stuff in the morning and now this. Go home. Take the car. Switch off your phone and sleep a bit. I too am leaving.'

Rupesh was surprised. 'Really? Rajiv told you to go home?' Abhishek nodded.

'Okay, fine by me. I'll go and hand in a few fresh shots for the morning bulletin.'

The driver was asleep and then irritated at being told that he would now have to go to east Delhi. 'My duty time ends in one hour,' he grumbled as he started the engine. 'It will take me at least two hours to get back to the office. I've been on duty since morning.'

Abhishek, initially apologetic, began to doze off, his head bumping against the car window.

Dhruv Kapoor, the morning input editor at News Today, was staring incredulously at the story list handed to him by Dilip. 'But where is the full report of the crash?'

'That's what I am trying to tell you, Dhruv. The guy just vanished. He never came back to the office.'

Dhruv did not understand. 'What do you mean? Where is he?'

'Well, Rajiv tells me he was feeling exhausted and went home,' Dilip replied. 'I've done the best I could, including a voice-over on the shots that the cameraman got. I also picked up snippets from the wire agencies.'

'He went home to sleep?' Dhruv could not believe what he was hearing. 'And we are using wire copies when we had a reporter on the spot? Who hired this idiot?'

'If he doesn't want to fuck you, there is no urgency. If there is no urgency, our opportunity will not be created. How could you let this situation arise?' Babloo had arrived late last night at Archana's flat in Panchsheel and stayed the whole morning. They were just finishing lunch, and she had explained how her relationship with the boy was developing.

'He's so in love with me, I think he's even happy to wait for sex,' she'd laughed.

Babloo was furious. Just when it mattered most, she was fucking up.

Archana agreed that things had slipped, but was unwilling to accept all the blame. 'Had you told me from the beginning how long this would take, I could have planned it better. I thought it would take two weeks; it's been close to two months.'

She had been forced to morph from the sexual Monika to the troubled one to prolong the relationship. That Amit Mahajan was overly sensitive and would fall in love with her, instead of simply fantasizing about her, was something they had not considered.

'The parents are back in February. Later than I expected,' Babloo told her. 'Do you want to extend the two-week break to a month? That will increase the longing. Call him and say that your father is unwell or something?'

Archana thought about it. 'If I lay off for a month, Babloo, he might go completely cold. How about doing what we did with

Rustom Modi? Phone calls. Get the fire stoking again and come back at the right time. What do you think?' she asked, lighting the second of Babloo's three daily cigarettes.

Abhishek had gone home and straight to bed. Four hours later he was back in the newsroom, trying to explain his disappearance. He'd realized immediately that telling anyone that Rajiv Bose had told him to switch off his phone and go to sleep would make matters worse. He would come across not merely as incompetent, but a simpleton.

In the canteen, Rajiv came over to him, all smiles and handshakes; not a trace of trickery showed on his face.

It astonished Abhishek to see how quickly gossip spread. By afternoon, everyone seemed concerned and came up to ask him what had happened. The first two times when he confided, conflated reports spread even faster. Shocked and lonely, he decided to hold his tongue.

Abhishek needed to understand what had happened, and why. So that evening he went to meet Vivek, who was still recovering from dengue fever.

'You idiot!' Vivek hooted. 'You committed the cardinal sin of making an anchor look silly. It was great! I couldn't sleep so I caught it. Hilarious.'

Abhishek scowled. He had only wanted to get the facts right.

'Look. The anchor is the face of the channel. He must always look like he knows. The channel's credibility depends on it. And you, you fool, chose to put down the biggest ego in the business – Mr Rajiv Bose. He's a prick. What did you expect?'

Abhishek thought that Vivek looked rather too well, given

his illness. As he consumed the excellent single malt – hand-delivered, Vivek told him, by his man in Customs – the young reporter tried to tell his senior about the awkwardness; the constant feeling that he did not belong.

'You are not the only one.' Vivek smiled ruefully. 'We are the eunuchs here; we fall in neither the Hindi category nor with these privileged English sons of bitches. The Rajiv Boses make us feel inadequate. We do not have their social graces, don't have their foreign degrees, our fathers are not top bureaucrats. The Hindi journalists see us as part of the English set-up and, therefore, somehow privileged. So where do we go?' Vivek poured himself another stiff peg. 'Forget you, I feel like a fucking novice. After eight years of journalism, kids at the desk who have never done shit, never been out on the field, talk back to me. It's amazing, their level of confidence.'

But more than his sense of dislocation within the office hierarchy, it was Vivek's disillusionment that struck Abhishek. 'Four years with Amir – and he is one cynical bastard – he still made you feel that it was worth it, that it was our fucking duty every bloody morning to get up and go kick someone's ass. And what's most important – he made it fun.'

Abhishek hardly needed telling. He missed Amir sorely. While Abhishek knew his old boss would have laughed at anyone ascribing any higher purpose to journalism, he managed to imbue the workplace with a sense of integrity that made the work fun and worth getting out of bed for.

'The thing about Amir is,' Vivek added, 'that you can look up to him. He was the best reporter in town. He earned that respect by doing story after story. Amir understands quality; in television it's all been reduced to rating. We're bloody accountants, jumping in the air with a one-point increase and distraught at a fall. This cannot be journalism.'

Finally Vivek admitted to Abhishek that he had lied to the office about the dengue fever and hospitalization. 'I was in a remote village in Bihar for six days, tracking men who rig elections. The bulletin producer wanted an early morning update and then ticked me off for appearing unshaved. I told him that where I was, there were no toilets or clean water. "Not my problem," the motherfucker replied. I came back and got my local doctor to give me a certificate. I needed time to think about what I am doing.'

'Why did you get me into this?' Abhishek questioned. 'If you knew this was such bullshit, why did you not tell me?'

'Oh, shut up. I had no clue you were joining. Samir asked about you and I arranged a meeting. You were the hasty one. You should have at least spoken to me, no? Or was the money that irresistible?'

After leaving Vivek's place, Abhishek went directly to meet Rahul. On the way, he made up his mind: He would leave television. He would beg Amir to take him back. He would sign a bond, if necessary; enslave himself. Amir would surely understand. From Rahul, he wanted to get a sense of how to approach his former boss. Once he had made the decision, Abhishek felt a surge of relief.

Rahul met him at the tea shop they used to frequent in the past. Both men hugged.

'Bastard, I haven't seen you – been more than a month.'

'Sorry, Rahul.' Abhishek smiled apologetically. 'Been really, really busy.'

'With the women, I am sure,' his friend joked.

Abhishek felt close to tears.

'I just met Vivek,' he said, taking a long drag of his cigarette.

'You did? Then you know Vivek is joining us, right? He's coming back to the crime beat. Amir is thrilled.'

17

Mishra-ji was delighted to see Abhishek. 'Come in, sir, come in,' he said, jumping up from his chair and proffering a box of sweets. 'Here, have some. My son just got engaged.'

Abhishek took one, and congratulated the friendly figure before him.

'It's not like the Bengali sweets. You must be used to better. But in Delhi, what can we do?'

'This is delicious, Mishra-ji, thank you. I'll have another.'

Abhishek had once asked this apologetic and affable man what he was doing in the police.

'Obviously nothing,' he had replied. 'I am a government clerk. Doesn't matter, police or railways.'

He now told the reporter that the DCP was busy. 'But let me go and tell him you are here. Is he expecting you?'

'No. But I can wait, don't worry.'

Mishra-ji ordered a cup of tea for Abhishek and, collecting an armful of files, bustled off to inform his boss. Abhishek let himself sink into the waiting-room sofa's sagging embrace.

The past four days had exhausted him. He was required to be in office by five each morning and, though the shift was meant to end at one, he was never home until late evening. He complained to the input editor once and was told that if as a television reporter he was clock-watching, he should find something else to do.

Abhishek had started dreading going to office. He slunk around the newsroom, hoping no one would notice him. But the longer he went unnoticed, the more miserable he became. He had been hired to join the special investigations team, but spent his days writing voice-overs for other people's stories. He was amazed at the alacrity with which his colleagues kicked him when he was down. The entire office, it seemed, was conspiring against him.

He sipped the lukewarm sugar syrup masquerading as tea, brought to him by the ever-pleasant canteen boy. Mishra-ji re-emerged from Uday's office. 'Sir will take half an hour. He really wants to meet you, so don't go away.'

Abhishek nodded tiredly. He too wanted to meet Uday Kumar. He was desperate for a story.

'This is dynamite,' Samir Saxena told Mohan Kapoor, the executive editor.

Abhishek felt it immediately: the elation of a scoop.

'Yes, but how will we execute the story? I don't think the police or anyone will give a quote.' Mohan got straight to practicalities.

Abhishek had anticipated the question. Or rather, Uday had. For the umpteenth time since meeting him yesterday, Abhishek offered silent thanks to the policeman. Not only had he given Abhishek a cracker of a story, he had also told him exactly how to do it.

Of course, the tip-off had been accompanied by the usual Uday theatrics. Abhishek had been called all sorts of names, told that he deserved every bit of shit that he was getting and, if Uday could help it, there would be a whole lot more. It was only after ten minutes of tongue lashing that Uday had asked what he was there for.

'A story, sir. I need a story.'

'Okay, note down,' the cop had replied, with a grin.

Ranjana Shetty, the senior additional commissioner of police, ran an NGO for street children called Koshish, Endeavour, which was organizing a Bollywood-themed fund-raiser. Shetty had asked every station house officer of every police station under her jurisdiction to sell tickets to business establishments in their areas. Those who sold the most, Uday explained, would curry the biggest favour with their boss. 'And in their zeal for approval, the bastards resorted to extortion. Racketeers, the whole lot. Do the story.'

Seeing Abhishek's delighted face, Uday had immediately proceeded to deflate him. 'Any idea how you will do it? Who will give you a quote? You can't say your newspaper crap about informed sources. What will you do, go to Madam Shetty for a quote?'

Abhishek, by now familiar with Uday, had waited patiently for the punchline.

'This is how you'll do it. I'll arrange for two businessmen in Sarojini Nagar to speak to you. They just coughed up five lakh each and are hurting. Go and meet them now.'

'Excellent,' Mohan said, once Abhishek had explained. 'So you've the businessmen and they've agreed?'

He nodded.

'Then there is no problem. Get their quotes, get shots of the invitation card. Try and meet Ranjana Shetty. If she agrees to meet you, great; if not, no worries. We can get the commissioner to comment and come on as a guest in the evening. Brilliant. This is the headline tonight.'

'Okay, Abhishek, let's get going. Let's get the job done.' Samir smiled at the elated boy beside him.

The businessmen spoke candidly about how the police had coerced them to pay money for an NGO they had never heard of. The choice they had been offered was simple: Their businesses could earn the goodwill of Madam Shetty, or they could pay later – far more and in worse ways. 'So much money to go and see Bollywood actresses sing and dance,' one of them, a restaurant owner, told Abhishek. 'For that amount, I could sleep with one.'

Listening to the tape now in the edit suite, Abhishek laughed aloud. There was a knock. 'Call for you at the input desk.'

'Hello, is this Abhishek Dutta?'

'Yes, who is this?'

'This is Ranjana Shetty. I believe you are doing a story which involves me.'

Somebody is fucking with me, he thought. How did she know? Who told her?

'Yes, ma'am,' Abhishek replied, collecting himself. 'I was going to contact you for a quote. I'm doing a story on the ticket-selling for your charity event.'

'First, you must come and see the work that we do,' she said.

'I will indeed do so. But the story will have to go on air this evening, ma'am, so I need a quote from you on this today. I can come to wherever you are now.'

'The story is not going anywhere. Why don't you first come and meet me and see the work my NGO does?' Shetty insisted.

He tried to argue and was rudely cut off. 'Look, the story is not happening. So come and meet me.'

Abhishek put the phone down and walked towards Samir's office in a trance. This story, he knew, was over.

'What?' Mayank leaned forward, suddenly realizing that his driver was speaking to him.

'Sir, madam had said that she wanted me to get some shopping done. Shall I go after dropping you at the club?'

'Which madam?' Mayank asked, his mind elsewhere.

'Your mother, sir.'

Damn ma, he thought angrily. It didn't matter how many times he insisted his office car must never be used for personal work, his family wilfully pretended deafness. 'No,' Mayank snapped. 'You stay put. Give me the list. I'll do it.'

Ritika called on his mobile to thank him for the flowers he had sent. Could they meet at the weekend? 'I have nothing planned right now, so yes,' he replied happily. 'But you know that something might come up?' It was best to be clear from the very beginning about the demands on his time and the pressures of work. She said she understood.

Mayank had agreed to the marriage and the delight expressed by both families confirmed that he had made the right choice. The point system he had devised with his counsellor had made the decision easy and logical, sure, but it did help that he was attracted to her. In a life consumed by duty, career and parents, Ritika was a charming and welcome addition.

He found Abhishek sitting in the lobby of the Gymkhana Club where the two young men had arranged to meet. He looked awful, Mayank thought. 'Sorry I am late. Last-minute meeting. You okay?'

Abhishek nodded. 'I need your help on a story.'

It seemed an innocuous enough request coming from a reporter to a policeman. 'Of course,' Mayank said, leading him towards the coffee shop next door.

'Tell me,' he said, as they sat down.

'Is Babloo Shankar coming back?'

'What?' Mayank looked flabbergasted. 'How do you know?' His reaction, and he would kick himself later, was an obvious mistake.

Abhishek refused to say how he had got the information and Mayank absolutely refused to give any more. They had reached stalemate.

Mayank tried one last time to dissuade his friend. 'A journalist has to go beyond a story. There is an issue of national importance here, do you understand?'

Abhishek remained quiet for a while and then said, 'You know, Mayank, Uday and Amir are great friends.'

The cop nodded, unsure of where this was leading.

'Amir told me their friendship was built on something Uday told him when they first started to meet. He said that whatever Amir found out, Uday wouldn't stop him from writing; whatever Uday could hide, he would. Perhaps we need a similar agreement.'

Samir was on the phone with the CEO. 'Abhishek is right,' he said.

'Excellent. That's great,' Ashok Desai said excitedly. 'I'm in a meeting. Shall we meet in half an hour? We need to plan this.'

'Yes, I'll come up,' the newsman replied and put the phone down.

As a general rule, Samir trusted his reporters but this story was big and the boy was new. Abhishek had refused to disclose his sources and, when told that Samir would have to do a fact check, had insisted that the police should not be approached. It had taken Samir a while to track down the two Interpol officers.

Uday Kumar, they had confirmed, had sent out an alert that Babloo Shankar had landed in Kolkata recently and was now holed up somewhere in the capital. The importance and scope of the story did not need reiterating. Samir was in college when Babloo had burst onto the crime scene. The kidnapper's rise to fame had caught the public imagination: his gangster brother, his glamorous cohorts, the high-profile kidnappings and then one day, his sudden disappearance. It was like a Bollywood script conjured up by an overactive imagination.

Abhishek was sitting in the newsroom and Samir beckoned to him through the glass of his cabin. The boy had a rough first month and Samir had failed him once. He wasn't going to do it again.

'Done, checked. You're right,' Samir said, as Abhishek walked in. The boy shook the proffered hand, unsmiling, apprehensive. 'Sit down and loosen up. We'll go big with this. Don't worry,' he said jovially.

Abhishek remained quiet.

'What's the matter?'

'Nothing, sir. I was told something similar a couple of days back.'

'I know, I know. Look, that was an anomaly. It doesn't usually happen, Abhishek. Editorial here is independent.' He moved on quickly. 'The initiation has been rough for you. Don't think I'm oblivious. I was aware of what our resident bastard did to you, but didn't intervene because I wanted to see how you manage. You stuck it out. We do that to people here: throw them in at the deep end. You are still swimming, so you're okay.'

Samir got up and walked towards the window. 'I met Amir three days back,' he said. 'He is one of my heroes, you know. I grew up reading his scoops and wanted to be like him. He told me that getting you here was one of the smartest decisions I ever made.'

'Really?' Abhishek felt a huge surge of pleasure, tinged with guilt.

Samir turned back to face him. 'He might be my hero, but we don't see eye to eye on television journalism. He only sees problems whereas I see areas to improve. I fundamentally disagree with him that print is some sort of utopia and television is kitsch. I've done both.'

'I think, so has Amir,' Abhishek ventured quietly.

Samir smiled. 'My print experience wasn't as disastrous. I think his is a personal problem rather than an objective evaluation. And I think you too are seeing things in a narrow way. You had a short, good run with print journalism and going by the stories you're doing, you'll have an even better time in TV. Hopefully, you'll even make some money.'

Samir returned to his desk and sat across from Abhishek. 'I know there are problems here, but remember that this is a very new industry; we are trying to set standards here as well as being a profit-making corporate entity. Amir says that a journalist cannot be an accountant. I say he needs to be accountable to the salary he is paid. And if I have anything to do with it, it should be a damn good one.'

'Amir once told me that in television there are just three topics: cinema, cricket and crime,' Abhishek said.

'Well, let me add another one, "crap",' Samir responded,

smiling. 'But seriously, television has done some great exposés in this country, and underpaid print reporters should not make a virtue of poverty. If you are poor, it doesn't mean you are a better journalist than I am. I think of it this way: The print industry has been around for nearly one hundred and fifty years; there is always precedence, something it can fall back upon. It grew with India's independence struggle, was an ally, a partner to the movement. It has a rich and amazing history. We are new, we are searching for a path, and you are part of this defining movement. You are as important as I am because we both don't know. We want to know, we want to set standards.'

'I thought the BBC was the standard,' Abhishek interrupted. 'At least, that's what I was told during my elocution lessons.'

Samir laughed and clapped his hands. 'Did they set Roopleena Bhattacharya after you? She is a mouthful and a handful.'

He got up. 'Look, I'm off to meet the CEO to plan your story. Wait for me here.'

As Abhishek waited, he thought about Babloo. The old gangster had made his career. Abhishek merely had to breathe the man's name, and the press and policemen jumped to attention. He wondered whether this sword he wielded would turn out to be double-edged; whether risking his friendship with Amir, Uday and perhaps even Mayank would be worth the story.

Samir came back with Ashok Desai, interrupting Abhishek's thoughts.

He stood up. 'Sit, sit,' Ashok said, taking Samir's chair.

Abhishek's boss sat beside him on the sofa.

'So we break the story this evening at seven,' Ashok announced. 'Tomorrow morning, the newspapers will be forced to mention us in their reports, but they won't be able to add much meat by then. Nor will the TV channels. And they'll be running around confirming the story while we're already screening follow-ups. Abhishek, Samir will tell you what to do. He says he is putting you in charge of the story and you have to milk it for as long as possible. This is good work, my friend. Congratulations.' Ashok shook Abhishek's hand solemnly.

Through the glass panel, he saw the entire newsroom watching the proceedings. 'Thank you, sir. I'll do my best.'

'You shall indeed. Samir, let me know how things go. Later, boys.'

Samir explained to Abhishek how to construct the first story. Using archive shots of Babloo and sound bytes of two former police commissioners, he was to create a voice-over with basic details. 'Retired policemen will give bytes on anything. Here, call these numbers. It's afternoon; let's get the story in by five. We'll talk about follow-ups later.'

Samir watched Abhishek walk across the press room, avoiding eye contact with his colleagues. The senior newsman had decided to lend his personal weight to the story. The police, Samir knew, would deny the report. The other news channels would echo the police line and, if not supported, the boy would be brutally attacked. Samir had confirmed the story and would challenge Delhi Police. A good confrontation meant drama and a week of high ratings. This was going to be fun.

Mayank was sitting with Uday when the story broke. It was just after 7 p.m. and the senior cop was lecturing him on the perils of marriage when the phone rang.

'What? What are you saying?' Uday sounded extremely agitated. 'Okay, I'll call you back.' He slammed down the receiver and turned to Mayank. 'Fucking News Today is running a story on fucking Babloo Shankar.'

He looked for the remote control, finally locating it by shoving a pile of papers off his desk.

It was the headline story: 'Dreaded gangster Babloo Shankar is back in India.' Mayank recognized Abhishek's voice. He looked from the screen to his boss.

'Must be Amir. Who else? Has to be him,' Uday muttered and then shouted, 'Motherfucker! But why? Why the hell would he do this to me?'

The intercom buzzed and Uday lunged for it. The call, Mayank surmised from Uday's quick change in tone, was from the commissioner. 'Yes, sir. I've just seen it. I am on my way, sir.'

Amir was at his desk when he saw the newsflash on his computer. It took him a while to register what his former protégé had done.

Rahul rushed in enthusiastically. 'Boss, have you seen what Abhishek is saying?'

'Rahul, please knock before you come in next time, and tell everyone this – no barging into my office.'

Uday's phone was engaged. Amir rang Mayank. 'I am on my way.'

Babloo called Archana. His instructions were sharp and simple. Maintain regular lifestyle. There must be absolutely no sudden changes. She should not call; he would. She must keep an eye on Imran and ensure that he didn't engage in loose talk. He would handle Salim Khan and all arrangements.

By midnight, when every news channel and Internet portal was giving him top billing, either confirming his entry into Delhi or denying it, Babloo Shankar started to smile. This was turning out to be an unexpected bonanza.

He called an associate. 'Get me something on this television reporter, Abhishek Dutta. Who is he? How did he get this?'

Samir shielded Abhishek from the immediate effects of breaking an aggressively contested story by putting him on follow-up reports: Why has Babloo come back? What is he after? The most plausible reason was to kidnap someone for cash. So what was Babloo's modus operandi in the past? What should the rich and famous do to protect themselves? Who are Babloo's competitors now?

'Don't let this story go, Abhishek,' Samir asserted. 'It ticks both the boxes: the public is interested and it is of public interest.'

For the next week, Abhishek was kept incredibly busy. He worked from early morning till late into the night, and often slept over on an office couch. It was wonderful. The work was exciting and he was spurred on by Samir's continuing support.

Samir delivered a masterstroke on the third day, when three other English channels had taken a position against his story, promoting the official police version. During the 9 p.m. news bulletin, after several denials from the police commissioner, the country's most respected news anchor had asked him, 'Mr Pratap, can you guarantee that your deputy commissioner of the Crime Branch, Uday Kumar, did not send messages to Interpol that Babloo Shankar is in Delhi? If you are wrong, will you resign? For if we are wrong, I will.'

The commissioner faltered; he mumbled excuses, and the battle was decisively won.

The story remained in the headlines for over a week. 'In these attention-deficit times of Twitter and Facebook, a remarkable achievement,' the CEO wrote to Abhishek in an email.

Abhishek had proved his point and finally, quietly, he gained admirers in the newsroom. In an environment where everyone made much of nothing, and loudly, here was a journalist who preferred to shy away from the limelight. The bosses had to push and cajole him to promote himself. It was a welcome change.

There was to be a Republic Day party on the last day of January at Samir Saxena's house to which Abhishek was invited. Rajiv Bose was not. Usually one to avoid pettiness of any sort, the blushing star of News Today couldn't help ensuring that his colleague noticed the slight.

18

Delhi loves February. The month brings relief from the ice-cold winds that sweep through Tibet and Ladakh, via Kashmir and the hill stations that lie between the troubled valley and the Indian capital. The torrid summer months, the incessant power cuts, baking tarmac and frequent fires that engulf the city's poorer parts, dry as a matchstick, are a while away. In between the severity of the winter and the ferocity of an angry sun god, there is festivity. The rich party on their penthouse rooftops; street kids dance at traffic lights to music tossed casually from passing cars. There are film and food festivals, literature and drama workshops. Delhi, screwed by the harshness of geography, rediscovers culture; people rise from the mediocrity of the daily grind and smile at the gyrating kid on the road. To egg her on, they pump up the volume. February allows Delhi to feel kind.

Even the law enforcers give in to the weather and take time out to celebrate the annual Police Week, a moment to reach out to the public they purport to serve. The officers attend all-night poetry sessions in Chandni Chowk, distribute sweets to school children and, if the local booze shop owner has the misfortune of a case hanging over him, then whisky and rum are distributed to remind the public of the munificence of its uniformed men.

One of the key features of the week, looked forward to by both parties, is the annual cricket match between the press and the police. Past enmities are washed away by the gin and tonic that flow all afternoon.

Abhishek used the day to attempt a reconciliation with Uday. He managed only a handshake, but even that was a start.

Commissioner Pratap turned out to be an excellent leg-spinner, and several of the police officers displayed similar age-defying skills, winning them the year's contest.

During the prize-giving ceremony, the commissioner was magnanimous enough to award the opponents with cricketing gear, bats, balls, sweaters and blazers, all procured by his men from a hapless manufacturer. The city's pressmen, defenders of free speech and crusaders against injustice, accepted this largesse without a qualm. Those with school-going kids would have the opportunity to be generous that evening.

On 18 February, the final day of the Police Week, Commissioner Pratap stepped out onto the spotless lawns of his Akbar Road residence to cast an eye over the evening's preparations. He was hosting a dinner for India's high and mighty. The prime minister, home minister and Delhi's lieutenant governor had all confirmed their presence.

Winning the annual contest had rounded off nicely what Pratap felt had been a decent year overall, despite the difficult circumstances. In a city of unplanned and uncontrolled growth, where the black economy rivalled the legitimate, where politics and power were synonymous with crime, where the police were shackled by corrupt masters and human rights sharks, he felt that the statistics should earn him another year at the top.

Manufacturing those numbers had involved a hell of a lot of burking, but one couldn't have everything, Pratap reasoned. There had genuinely been a fall in murders, petty thefts and armed robberies. Besides kidnappings and rapes, most other categories remained constant. There had been no attention-grabbing terrorist strikes or bomb blasts in railway carriages like in Mumbai, where his colleague and batchmate Commissioner T. Krishnan felt his days were numbered. Pratap permitted himself to feel cautiously relieved.

Not very far from the commissioner's residence, in one of Golf Links' most ostentatious bungalows, a young man sat quietly at the breakfast table after a sleepless night. His parents, Brigadier Devinder Mahajan and his wife Radha, were early risers and were already immersed in files and paperwork, oblivious to his presence.

Since their arrival from the US, the couple had started to leave the house early in the morning and return late. Amit had learnt from the newspapers that his parents spent the long days being grilled by the CBI at its Lodhi Road offices.

His father refused to speak to him about it. His mother tearfully confided that things would soon be set right and that Daddy was a victim of political conspiracy. Amit had no opinion in the matter, nor did he feel strongly about it. That his father was crooked he was certain about, but it caused him no outrage. His friends didn't seem to mind and his only worry had been what Monika might think. His fears had been assuaged by her gentle, measured response.

She had been away for more than a month. Her father had suffered a heart attack and she had been forced to stay back in

Chandigarh to look after the family. They had spoken on the phone almost every night she was gone.

'What your father might have done doesn't affect how I feel for you, Amit. Not in any way,' Monika had told him softly.

He was certain that they had become much closer after his confession. Their conversations had improved when her fiancé had to go on an extended business tour to the US. She brightened considerably and they spent long hours chatting late into the night. Sometimes Amit felt he could barely control the physical urge to hold her, kiss her, touch her skin.

Monika had arrived in Delhi last night and he was finally going to see her – she was coming over that afternoon. Till then, it would be hard to get through the day. He asked, and his parents confirmed again, that they would not be back before six.

Archana smiled and shuddered as a slow, pleasurable tremor spread through her body. She gripped the steering wheel tightly. The telephonic exchanges had become increasingly arousing, and Imran had found himself at the receiving end of her lust on several nights.

Archana turned her thoughts to the plans for the afternoon. She would meet the boy at his residence after 2 p.m.. That gave her four hours before the parents returned. The last hour would be the most difficult, but she had devised an audacious plan.

At 2.15 p.m., Archana rang the bell at the gates of the Mahajan residence. There were two security guards who, apparently forewarned of her arrival, let her in without question. She did not expect to meet anyone in the house besides Amit. The boy had said he would send away the domestic help, and Babloo had double-checked that there was no sudden cancellation of the parents' CBI session.

Archana parked her car and waved at Amit, who rushed towards her from the house.

Just after 4 p.m., Amit started to feel tense. He looked at the sleeping woman by his side. How long could he wait before waking her? Oh, he didn't want her to ever leave, but his parents would be home at 6 p.m. and the house staff was due back soon.

Maybe another ten minutes, Amit thought as he closed his eyes. He wanted to re-enact in his head all that had happened in the past hour, savour it, understand its delights. He was in love with this woman, in love with her beautiful body and what it could do to him. She had come to him like a storm, a dark whirlpool of energy and emotion and he had been swept away by her.

Amit woke up with a start. It was 4.30 p.m. Outside, the sky was already preparing for night, and he could see the golden rays in which their bodies had basked in the afternoon, retreating through the windowpanes. He looked at her face again and smiled, gently nudging her.

Monika awoke immediately and sat up, pulling the sheet to her chest. 'What time is it? Am I late?'

'No, no,' he said hastily, not wanting to hurry or offend her. 'Just that my parents will be back soon.'

'Yes, okay. I should get ready to go,' Monika said, leaning forward for a brief hug. 'Will you make me a coffee, darling?'

Amit didn't remember anyone calling him darling before. How sweet it sounded. There was so much he wanted to tell her. He knew that he wanted to be with her for ever, protect her, rescue her from that boor of a fiancé, but now was not the time. Now, she needed to leave.

She picked up her clothes from the floor and went into the bathroom.

Monika liked fresh coffee, Amit knew, and he was just about to start the grinder when he heard a scream and a terrible crash. He froze for a moment and then rushed back to his room.

Monika was face down on the bathroom floor. There was a small, steady trickle of blood on the white marble by her head. The mirror was cracked and there was glass everywhere.

Amit's knees gave away and he had to support himself against the wall. He took a few deep breaths. She must have slipped and crashed into the mirror.

He crouched down and gently turned her over. She seemed to be coming around and was moaning softly. He splashed some water on her face. Then, taking a towel, he wiped her forehead. There was a lot of blood and glass. Amit's stomach churned.

Brigadier Mahajan was in a foul mood. On the short drive from Lodhi Road to his house, he berated his wife for her indiscretions. 'That officer is not your friend. He doesn't think you are sexy. What were you thinking flirting with him?'

The usually domineering Radha Mahajan kept quiet. She knew when not to push her husband. It was true that she had taken a bit of comfort in the smiling face of the young man. His boss had been so harsh and cruel. Her husband, she realized, was right. Her brother-in-law should not have been mentioned.

'Did anyone come?' Brig. Mahajan asked the security guard at the gates.

'Yes, sir. One madam. She is inside.'

The Brigadier looked at his wife, who shrugged; she was not expecting anyone.

The woman was lying on the sofa, her forehead bandaged, a dark patch of blood congealing on her cheekbones.

Seeing his parents, Amit nervously stood up and spoke in a rush: 'Daddy, she's my friend Karan's cousin. She had come to drop off something Karan sent me from Mumbai. She fell down in the bathroom.'

The woman, Brigadier Mahajan noticed, had opened her eyes and was looking at him. He decided to take charge. 'Please don't get up,' he said. 'Amit, have you called the doctor?'

'Please don't bother, sir. I've called my driver and he'll be here soon. I feel fine. It's just a cut, really,' the woman said gently.

'Are you sure?' the Brigadier asked, concern lining his face.

She nodded.

The painkillers she'd popped before crashing her head against the mirror were taking effect and except for a dull throbbing ache, Archana felt fine. She quickly assessed Brig. Mahajan: overbearingly male, protective and leery. It was amazing how similar rich middle-aged Indian men were. All of them seemed to originate from one single gene pool of sleaziness. In many years of a remarkably singular profession, she had never met one who refused to return her gaze. This was going to be simple. She was already bored.

Half an hour later, Archana was trying to keep her eyes averted from Amit to stop herself from laughing. She could feel his astonishment as she flirted with his father. There had been times in the past when she wondered at this unnecessary and unprofessional cruel streak in her. It surfaced now as the Monika that Amit knew and adored climbed into a different skin.

It was 7 p.m. and the four of them were having tea when the intercom rang. Her driver had arrived and she requested that he be called in to escort her to the car.

She then reached into her handbag and took out a piece of paper that she smoothed onto the table and placed in front of Brig. Mahajan. He looked at her enquiringly, and she smiled. 'Read it.'

Archana focused a steady, unblinking gaze on the Brigadier as he put on his glasses and read the note, the initial astonishment quickly turning into terror. Amit saw her leaning close to his father. 'Tell them to be calm,' she said.

Brig. Mahajan tried to speak but no words came out.

Amit finally asked, 'Monika, what's going on?'

She turned to look at him and his mother. 'I have a gun pointing at your father's balls, Amit, and if you so much as make a sound, I'm going to plug a little bullet into him. Now listen very carefully.'

By the time the man supposed to be Monika Mathur's driver came into the large living room, Amit was crying in mute terror. Radha stared helplessly at her husband who, after the initial moment of shock, was trying to maintain a brave face. The driver, they saw, had a huge mop of hair and was wearing absurdly large glasses on his prominent nose. He approached them in rapid strides.

'All okay?' he asked Archana.

She nodded.

The family looked on, astonished, as the man took off his wig, glasses and false nose and handed them to Brig. Mahajan. 'Put them on. Quickly.'

Archana got up and stood behind the Brigadier. 'My friend here will now tie up your wife and son,' she said, letting him feel the pistol against his neck. 'Then we'll go out and get into my car. You'll drive it to the front gate for my friend. And we'll leave without any fuss.'

Archana turned towards Radha, whose hands were being tied to the chair. 'Your servants will be here soon and will untie you. You can then call the police and the fire brigade and whoever else you want. Just remember this: Your husband is with us and this pretty face could be his worst nightmare.'

Ten minutes later, the security guards at the gate let out the steel-grey Maruti Zen. Both of them laughed again at the driver's hairstyle and strange face. The sexy madam, they saw, was in the backseat, leaning forward and chatting with him as they drove out. They wondered for a moment at the third person in the car. 'Must have come with sahab and madam earlier,' one of them said disinterestedly.

Shortly after, the gardener and the cook were knocking on the gate, dishevelled and frightened. They narrated a harrowing story of having been detained in the back of a van for two hours.

'Bastards – making excuses because they are late,' one of the guards said, as the duo proceeded towards the house. 'Spicy story though, better than his bloody cooking.'

They went back to the tiny outpost by the gate and settled into their chairs. Soon after, the intercom started ringing. It was a call from the main house.

Hearing of the invitation to the police commissioner's annual dinner, Samir had graciously offered Abhishek the night off. The evening would receive a lot of press attention, but News Today could send someone else to join the crowd of journalists and cameramen who would gather outside the house, catching shots of the dignitaries and reporting on proceedings just out of their reach.

Abhishek had refused. He would go to the dinner, but would come out and give hourly updates from the OB van. 'I'll have more insider details.'

He was on his way to the party in a News Today – sponsored suit, when his phone rang. It was from a private number.

'Abhishek Dutta?' the voice asked.

'Yes,' he said. 'Who is this?'

'This is Babloo Shankar.'

There was a touch of mirth in the voice, as if the speaker knew the incredulous reaction this might provoke. Yet it did not seem that the caller was joking.

'What?'

'You heard me, Abhishek-ji. Why are you surprised? You said I was in town, did you not?'

Abhishek's journalistic instincts snapped into motion. 'Yes sir, I did. Can we meet?'

'We'll meet soon, tonight in fact. For now, I have kidnapped that corrupt wheeler-dealer son of a bitch, Brigadier Devinder Mahajan. You can go on air with this information. Go to 107, Golf Links. You'll know I am speaking the truth. I'll call in an hour.' The line went dead.

Samir was at the input desk and could barely hear amid the noise of the several television sets and chattering journalists. 'One second, Abhishek,' he said to the nearly incoherent boy at the end of the line. He put his hand across the mouthpiece and screamed, 'Shut the fuck up everyone.' The newsroom immediately fell silent. 'Yes, go on, Abhishek.'

Rajiv grimaced and nudged his producer, who rolled her eyes. 'The golden boy again.' Rajiv watched Samir as he strode to a corner, listening intently, and then suddenly rushed to his cabin. Through the glass partition, they could see him bending over his table and noting something. Moments later he emerged and the look on his face told Rajiv that they were in for a long night ahead, and Abhishek would be its protagonist.

'Dilip,' Samir yelled to the input editor, 'who is in charge of output tonight? Bring him to production control right now. Hurry.'

Samir had already redirected the OB van from the police commissioner's party to the Golf Links address Babloo had given. As he put on a tie and prepared to go on air, he briefly explained to the editors what Abhishek had told him. 'This might be the biggest thing we have done,' Samir said, then more to himself than the other two, 'Fuck me, I hope to God it's true.'

Abhishek found 107, Golf Links without any difficulty, and the four police cabs parked outside immediately confirmed what he'd been told. He gripped the cameraman, Ankur Bhasin, in excitement.

'Boss, the OB van is behind us. Look,' Ankur told him.

'Stop the car.' Abhishek put his hand on the driver's shoulder. 'Ankur, keep the OB van at a distance for now. I'll go to the house, figure this out and be back. Get ready to upload.'

He almost ran the hundred yards to the gate where Inspector Tiwary from the Crime Branch was standing with four other policemen. As Abhishek walked up, he looked around, surprised.

'Boss, is Uday sir here?'

The inspector shook his head, looking unsure. 'No, sahab is on his way.'

'What time was the incident?' Abhishek asked. Seeing the policeman hesitate, he prodded, 'Arre, what time did the kidnapping take place? Has it been an hour?'

'Around six thirty, they are saying. I haven't gone in. Our assistant commissioner is inside.'

'Yes, Mayank told me.' Abhishek was guessing that his friend would be working on the case if the Crime Branch was involved.

'Oh.' The inspector looked relieved. 'Sir told you?'

'Yes. Okay, I will be back in a minute.' Abhishek walked back rapidly towards the OB van.

At the prime-time hour of 8 p.m., just as the home minister was shaking hands with the police commissioner at his residence, News Today broke the story: Brigadier Devinder Mahajan, an accused in the Commonwealth Games corruption scandal, had been kidnapped. The perpetrator was the infamous Babloo Shankar, on the run from the police for the last fifteen years. His recent and secret return to India had been revealed by this very television channel.

The journalists were the first to flee the party. Golf Links was close by and even senior editors were instructed to get to the spot as fast as humanly possible. Commissioner Pratap, his party decimated, retreated to the back of his residence with the home minister. The rest, Delhi's elite and those waiting on them, gathered around a large-screen television in the living room. The prime minister and the lieutenant governor, minutes from the commissioner's residence, turned their convoys around.

As news channel after screaming news channel began to pick up the story, crowds formed outside television showrooms. Waiters, forgetting their hungry customers, clustered around portable TV screens in smoky kitchens. Returning commuters received calls from hyper wives. Auto-rickshaw drivers heard the story from their passengers and shared it at the traffic lights. Wire agencies, Twitter and Facebook joined in: The ransacker of public coffers had been kidnapped by a public enemy.

19

'Come to Chhatarpur temple. Bring your cameraman,' Babloo instructed Abhishek in the midst of the prime-time pandemonium they had caused.

The two young men drove south, excited but saying little to one another.

At the temple gates, a man approached their car and knocked on the passenger door. 'Abhishek Dutta?'

The reporter nodded, and the man got into the front seat. He did not speak another word, except to direct the driver along an unlit lane which snaked its way off the main road for several kilometres.

They pulled up by a tall wooden gate where another man was waiting with what looked like a large rifle. There were few lights and it took Abhishek a while to get used to the darkness. As they shook hands, the man muttered an introduction. 'Imran,' he said, and led them across a neatly kept front lawn to a two-storey wooden house.

They trooped up some stairs, Imran lending a hand with the camera equipment, to a large living room in which sat two older men: one in a wheelchair, and the other tied securely to his seat.

Babloo Shankar greeted the young reporter with a firm handshake and asked him to pull up a chair. 'Thank you for coming, Abhishek-ji. I have heard about you. Tonight will be busy, but I hope we will get to talk later. Perhaps you'll come and see me in jail.' He smiled and then asked Ankur to switch on the camera and focus it on the Brigadier.

Once the equipment was positioned, Babloo asked both journalists to leave the room. Imran accompanied them downstairs where they stood silently in a slightly damp kitchen, drinking warm Coca Cola until Babloo summoned them back.

'Brigadier Mahajan has told us a story better than the Mahabharata. The high and the mighty will lose a few hours of sleep tonight.' Babloo grinned at Abhishek.

The reporter tried to make eye contact with the retired army man, but he stared at the floor miserably.

Babloo instructed Ankur to edit a tape on their OB van's editing machine.

How did he know so much? Abhishek wondered.

'Just keep his words and cut the rest. Show it to me when you are done,' Babloo said.

Abhishek nodded to his colleague to go ahead.

After Ankur and Imran left for the van, Babloo explained to Abhishek how he wanted the evening to play out. During their conversation, Brig. Mahajan spoke only once. 'Sir, why me? There were others too.'

Babloo looked at him wryly. 'Bad luck ... kismet. And then think about this – why not you? Which kingdom are you the fucking king of? Now, and for the last time, you will not speak a word till I say so. Next time you do, I will shoot you in the knee caps.'

It appeared by some sleight of hand and was sitting on Babloo's left palm: a shiny black metallic object, menacing and smooth. And then it was gone. Abhishek wondered if it was also a subtle way of telling him to behave. He, of course, had no plans to do anything rash. There was nothing subtle about the shotgun that Imran was carrying.

Mayank sensed the change in the man sitting beside him in the car. The bravado that his boss usually wore like a protective coat had vanished, and he looked crumpled and defeated.

Uday was on the phone to the home minister. 'Absolutely, sir ... I'll take care of it, sir ... Please don't worry, sir.'

Putting the phone down and staring out of the window, the DCP said, 'All top bosses are in agreement. No force to be used ... I'm just the fucking nanny bringing the baby in.'

He paused, shaking his head, then continued, 'What the fuck is this about? What's going on in that motherfucker's head?'

Mayank, wondering the same thing, silently scrolled down his phone screen, reading the latest updates. He had tried to get a live streaming of News Today, but the signal was weak in the moving car.

'Anything new?'

'Checking, sir. The page is taking some time to load.'

Uday shook his head. 'Updates from a television channel on a damn mobile phone to do my work. I don't know anything any more.'

The radio crackled constantly. Police contingents had been deployed all around Mehrauli. Road blocks were being set up.

'Turn it down,' Uday told the radio operator and sat back to look at Mayank. 'Can't you give me something?' he asked impatiently. 'You've been glued to that News Today nonsense for the last half-hour. Just let's go over what we have.'

'Yes, sir.'

According to the channel and its reporter Abhishek Dutta, who seemed to have exclusive access to Babloo Shankar, the kidnap victim was being held in a Mehrauli farmhouse. The police had surrounded the building, though no attempt was being made to force entry. Babloo, through Dutta's phone updates to the channel, had announced his intention to hand the victim over to the police. He had one condition: that DCP Uday Kumar conduct the negotiations along with the chief reporter of the *Express*, Amir Akhtar. Dutta also said that News Today would be a witness to the process and would bring it live to its viewers.

Uday nodded. 'He just wants to humiliate me. He's settling old scores. Who would think that he would go this far and after so long? You know that he's in a wheelchair because of me, right?'

'Yes, sir,' Mayank said, 'but what's the connection with Amir Akhtar?'

'I imagine you'll find out very soon, Mayank. Till then, let's discuss what options we have.'

'Very few, it seems, sir,' the ACP replied. 'The use of force has been ruled out. Abhishek and his cameraman are already sitting with Babloo in the farmhouse. So there is no way to pull off a surprise encounter. Also, it seems to me that he has brilliantly caught on to the public mood by saying he is an anti-corruption crusader and wants to clean up the system. Something happens to him now, everyone will say it was politically motivated. I expect that's what the government is thinking too.'

Uday smiled. 'Brilliant, isn't he? I've been outsmarted again.'

Abhishek turned to the man in the wheelchair. 'We are ready to go on air when you want, sir. We have a direct link to the OB van.'

Babloo nodded and asked Imran to take a look outside the window.

'Bhai, it's like a carnival outside. Police, public, press – they're all there.'

'Abhishek-ji,' Babloo said, looking at his watch, 'it's ten p.m. Time to give our prime-time viewers some masala. We have kept them waiting.'

Moments later, News Today began its broadcast of a confessional statement from Brigadier Mahajan. It was a six-minute recording in which the kidnapped man accepted that he and his company had swindled Indian taxpayers out of millions of dollars from the Commonwealth Games budget. He mentioned names of politicians, bureaucrats and contractors who were on the take. The home minister, who had just ordered the police to ensure no harm be done to Babloo, was among the damned.

Abhishek glanced at his notes nervously as he stood by for his cue.

'Coming to you in fifteen seconds, Abhishek,' he heard through his earpiece. 'Four … three … two …'

'Abhishek, you are now with Babloo Shankar and Brigadier Devinder Mahajan. Can you tell us the situation?' Samir Saxena sounded over the moon.

'Samir, that is correct. We have been granted exclusive access to the kidnapping situation and to Babloo Shankar. He has asked me to let our viewers know that he demands no ransom; that this was his way of forcing the corrupt to be brought to book. He has a few demands for the safety of his associates and he will make these to DCP Uday Kumar of the Crime Branch. He has also asked for the presence of veteran journalist Amir Akhtar. I believe both are on their way.'

In the forty minutes that he had spent with the kidnapper, this request for his former boss had caught Abhishek by surprise. Babloo was cryptic. 'There is much history between us, Abhishek-ji. I hear you worked for Amir?'

Initially shocked by how much Babloo knew about him – his work, parents, schooling – Abhishek soon realized the meticulous groundwork that had gone into this operation. Apart from chain-smoking, Babloo showed no signs of anxiety. The outcome seemed foregone.

Abhishek was careful not to offend. He was aware by now that he had been called in for a purpose: to convey the kidnapper's message and prevent a shoot-out. This was no time for heroics. Tomorrow he could say anything he wanted; today he was sticking to Babloo's script.

Uday and Amir entered the room together, escorted by Imran.

'Uday-ji, we meet for the second time! But this time round, I have the gun.'

Abhishek saw that the object of conversation was now clearly displayed. Two chairs had been placed in front of Babloo and he indicated to the new arrivals to sit. Behind the thick glasses, his eyes danced with mirth.

Uday looked at the Brigadier.

'Don't worry. He is fine, Uday-ji. Let us finish our business first.'

'I do not conduct business with criminals, Shankar,' the policeman replied, scrambling to salvage some authority.

Babloo laughed, a low growl of a laugh. 'But we all know that you do, sahab. Do you want me to say it all on national television?' He gestured towards the camera, which for now was switched off.

'Okay, let's all act like grown-ups,' Amir intervened. 'We have a situation and let's resolve it as smoothly as we can.'

Babloo's eyes settled on the newsman. The smile that had been playing across his jowly face disappeared. 'Have you grown up, Amir Akhtar?' he asked slowly.

For the first time Abhishek understood the menace that this man might be capable of.

'Doesn't seem like fifteen years – you're looking well. Like someone who sleeps peacefully at night. Not what you would expect of a man with blood on his hands.' The room was suddenly still. 'Seems like you need reminding that a girl died because of you.'

'You killed her. I did not.' Amir's voice, quiet, seemed shorn of its usual confidence.

'And who will prove what happened?' Babloo signalled to Imran for a glass of water. 'Uday-ji fired several bullets that day. One is in my spine. Have you accounted for the rest? Because of you heroes, I had to spend fifteen years in exile. You gambled with that girl's life for a story, Amir sahab. Wasn't she your friend's daughter?'

Abhishek listened, astounded. Amir's eyes remained lowered. So here was the link.

Babloo paused to drink. 'But enough about the past. Today you will orchestrate my return.'

He laid down his demands. Archana Pandey would get safe passage to Singapore. She was at the airport and would board a Singapore Airlines flight which was due to leave in an hour. As soon as she landed in Singapore and left the airport without being stopped, Babloo would give himself up, along with Imran. The whole thing, he said smiling, should not take more than four to five hours. Till then, they were his guests.

'Uday-ji, your government won't mind the deal. They have given up terrorists before. Here they're getting one.'

He's toying with them, Abhishek thought, and wondered if he could somehow switch on the camera.

Babloo waved at him to join the group. 'Abhishek-ji, I expect you have met Amir Akhtar and Uday Kumar – venerated, lofty men, these. But now you must update the world, no? No more cameras though. Phone updates from now on. Okay?'

Abhishek nodded.

'You can only talk of my demand that my friend goes free. Nothing of where she is going or what she will do. Now call your office.'

Samir came on the line immediately.

Abhishek briefly explained the situation.

'Are you all right?'

A meaningless question given the circumstances. 'Yes,' he said. 'Let's go on air.'

The policeman asked for some privacy to make a call to the home minister.

Babloo laughed. 'You can face the other way and know that Imran is watching you.'

Uday dialled the home minister's personal number. The minister was clearly surprised by how minimal Babloo's demands were and they were acceded to without fuss, just as the kidnapper had predicted.

'What is this about, Shankar?' Uday asked after a while, reclaiming his chair. 'Why did you come back? To be arrested?'

'I am a patriot, Kumar sahab – love for my country.' Babloo grinned.

'Well, you'll die in an Indian jail.'

'You think so? At the most, five years for attempted

kidnapping. I cooperated, didn't I? And public opinion, what about that? I've got this looter of the national treasury to confess. You and your entire state machinery couldn't do that. And look, not a scratch on him. Who will stop me from contesting the next general elections? The parties will scramble to give me a ticket. In my home town, you think I can lose?'

Abhishek stared at Babloo in amazement and then at Amir and Uday. Both men appeared stunned at the sheer audacity, and plausibility, of what they were hearing.

Abhishek couldn't hold back any longer. He desperately needed permission to leave the room to pee. Babloo looked momentarily annoyed, then he wheeled around and followed Abhishek down the corridor. 'No, leave the door open,' he said.

Abhishek splashed water on his face repeatedly and took his time. Babloo seemed relaxed and nonchalant, but his eyes never left the reporter.

'Was it Amir who asked Uday to come after you?' Abhishek couldn't resist asking the question any longer.

'Yes. The girl's father was an industrialist. We had agreed on the payment. The money meant nothing to him. But your boss wanted a great story; a story that would make his career. The idiot went to Uday and look at what happened.' Babloo pointed towards his legs.

'What happened to the girl?'

Babloo shrugged and indicated that they should get back.

In the room, Amir and Uday were speaking to each other in hushed tones. Brigadier Mahajan had not moved his eyes from the floor. Abhishek looked at his cameraman, who seemed to be enjoying the evening and flashed him a grin. Imran moved back to his position at the window from where he would occasionally peer outside and inform his boss of any developments. Choppers intermittently circled the house. Imran produced a carton of cigarettes and Babloo offered Amir a packet.

Abhishek sat across the floor from his former boss and stared at the man he had so admired. Since the day he had broken the story of Babloo Shankar's return, Amir had refused to have any contact with him, ignoring his calls and messages. Despite the headiness and the attention, Abhishek had felt a sense of terrible guilt. And for what, he thought now. A legitimate story which any reporter would have done.

It was more than three hours before Babloo received confirmation of Archana's safe arrival at Singapore. He signalled to Imran. 'Okay, Uday-ji, you can arrest me now. But I will give you my gun outside, in the presence of the world. You can take this asshole too,' he said, gesturing towards Brig. Mahajan.

Uday began to untie him. 'Come,' he said, helping the man as he struggled to his feet.

Just before they reached the main door, Uday turned back to look at Babloo. 'Tell me, Babloo Shankar, why are you back?' he asked, in a not unfriendly voice. 'You haven't told me the real reason, have you?'

Babloo smiled. 'Uday-ji, I have great respect for you and your powers of deduction. Now, arrest me and claim your glory. We are even.'

This must be what fame feels like, Abhishek thought as they made their exit into the garden, now alive with flashing cameras and eager television crew hurling questions at the emerging group.

The police tried to bundle Babloo into a waiting van, but the press resisted fiercely. They had stood outside and watched someone else's reports for too long to let the mastermind of the evening disappear. Scuffles broke out with the police, cameras were smashed, but a determined press would have a statement. Babloo Shankar was more than obliging.

When the police finally managed to move him and Brigadier Mahajan, the press turned to Abhishek: 'Boss, what happened? What did you see? Tell us, were you scared?'

No, he had not been scared, but just before leaving, Babloo had given him a few words of advice. 'You are an intelligent boy, Abhishek-ji. So be careful. We know where your parents stay, where your father works.'

Abhishek refused to offer any comments. 'Can't say anything till I talk to the office,' he said, beaming at his colleagues. 'I'm sure you understand.'

They smiled back at him. Yes, they did. He was their newest celebrity.

'You'll have to come to the police station,' Mayank said gently, his hand on Abhishek's shoulder. Abhishek turned around and nodded, happy to be led.

ACKNOWLEDGEMENTS

First drafts are notorious killjoys; a few select friends were subjected to such torture.

Greg and Joanna Falkoff's immensely detailed notes rivalled the manuscript's word count. Debashish Mukerji read various versions and made painstaking edits. Arkaja Singh, James Boyd, Lena Michaels, Madan Oberoi, Matti Pohjonen, Srinath Raghavan, Rosamund Hutchison, Jonathon Page, Rikhia Guha, Nada Jung and Paul Webley gave their valuable time and comments. My agent, Jessica Woolard, worked tirelessly through each draft. I am very grateful to all of you.

This book was written primarily in two locations, Heidelberg, Germany, and Mandrem Beach, Goa. Katharina Weiler was a perfect housemate, leaving me to work through the day and lighting up the summer evenings with red wine, food and friendship. The boys at Dunes shack built an office space on the beach and ensured endless cups of black coffee, extra strong.

I am grateful to my editors at HarperCollins, especially Shantanu Ray Chaudhuri.

This book would not have been possible without my publisher and dear friend, V.K. Karthika. To Georgina Pope, who bore the brunt of being with a first-time novelist and his ghosts, the debts are immeasurable.